Country of Red Azaleas

ALSO BY DOMNICA RADULESCU

Train to Trieste

Black Sea Twilight

Country of Red Azaleas

A NOVEL

Domnica Radulescu

TWELVE

NEW YORK BOSTON

The excerpt from "heart heart heart" by Stella Vinitchi Radulescu is reprinted from *I Scrape the Window of Nothingness: New & Selected Poems* (Orison Books, 2015), copyright © 2015 by Stella Vinitchi Radulescu, with permission of Orison Books, Inc.

Twelve
Hachette Book Group
1290 Avenue of the Americas
New York, NY 10104

www.HachetteBookGroup.com

Printed in the United States of America

RRD-C

First Edition: April 2016
10 9 8 7 6 5 4 3 2 1

Twelve is an imprint of Grand Central Publishing.
The Twelve name and logo are trademarks of Hachette Book Group, Inc.

The Hachette Speakers Bureau provides a wide range of authors for speaking events. To find out more, go to www.hachettespeakersbureau.com or call (866) 376-6591.

Library of Congress Cataloging-in-Publication Data

Names: Radulescu, Domnica, 1961- author.
Title: Country of red azaleas / Domnica Radulescu.
Description: First edition. | New York : Twelve, 2016.
Identifiers: LCCN 2015044687 | ISBN 9781455590421 (hardcover) | ISBN 9781478964483 (audio download) | ISBN 9781455590438 (ebook)
Subjects: LCSH: Female friendship—Fiction. | Self-realization in women—Fiction. | BISAC: FICTION / Literary. | FICTION / Contemporary women. | FICTION / Coming of Age.
Classification: LCC PS3618.A358 C68 2016 | DDC 813/ .6—dc23 LC record available at http://lccn.loc.gov/2015044687

For my sons: Alexander and Nicholas

Motto

"I remember
the town, the street,
something called past
better than the unbleached sun,

the broken sounds
heart
heart
heart

sit down angel, I am desperately alive."

From "heart, heart, heart"
by Stella Vinitchi Radulescu

Sarajevo, My Love

1980–1985

I started out in life under a Communist leader and a Hollywood name. I was named Lara, like the heroine from the story of *Doctor Zhivago.* "It's going to open doors and conversations for her when she grows up, darling Petar," my mother was heard telling my father after my birth. "Beloved Anica, it will be a burden carrying the name of a famous heroine," my father was reported having told my mother in return. My parents always called each other sugary names and diminutives even when they were having fierce arguments. "It will distract people from the person she really is and always force comparisons. Do you know anyone called Cleopatra, my precious love?" "As a matter of fact I do, darling Petka," my mother apparently answered unfazed. "The daughter of my boss." "Exactly my point, my precious dove, and she is the strangest girl I've ever known. She has a snake for a pet." "That's because Cleopatra is the wrong name to

give. Lara is perfect for our little jewel—just look at her!"
And the story goes that the second my father took a look at
my scrunched-up face from a thirty-hour delivery with three
blond hairs stuck to my round skull, he melted and called me
Lara and Larinka.

Those comparisons would indeed disadvantage me, for
who could compare herself to that vision of luminous beauty,
grace, and quivering passion that was Lara from *Doctor
Zhivago*? Even in Communist Yugoslavia, people knew the
story of *Doctor Zhivago* better from the mega Hollywood hit
with Julie Christie and Omar Sharif than from the original
novel by the Russian author Boris Pasternak. My father's vote
of no-confidence of course added to my onomastic embarrassment once I was old enough to hear and process for the
millionth time the story of how I ended up being called Lara
Kulicz. Why hadn't my father said something like: "This girl
will shine and outshine all the Laras in the world," or: "She
will be smarter and more beautiful than that Lara from the
movie." My father was a realist and my mother was a hopeless sentimental who cried even at the sound of the Communist tunes that were played whenever President Tito made his
appearance in some public place, a factory, a school, or on
television. Once I saw the fateful movie myself, at the fragile age of seven, Julie Christie's Lara filled my dreams and
nightmares alike. Not only did I want to look and act like
Lara, but I wanted Lara to look and act just like me. I didn't
just want Hollywood stars to be branded on my physique

and psyche forever but I fiercely wanted to brand myself onto Hollywood. I wanted Vivien Leigh, Marilyn Monroe, or Elizabeth Taylor to be me, Lara Kulicz, as revenge for my having to own for the rest of my life the character name that a stunning Hollywood star carried in one of her shiniest roles. I wanted to impose my grayish-blue eyes onto the famous mauve eyes of Elizabeth Taylor and my thin ash-blond hair onto the undulating golden waves of Julie Christie. In the Yugoslavia of my youth and in our family, Hollywood was more important than the Communist Party. It was our refuge and our guilty delight that made up for some of the boredom of the uniforms we had to wear, the lack of pretty clothes, the monotonous sound of the Party language we heard in school. However, unlike the surrounding Communist countries, we had the special fortune that our own President Tito was in love with Western movies and saw himself as a rugged leftist version of John Wayne who had fought the Nazis instead of the Apache Indians. His love of movies drove him to create the mega film studios Avala in the middle of Belgrade in a utopian hope that someday they would match Hollywood. In that hope, he even had Richard Burton play him, Josip Broz Tito, as a war hero valiantly standing up to the Nazi invasion in *The Battle of Sutjeska*. The educated Yugoslavs like my family, however, scoffed at domestic movies and greedily swallowed the real Hollywood features with all their irresistible glamour and magnetic stars. I didn't care either way but was guided by my parents into the cult of American movies from the age when I should have been rolling hula hoops with the neighborhood children.

The day I was made a pioneer and had to wear the red scarf and the navy-blue hat called Titovka from the name of the president of our country himself was also the day when my parents took me to their friend who worked at the Kinoteka, the special movie theater in Belgrade that showed classic foreign movies, and asked him to give us a private showing of the *Doctor Zhivago* movie. We went late after the theater closed down and my father's friend gave us indeed a private showing of that mythic movie that freaked the hell out of me. After the movie my father's friend and my parents had the greatest time comparing Lara from the movie with my own seven-year-old puzzled self and calling me all the nicknames and diminutives derived from that cursed name—Laricka, Larinka, Lari, Larika—until I would have rather been called Bob or Josip instead of the fated Lara. At the end of that day I decided that having become a pioneer had been a more cheerful experience than seeing the movie *Doctor Zhivago* at a private showing with my mother sobbing hysterically through most of it, and my father whistling the "farewell my love" tune all the way home.

The age of seven was also when I fell in love with Marija, "the girl from Sarajevo." Her parents had moved to Belgrade because her father was a flute player and had gotten a position in the Belgrade philharmonic. Her first day of classes, she stood in the doorway with a mischievous smile and dark waves of hair that fell smoothly onto her shoulders. She was both self-assured and dreamy. I was stunned by her beauty, and the second I saw her I wanted nothing more than to be friends with her for life. I felt that as long as Marija was in my life, everything was going to be all right. I would even get over my name hang-up if she were the one to pronounce it. I went straight to her and asked her to share my school bench with me. I was always seated by myself because the teachers said I disrupted my desk mates with my constant talking. But I was not going to let go of Marija. She looked straight at me with a clear smile and followed me to my desk as if it was the most obvious thing in the universe: that we were going to be desk mates and friends for life. She carried almond sesame and honey desserts in her backpack and little sparkling trinkets, some jewelry, some simply for the fun of the jingle and the sparkle. She put some on our desk and suddenly we were no longer in the drab classroom with the picture of President Tito hanging on the wall in front of us, but in an enchanted castle in Persia or Morocco, somewhere with orange trees, sparkling beaches, and flashy belly dancers. One day she pulled out of her backpack a miniature pair of Turkish toy slippers made from fake gold and red velvet. Whenever the lesson became too boring, Marija told me to take one slipper on my pinkie; she would put the other one on her pinkie, and we imagined we flew away to an enchanted place in Persia. There were suspended gardens and fountains sprinkling crystal-clear water and we were belly dancing. She directed our fantasies and I went along.

We made the most feared team in the school at everything: reciting patriotic poetry with an undercurrent of irony, playing volleyball in the school yard, getting ahead of everybody in the cafeteria line to get the fresh slices of bread before the stale bread was brought in surreptitiously by the kitchen workers, cheating on math tests, getting away with making faces behind the teachers' backs, being first at reading and writing contests. We were always both first. We didn't want to use the expression *a tie*, but we always said: "We are both first." The only area where Marija was the real first was running. Until she came into the school, I thought I was the fastest runner around. At first Marija let me think so for a while, until one day in physical education class when she took off like a flash on the track field in our school yard and my mouth opened wide in awe. She was faster than any of the boys and girls and even faster than the teacher herself. Her hair opened up like a set of wings when she ran and it made you think she might have been a creature of a different kind, supernatural or magical, a witch of sorts. At least I thought so all through our school years.

When Marija and I learned about the process of parthenogenesis in our biology class we were ecstatic: Some birds, reptiles, amphibians, and even bees could reproduce through asexual reproduction, by a process of cell division that did not involve the sexual act between a male and a female. That meant, said Marija stuffing her face with one of her delicious honey almond desserts and giggling at the same time, that she and I could have children together without needing a man. All we needed was the love and willpower to divide our own cells and produce offspring. If frogs could do it, so could we, said Marija triumphantly. We were nine years old and everything was possible, producing children through asexual reproduction, battling villains with our sleek shiny swords, and living in a tiny castle at the very top of a snowy mountain somewhere in a place called the Wild West.

We were inseparable. We cried at the end of school on Saturday because it meant we wouldn't see each other until Monday. And when she first invited me to her apartment on a Sunday afternoon one April after Easter, I thought I must have entered the gates of heaven through some unheard-of miracle. Her apartment smelled divine, like the desserts she always brought to school and shared with me alone. Their apartment was in the Dorćol area near the Belgrade Fortress at the confluence of the Sava and Danube Rivers, near open parks and old ruins. It seemed like a different city, a different Belgrade to me, with its old elegant residential streets compared with the drab area near the Square of the Republic where we lived in a grey modern building, made of cement blocks, cold steel, and clamoring glass. Her father's flute music rose in such delicate melodic trills that it made you want to slide out of your body and glide through the open window and into the blue ether. Her mother moved around the house effortlessly wearing a brown velvet dress and offered us orange preserves. For some reason nothing seemed polluted and drab any longer, and the world suddenly had a tangy delicious taste.

Marija fed my family-induced obsession with Hollywood movies and stars, only in her own humorous and enveloping way that made you want to follow her to the end of the earth. Her parents were able to miraculously obtain videotapes of classic foreign movies that sometimes we all watched sitting on the edge of the bed in her parents' bedroom where the small black-and-white TV and the enormous video machine were placed. Next to Marija I loved absorbing the teary-eyed shimmering faces of Julie Christie, Katharine Hepburn, Marilyn Monroe, or Vivien Leigh to the point where it was me, Lara Kulicz, on the screen being embraced or kissed passionately by Clark Gable, Alan Bates, or Cary Grant. Marija and I held hands throughout the movie and smiled at each other at all the romantic scenes. Sometimes after the movie was over, if it was too late and if it was a Saturday night, her parents would invite me to stay over. Staying over at Marija's and sleeping in the same bed with her was another delicious slice of heaven. Marija's mother made the bed for us, tucked us in, and kissed us both good night as if we were both her beloved daughters. Sometimes Marija and I tried to kiss each other like we had seen the actors in the movie do it. Marija's lips were velvety and tasted bittersweet like the desserts her mother made. We fell asleep holding hands and I traveled to colorful sugary lands where Clark Gable was the president of our country and the First Lady was none other than Marilyn Monroe. The president and his wife lived in the Beli Dvor, which was where President Tito normally resided, but now it was occupied by Clark Gable and Marilyn Monroe. Marija and I were ladies-in-waiting for the First Lady and we wore poufy magic dresses with hoops that swirled and swished and that even made us swoop over the marble stairways and banisters of the palace like weightless balloons. In the morning Marija and I shared our dreams. Hers were always about chases and fights. She would save me from pirates and gangsters and Apache Indians while riding a wild stallion and swishing above her head a glittering saber that shone and sparkled in the setting sun and blinded all the enemies into submission. She carried me off on her stallion and we rode into the sunset.

In the summer she invited me to her grandparents' house in Sarajevo, together with my younger sister, Biljana. I didn't really want my sister to come along because that meant I had to share Marija and babysit Biljana and worry about her stupid pranks and whims. But it was the only way my parents were going to let me spend part of the summer in Sarajevo. My parents were high on sisterly love and wanted us to be together all the time, because "when we are dead and gone, you'll have each other," they always said. I didn't know why I had to drag my sister with me everywhere I went in preparation for the times when my parents were going to be dead and gone, but I decided I was going to go along with anything, just to be able to spend the summer with Marija in Sarajevo at her grandparents' house.

Sarajevo was an enchanted garden that shimmered and sang. With Marija in Sarajevo I fell inside a fairy tale, the movie that hadn't yet been made, the Balkan-Hollywood film with Marija and me as the costars. The creamy white mosques with the half-moon on their towers looked like wedding cakes as we chased each other in and out of their coquettish gardens until a bearded man disturbed from his prayers would come after us and threaten us with bodily harm like a scary ogre. The Ferhadija mosque in particular with the honeyed glow of its illuminations at dusk sparked in my mind fantastical images in dreamy pastels. In the old center the copper pots glinted with reddish sparks in the sun, and red azaleas and geraniums cascaded from balconies and fences everywhere. Marija was a brave and knowledgeable captain who knew her way around every back alley and knew more people than there were letters in the alphabet. Here is the bread store of Mr. Novic, the fat man with a huge mole on his nose, here is the big house of Mrs. Drakulic the crazy widow who feeds the pigeons in the big square, here is the coffee shop of Mr. and Mrs. Moravic who could never have children and always gave coffee beans soaked in honey to children who stopped by. "Let's go in and see." The Sarajevo around the times of the Winter Olympic Games seemed to have escaped the Communist rules and flags; everything was dripping with red azaleas, honey, coffee, and apricots, and the silks in the store windows undulated lusciously. Sarajevo of those years was a delicious secret nestled in the cradle of the heavy wooded Dinaric Alps. The bus that had taken us into the city seemed to be hanging on a hairpin road flirting with the rocky edges on one side and the dizzying drop on the other. We flew recklessly on the road, but I didn't care, Marija made everything look both magical and safe. Even dangerous things felt safe next to Marija, little more than a suspenseful game; you had the thrill, but nothing bad ever happened. You didn't fall over the immense drop at the edge of the road, you weren't beaten up by the angry man in the mosque. You just kept on playing and playing until twilight enveloped you.

Our favorite game was stealing fruit from the open markets in town and running away as fast as we could. On some days Marija was Robin Hood and Biljana and I were her army of thieves. Marija would whistle or wink and we would all rush toward the stands with apricots, pears, or cherries and pick as many as we could while on the run. The vendors yelled after us but before they had a chance to come after us, we were already on a different street, in a back alley, devouring our spoils. Stolen fruit tasted delicious. In true Robin Hood spirit, we gave some to the Gypsy children in the street who were adding them to their own stolen foods of the day. All the tartness and sweetness in the world was gathered in

DOMNICA RADULESCU

our puckered mouths as we crouched against the stone wall of a hidden house in an alley in Sarajevo. We were our own little Yugoslav girl movie and had yet to be discovered by the real moviemakers in America. With Marija I often had the feeling I was in a magical yet very important reality that was going to one day become immortalized on screens all over the world. At the end of the day, we ran back to Marija's grandparents, elated and queasy from all the fruit.

Marija always ran ahead of us like a firebird. We raced up the hill without stopping. She would run faster than Biljana and me with her raven-black hair that moved in waves and she never stopped until she reached her grandparents' house. Biljana who had comparably rich waves of curly red hair came in second, and I was always last. My best friend and sister were the striking Amazons I was never going to be.

"Wait for me, Marija! I'm tired and thirsty!"

"Come on, Lara, give it another push, you can do it," Marija always said.

"Yes, Lara, run faster!" my sister Biljana would add.

Marija would stop for a second to catch her breath, tidy her dress, and grab my hand. She was a vision of unparalleled beauty as we stood on the hill above her native Sarajevo, in front of the white stone house with the red azaleas in the window, her face flushed from the run, her green eyes sparkling like an emerald fire, her hair a dark wavy crown framing her face. But mostly it was the deep raspy voice and laugh that gave me a jolt of joy and melancholy as she would tell me to go in and not tell her grandparents we had been stealing apricots from the neighbors' yards and the city markets. Biljana danced her way into the house behind Marija and supported all of Marija's lies and stories, which she spilled out with unbridled passion and trickles of irrepressible laughter. Then Biljana would start dancing for Marija's grandparents and go through all the ballet poses she had learned in ballet class as they would both go "ooh" and "aah" from their worn-out peachy velvet armchairs, setting their rimmed glasses straighter on their noses. I was in the shadows, panting and embarrassed for something I hadn't done.

"Here is fruit from the garden, have some, girls. You must be thirsty after all that running around," Marija's grandmother Farah would say and tidy the colored scarf she always wore on her head, tied underneath her chin like a babushka. Marija and Biljana would burst out laughing because our stomachs were already full to the limit with the apricots, cherries, and gooseberries that we had stolen and eaten from every garden in that neighborhood facing the Muslim cemetery with its white stone columns and tombs. The house stood on a slanted narrow street like many on the hilly neighborhoods of Sarajevo, and I invariably experienced a sense of joy at the sight of the overlapping red tile roofs and the entanglements of fences and gardens that led to the house. My embarrassment knew no bounds once I was confronted with Farah's hospitality. I was the only one who actually went ahead and had more apricots and more watermelon and cherries from

Farah's fruit bowl, only to become miserably sick in the next half hour. Marija and Biljana laughed in big gulps at my stoic fruit gorging and then kissed and tickled me. Farah would scold them and ask them to stop tormenting "the poor girl." I loved Farah and my heart always melted with gratitude and self-pity every time I heard her call me "poor girl." That was the best vindication from the shame of always lagging behind Marija and Biljana, of being too scared to steal as much fruit as they did, even though I still ate just as much only to keep up with them.

Farah smelled like cinnamon and something else sweet and spicy that I could never figure out. I buried my head in her bosom when she hugged me and I wanted to be there for a long time smelling her and being called "poor girl." To me that sounded almost like "beautiful girl with beautiful curls." Kemal would get up from his chair with a slight bend of his back and walk across the room to look out the window and check on the sky and the weather. Then he took his pipe from the little table next to the window and smoked it, producing a fragrance that was to me at least as delicious as Farah's spicy sweet smell. It never smelled like that in my parents' apartment in Belgrade, it always smelled sour and heavy, like burnt cabbage, and then sometimes my mother's heavy perfume got mixed in with the smells coming from the kitchen making the air even heavier to breathe. I always felt our Belgrade apartment was a temporary thing, something we would get over and move to our "real" habitation, some kind of a

utopian spacious and luminous apartment in Sarajevo over-
looking rolling hills, tile roofs and white stone houses.

My return to Belgrade and to my parents' apartment was
wrought with a wrenching sense of yearning and a growing
repulsion for the smells in our kitchen, the sounds of people
fighting in the apartment next door, or of the folkloric music
that our other neighbor felt compelled to play at its highest
volume, filling me with a lifelong dislike of traditional Serbian
music. The only thing worse than that was when my parents
played the music from *Doctor Zhivago* on their reel-to-reel
tape player for the millionth time, smiling knowingly and
sometimes dancing with each other and shuffling their feet
on the kitchen linoleum. I fantasized of Marija and me gal-
loping across velvety fields sprinkled with blood-red poppies,
the sight of snowcapped mountains looming in the distance,
and a small castle built just for us out of white stone and red
tiles on the exact top of the highest peak. At the height of my
fantasy my mother would barge into my room to remind me
to do my homework or write the letter to President Tito that
we were supposed to write in our civic education class. Or
my sister would burst in practicing her pointe walking and
pirouettes to my mother's great amazement and admiration.
At least one of us was always admired by our parents and it
wasn't me. Biljana was going to ballet school and talked of
little else but becoming the greatest dancer of the century.
My mother was in awe at every one of her turns and agreed
that one day she would become the Serbian Ginger Rogers.

I didn't care as long as I was admired by Marija. We wrote to each other daily letters in which we complained about the inanity of our school and the stupidity of our teachers and analyzed various characters from the films we had seen together the previous summer. Sometimes we mailed them to each other and at other times we exchanged them in school, or left them on each other's side of the bench like a secret and sacred ritual. In our letters we counted the days and the weeks that were left until our next vacation when I would go back to Sarajevo and when life would start all over again in the cinnamon and cumin smells of Kemal and Farah's kitchen and in the wild races for tart fruit from the orchards and gardens on the sloping alleys of my beloved city.

All throughout my college years in Belgrade, throughout my later years on a different continent, throughout the years of the war and after the war, the image of us racing through the back alleys of Sarajevo with our mouths puckered from stolen fruit, our hearts booming out of our chests, the cupolas of the mosques glistening in the sunset, and the hills of Sarajevo sprinkled with white houses and red azalea bushes like a huge colorful and throbbing nest of life was always with me as a reminder that I had once held a corner of heaven in my hands. Even the afternoon, years later, when I saw Marija emerge from her red Corvette convertible, strangely and disturbingly beautiful, completely changed and yet still Marija, proud and desperate, touched by an indelible sorrow in front of the white hotel inundated in red azaleas on a sunny and quiet Los Angeles side street, that image of us running in the Sarajevo of my childhood flashed through my mind with dizzying vividness. It wasn't like a memory but more like a persistent clip of our past that refused to be erased and that encrusted itself stubbornly into our present. It was a sliver of life that kept rolling through the years and the many wrecks of our lives. That sliver that I carried with me throughout the years emerged in my conscience at unexpected moments with clusters of scarlet flowers and a taste of apricots that shifted the past into the present.

Belgrade Revolutions

1989–1992

In college, Marija studied world poetry, anthropology, politics, art, everything. She wore the darkest eyeliner in Belgrade around her green eyes, and big shiny jewelry. Not a lot of jewelry, just one striking pendant or a pair of long earrings, but it always looked like she gave new meaning and color to the piece of rock or metal wrapped around her neck or dangling from her ears. On some days she looked like an Indian deity or like Cleopatra. I had never stopped being in awe of her. When we were at the University of Belgrade in the late eighties and early nineties we competed with each other in every domain and even dated the same man for a while. I wasn't half as versatile as Marija at juggling different fields, disciplines, and brooding lovers but I shone at the social sciences and became a better runner than I had ever been in my childhood. In the fall of 1989 when Communism fell throughout Eastern Europe and our country was breaking at the seams and dividing itself into its many ethnic constituencies, Marija and I both shaved our heads as a sign of protest. We wanted to believe that the object of our protest was Serbia's growing nationalism against Albanians, Bosnians, Croats, everybody who was not Serbian Christian and sought their independence, but truly we just wanted to shave our heads and get attention in the restless atmosphere that was bubbling around us in those years. While everybody around us was deploring the breaking of the former "mother Yugoslavia," Marija and I cheered for the dissenting regions and provinces that claimed their independence and asked for separation from that utopian national mother. Tito's Socialist Federal Republic of Yugoslavia had been an untenable utopia of tying a nationalist ribbon around six different little nationalities and countries all crowded under the same flag and Party. Now they all squirmed and wrestled for their independence.

While our neighbors throughout Eastern Europe were ablaze in their anti-Communist fervor and avid to play with Western values, commodities, and democracies, our country, once the freest and most liberal of those that had been placed under Soviet influence after World War II, was now relying on the League of Communists of Yugoslavia. The speeches of the new Serbian leader Slobodan Milosevic and his supporters, with their "Rally of Truth," made us sick with fury and our heads glowingly bald. We were part of an anti-nationalist minority at the university, as most Serbs supported the unity of the former Yugoslavia at all costs and thought Albanians were all "traitors." Since the days of our fruit thieving Marija and I had always been on the side of so-called traitors: "traitors" to Communism, "traitors" to the slogans of "brotherhood and unity," "traitors" to the notion of a "Greater Serbia." We smoked foreign cigarettes, wore dark eyeliner, talked about postmodernism and feminism, listened to Dire Straits, watched American movies, and dated Milko Dubravic, a thin, feminine-looking student of philosophy who was made fun of by his more masculine Serbian colleagues because they all thought he was homosexual. This worked out well for Marija and me, because nobody imagined that Milko would actually have not one but two female lovers and that the two weirdest women in the university, with bald heads, freaky eyeliner, and secessionist ideas, were exactly those two lovers.

Marija and I shared Milko in the most sisterly manner possible, without jealousy or rivalry, and called him "our brother." We took turns spending the wee hours of the morning in Marija's one-room apartment near the university and gorged on Swiss chocolates and Milko's creamy body. We called the Milko period our "white velvet Revolution," inspired by Czechoslovakia's nonviolent anti-Communist revolution called the Velvet Revolution, because Milko's body was so white and quite velvety to the touch and it was sort of radical to share the same man with such ease and comfort. Since Marija's parents were mercifully back in Sarajevo at the time of our college revolutions, they didn't have the fortune of seeing us in our bald countercultural glory. My parents, on the other hand, expressed profound signs of embarrassment, shame, and revolt all in alternating order whenever Marija and I visited them in the same three-room apartment that smelled like a vicious mixture of burnt cabbage and heavy Russian perfume. If a neighbor happened to be close by when my parents, Marija, and I entered the building or came out on the balcony, my father started talking about the weather, the most recent news, the fall of the Berlin Wall, or the World Cup to draw their attention away from us. My mother became meek and embarrassed and acted in a sickeningly apologetic way, as if we had just been released from the local asylum and were still in some kind of recovery or as if she had no idea how those two strange-looking women ever landed in her apartment. Seeing the painful ways in which my parents dealt with my rebellious period, I stopped going home for a while and spent most of my days and nights with Marija, Milko, and the other handful of students of politics or philosophy who tried to be either Goths or simply off the mainstream of the patriotic Serbian youth populating our university.

Marija wrote a brand of pornographic philosophical poetry that she pasted on the walls of the university hallways as another sign of protest. I thought her poetry was stunning, like the French surrealist poems, raw and disturbing, mixing body parts with political concepts and foods. She called it postmodern. Whenever we found ourselves in the most brooding and darkest of moods, out of sync with our

surroundings, or whenever we became bored with our collection of Hollywood movies, poems, postmodern theory,
and politics, Marija would pull out of her bag her leather-
bound edition of Dante's *Inferno*. We would jump into one
of the Infernal circles at random, read it out loud, and then
discuss at length the atrociousness of the punishment, which
was our favorite and which we would have preferred in case
we did happen to fall into a situation like one of those that
Dante's souls found themselves: Would we choose the howling winds that pushed the lustful mercilessly from place to
place like Francesca da Rimini forever tied to her adulterous lover Paolo Malatesta or the deep muddy swamps of the
sullen and keep gurgling in thick dark waters for eternity?
Would we have preferred running on burning sands like the
blasphemers and the sodomites or having our heads stuck
inside burning tombs like the heretics; would we have chosen
Ulysses's cloak of fire or the frozen place of the traitors of kin
whose tears froze in their eyes before even having the chance
to be fully formed? Marija always chose the waters and the
ice, I chose the fires and the burning sands. She said it was
because of our natures, we each chose the opposite of what we
were. That meant that I was ice and Marija was fire and there-
fore we each chose the opposite element. The punishment of
the fortune-tellers and the diviners whose heads had been
turned around so that they looked down at their asses always
made us laugh for hours. Still, our favorite was the punishment of the suicides, who had all been turned into trees that

bled if you broke off a twig. "I would commit suicide just to get that punishment after death, to become a bleeding tree," Marija would say. And then I would see her face scrunch in mad laughter and she would say: "A good thing it is we don't believe in the afterlife!" And then she would add with wicked irony: "Maybe the circle for sinners like us hasn't yet been invented: lust, treason of country, blasphemy... Our circle would have to contain fire and ice in simultaneity with one another," she would conclude proudly.

Marija also had very definite ideas about the political confusion in our country, which in her view was not a random confusion but a very deliberate one to distract people from what was "really going on." She said that the new Communism of Milosevic was a fascist Communism, which indeed was an oxymoron, yet it wasn't like the old idealist Communism of Josip Broz Tito or the one of the chairmen of the presidency in the post-Tito period or even like the old-fashioned Soviet Communism. The nationalist and religious part was what made it fascist, she said in between cigarettes and shots of vodka late at night in a café in the old cobblestone area of Belgrade, the famous Skadarljia. Finally, we had gotten to the point of being nostalgic for the good old days of "real Communism," she added laughing wholeheartedly, her eyes sparkling. We spent Saturday nights in a café, just the two of us, no Milko and no other underground elements from the university. We exchanged notes on Milko's lovemaking abilities and laughed ourselves to death until one evening when

Marija literally fell under the table because she was laughing so hard. The waiter had to come and ask us to leave because he thought we were too drunk to be in the café. Marija came back up from underneath the table with her eyes shining and her face dead serious and said they never threw out the men who got drunk to a pulp there every night and then pissed against the telephone poles across the street. The waiter left mumbling the words "goddamn bitches," and Marija went ahead and ordered another set of shots from the next waiter. Marija had other lovers, and I only had Milko, so her notes were always longer. She had so many points of reference with which to compare Milko, while my points of reference were scarce and not much to brag about. Marija never fell in love with any one single man. She just glided through love affairs with short periods of infatuation after which she invariably became bored. "There's got to be something better for me out there in this whole fucking world," she would say casually, as if it didn't really matter much. Strangely, she seemed more enamored of the feminine Milko than she had been of any of her dark-haired brooding knights from the different disciplines and departments of our university. Maybe it was because she and I shared Milko and that seemed to excite Marija more than just the simple affairs with the other men. It brought us closer together; she would say, "It's the closest two women can ever be together, sharing the same man." She dragged from her cigarette and through the smoke her eyes seemed teary and languorous as they smiled at me.

During those years the old section of Belgrade was throbbing with Serbian music, accordion and fiddle, mostly for Western tourists eager to find out what that whole region behind the so-called Iron Curtain was all about: Were we really human, were we primitive or Old World sophisticated, did all the women wear "babushkas" on their heads and the men exude that Old World masculine charm as they gallantly kissed a woman's hand? The Serbian musicians gave them what they wanted: hot-paced music and wide flirtatious smiles sprinkled with loud "oopas" and impertinent winks to the women. French women in particular couldn't get enough of that stuff and often they got up and danced in the middle of the restaurant some kind of imagined Serbian or Gypsy dance they must have seen in a Kusturica movie. Marija sometimes spoke to the tourists, seeming to know all their languages. French, English, Italian, German, glided off her tongue effortlessly.

One Saturday at the very beginning of April 1992, an American woman by the name of Sally Bryant sat down next to us and Marija started talking to her as if she had known her forever. My English was pretty good, too, so I joined in the conversation. The three of us got entangled in endless debates about nationalism, racism, the role of women in the world's governments and leadership, violence and political activism. The American psychologist Sally had a certain smoothness and intellectual sharpness about her that both Marija and I fell immediately in love with. She had come to Serbia to

COUNTRY OF RED AZALEAS

see her boyfriend. He had told her he was single and eagerly waiting for her to visit him at his summer house in the country, yet when she got to Belgrade he said he first had to square out his vacation plans with his wife and kids. Marija said that was the norm for many of "our men" to have a wife and lovers, "no big deal," she laughed sarcastically. "You should feel flattered, he wanted to go on vacation with you." Sally didn't seem particularly upset about the boyfriend episode and said it turned out to be a great experience anyway: "I got to meet so many interesting people, and now the two of you. I have the feeling this is the beginning of a beautiful friendship," she said with a quick laugh, quoting the last line from the movie *Casablanca*, which left both Marija and me speechless for a few moments, as that happened to be our favorite American movie. She lived in California, in Santa Barbara, and worked with victims of sexual and domestic violence. Santa Barbara sounded like the planet heaven. "What are the rates of sexual and domestic violence in your country?" she asked us as if we were up for an interview. Marija and I looked at each other with a grin. "From our having grown up in this blessed country of ours," Marija said between shots of vodka. "We know that indeed some men beat and rape and generally abuse their wives and children but not much is done about it, there are no shelters for the women, and the law doesn't offer the proper protection to the victims of such abuse. It's just how things are around here, the fucking culture, the macho-masculinist-nationalist, patriarchal bullshit society," Marija blurted out after her fifth shot of vodka. Then Sally wanted to know about the conflicts starting to emerge among Albanians and Serbians, Croats, Bosnians, what did we think about it? "We think it's all fucking bullshit nationalist crap, that's what we think about it," we said in an uproar of laughter around two in the morning after even more shots of vodka than we could remember. Sally gave both of us her business card when we parted at three in the morning and told us to look her up if we ever came to California. She asked for our addresses and phone numbers in case she came back to Belgrade. We staggered out of the restaurant and into the cobblestone street laughing loudly and kissing each other good-bye. An air of ease and lightness trailed after Sally as she silently disappeared into the Belgrade night. Marija and I looked at each other puzzled, wondering whether we shouldn't have held on to Sally, asked her to come stay with us at one of our studio apartments, gotten to know her better, developed a lasting relationship with that American from California who didn't seem to mind having come all the way to Belgrade only to be heartbroken and deceived. In our early-morning drunken stupor we elaborated out loud on visions of the two of us visiting Sally in Santa Barbara, which was close to Los Angeles, and being discovered by a talent and beauty scout from Hollywood who was interested in stories from the "newly freed" Eastern European states. We would become overnight stars, our stories and our personae the rave in Hollywood; we would make millions, order the assassination of Milosevic and all the nationalist pigs who wanted to start a war, and bring everlasting peace and independence for Bosnia, Croatia, Slovenia, Kosovo, everybody. We became international heroines and revolutionaries and the title characters of our own show that was broadcast all over the world and even in our country, dubbed from English into Serbian: Lara and Marija—our faces hanging on huge billboards above American highways and on small posters in Belgrade taverns.

That night Marija and I slept in her room in the same bed. The forsythias were in bloom and it smelled like jasmine. The air that came through the half-open window felt fresh and hopeful. *Who could start a war on a beautiful fragrant spring day?* I thought as I was coming out of my inebriation. In the morning we had a vague memory of the American Sally and were surprised to each find her card in our pockets. That morning Marija made the strongest coffee I had ever tasted to jolt us out of our hangover and when she turned on the radio in her tiny kitchen we found out the war had started. Sarajevo was under siege. Two women had been killed by snipers in the street—the first victims of the war. Marija was beside herself, she cursed at everybody and even got short with me when I told her there was nothing she could do right now. That was not something Marija could stand hearing: that there was nothing she could do. She wished she were there in Sarajevo taking part in the peace march with the other tens of thousands of Bosnians; she worried about her parents and grandparents and her native Sarajevo and about the world in general. Marija was the only person I knew who literally suffered deeply about the world and its miseries, who screamed in pain whenever she heard of atrocities and violence across the globe. Then she would start a political group, a literary circle, a discussion session, write letters to the student newspapers and to every paper in town, start chains of letters to help victims of earthquakes or of genocides, Rwandan women or Palestinian children. Her writing flared in quick colorful but precise sentences that woke you up from whatever state of moral turpitude you might have found yourself in on that particular day. When the news on one radio station referred to the Serbian armies claiming their rights to the territories of Bosnia-Herzegovina, Marija and I stared at each other: She and I were now part of enemy ethnic groups. It was the first time ever in our lives that we thought of each other as part of two separate ethnic identities. We had never even considered our Serbianness or Bosnianness other than she was born in Sarajevo and I was born in Belgrade. Struggling with our excruciating hangovers that morning, putting on makeup in the tiny mirror hanging above the sink in the half bathroom of her apartment and trying to cover up the deathly-looking circles around our eyes, Marija and I burst into tears and held each other for a long time. Our makeup ran down our faces, making us look even scarier, and we vowed we would never let any ethnic, political, nationalistic, or ideological powers come between us. "You know what? I am Bosnian, too, Marija, and I will forever be Bosnian, for as long as your people, that is our people, are under attack," I said between sobs. "We shouldn't even think in terms of our people or their people, that is part of the problem. You know what?" she said wiping her tears with the back of her hand. "I'm fucking American, that's what I am." We laughed and I said I was "fucking American, too," and we would eventually join Sally in her Santa Barbara Pacific heaven one day. Only now there was work to be done, Marija said. She was going to Sarajevo soon, immediately after exams. She wanted to get her diploma and work as a journalist in Sarajevo. "I would move with you to Sarajevo in a minute, Marija," I said breathlessly. "No, you can't, you need to stay here and act against the war from the inside," she said as if she was already planning an antiwar underground movement. Although that statement left me aghast with confusion, for I had no idea how I was supposed to work from the inside, I told her that yes, I would do just that, stay in Belgrade and engage in some kind of antiwar activism.

That night and the nights that followed, Marija and I did the rounds of the best-known student hangout places, taverns and seedy cafés, distributed antiwar leaflets, and engaged in fierce debates with our compatriots over the state of our country, region, and people. As I watched Marija unfold in all her physical and intellectual brilliance I thought she could be the president of Serbia, Bosnia, of the whole world. Why did we just have fat, old, obtuse, fanatic, and not very smart presidents in that wretched world of ours, for centuries? I thought that even war was really fun next to Marija. So apparently did hundreds of Serbian, Croat, Bosnian men who swarmed around her and brought her one drink after another even when they totally disagreed with her political views. Milko accompanied us at some of those political drinking bouts around Belgrade and faithfully stood by us, until one evening when a stout Serbian patriot and soccer player called him a faggot and punched him in the face. He fell on the floor unconscious in a puddle of his own blood. Marija and I had to drag him out of the tavern at midnight, and had him transported to the nearest hospital. We stayed with Milko until we were certain he was all right and walked to my parents' apartment.

Surprisingly my parents were genuinely happy to see us even at that ungodly hour of the night, and made no comment about our disheveled appearance, alcohol stench, and clothes stained with blood from Milko's injuries. My mother quickly made the bed in my old room and asked if she needed to pump the inflatable bed or if we were fine sharing my bed. If only my mother had known we were sharing not just one bed but the same lover, I thought. Marija smiled and I knew she thought the same thing. Biljana came out of her room curious about what was going on and eager to tell us about the dance show she had been cast in at the high school—she was going to be Maria in *West Side Story* and twirled around the apartment singing "I feel pretty, oh so pretty." Who said we weren't Westernized in old mother Yugoslavia? Biljana was wearing as always bunches of ribbons in her hair and scarves not just around her neck but also on her thighs and waist; she was a flowing nymph with irrepressible red hair flying in all directions. Biljana and Marija always got into friendly arguments the second they saw each other in a way that seemed sisterly and familiar. Marija made fun of the overly romantic tale in *West Side Story* and Biljana came right back telling her that was overbearing feminist crap, it was a beautiful story, it was the Romeo and Juliet story after all, what was wrong with Marija, why was she always so bitter about everything that involved romantic love? Marija laughed and said joyously: "I just don't believe in romantic love, it's beautiful in the movies, but in reality it is overrated and hardly ever lasts, but I'm sure you are going to shine in your role as Maria. Could you get me a ticket to the show, Billjie?" While my mother was preparing one of her unpleasant-smelling meals for us in the kitchen, the three of us chatted and teased each other and felt like three sisters. For that short period the war that had just started seemed inexistent, impossible, and immaterial. Only our girlish chatter mattered.

My father came into the room looking exhausted and unwell. Something heavy fell amid us like a thud: the news of the war. He had been asked to retire from his position as diplomat at the Greek embassy because he had expressed antiwar sentiments at work. Apparently the Serbians were interfering with the affairs of the Greeks and the latter gave in just to avoid any trouble. The news was shocking to me but apparently not so shocking for Marija. She was expecting all that.

My mother came in with a questionable-looking mixture-pudding of sorts, and Marija and I tasted out of politeness and because we were curious to hear more. My mother, too, had been reprimanded at the glass factory where she worked as a chemist because she had expressed an indignant stance against the beginning of the war. "Who starts a war in the middle of Europe in this day and age, less than fifty years after the horrors of the last war? Can our people be such idiots?" asked my father, puzzled. His usual show of manliness and effervescent spirit were drained. I felt sorry for my parents and apparently so did Marija because she tried to comfort them for their recent blows and she praised their courage to stand up to the shows of nationalism and to the new war.

"There isn't going to be much dissent allowed," said my father, "mark my words, we'll be going backward, we'll be thinking nostalgically of the Tito years and of Communism." It was exactly what Marija had said to me earlier and now the gloom of it all fell on us with that same threatening thud again and again. We sat around the table in the heavy-smelling apartment at an ungodly hour of the morning as Biljana swirled around the room in a cavalcade of ribbons and scarves and humming the tune of "I feel pretty." We did our best to process my mother's attempt at a rice pudding and the new political developments rushing at us from all directions. My father was wondering if Marija was going to leave for Sarajevo right away and my mother shushed him saying she would go when she felt the moment was right. "Maybe you should wait a bit longer, isn't it dangerous with the siege that just started?" asked my father, showing genuine concern. "If my parents can take the danger, so can I," she said abruptly. Who knew when she would be back again? Marija spoke as if she had already gone through several wars and was a pro at dealing with war situations. But the truth was that she was always a pro at dealing with a variety of mind-boggling circumstances from messy love affairs, to the politics of student organizations, to the beginning of a terrifying war. Yet there seemed to be another reason why Marija was delaying her departure, and the exams somehow didn't seem strong enough. There was a mysterious shadow moving back and forth on her face. When I looked at her straight she seemed to have a forced smile, as if trying to say she was all right, don't any of us worry about her. My mother mustered enough courage to ask the reason for our late-night appearance in bloody clothes. Marija and I stumbled in our explanations and then told my parents that a friend of ours from the department of philosophy got beaten up in a bar because of expressing antiwar sentiments.

. That night Marija and I stayed up in my bed talking about everything from the men we'd known to the state of the world, to our future with the war in it, to our careers, to our favorite movies, and fell asleep on memories of our childhood in Sarajevo and in Farah and Kemal's sweet-smelling house. It felt like a farewell night but neither Marija nor I said anything about a parting of any kind. We delved into the delicious illusion that we would be together forever like one delves into the illusion created by a Hollywood movie on that magical silver screen. Even as personal destinies were crushed by wars and irrevocable separations, the characters in those movies that Marija and I had watched wide-eyed in our early teenage years all seemed unperturbed, glossy and immortal, elegant and witty under the worst and most painful circumstances. A quick glance as a plane was getting ready to leave, a faraway war whose din had made itself heard nearby, the brim of a hat turned just right for us to see the soulful teary eyes of the heroine, all perfectly contoured and timed. I thought Marija fell asleep before I did. I remembered thinking that she must have been so tired since her breathing was inaudible. Just something in the way her head shifted off the pillow and her hair fell on her face made me think she had fallen into a deep sleep. I almost felt like I could hear hoarse whispers from the dark dreams that Marija was struggling with. Before falling asleep I had a sharp pang of fear for her, not knowing what the future would bring in that war zone she prepared to launch herself into as soon as exams were over. I felt a need to protect her and to tell her she could always count on me. But the heavy and precipitated events of the day must have weighed on my psyche, too, and sleep lulled me before my own dreams of empty labyrinthine streets pushed their way into my subconscious. Danger lurked at every corner in my dreams but despite the sense that people with guns and grenades were swarming all around the vicinity, everything was maddeningly quiet. Milko appeared in the middle of the street wearing a white hospital gown and with a deep gash in his forehead. He was offering Marija and me a pot of azaleas. Marija told me not to take them because they were dangerous, they were evil dangerous flowers, not all that looked pretty and fuchsia was safe, she said. Still, I so much wanted the pot of azaleas and I did not listen to Marija. I took the pot of azaleas from Milko and in that same second everything blew up. We woke up to the sounds of snipers and explosions on the TV in my parents' living room. The war was getting on and people and buildings were being blown to bloody shreds and it was not a dream and it was not a Hollywood movie.

Several days after the ruthless beginning of the war in April 1992 I met Mark Lundberg, a suave American intellectual pursuing a combined journalism and English literature doctorate at Harvard who had a touch of Gary Cooper and Marlboro Man combined. Even before completing his doctoral dissertation he had landed a teaching job at a university in Washington, DC, and for now he was going back and forth between Boston and Washington, he said with a smile that tried to be shy and unassuming. He had come to Belgrade to gather material for a humanitarian journalistic project back home, and miraculously dropped into the middle of a seedy Belgrade tavern at the shocking start of a war of nationalistic aggression. The word *humanitarian* sounded sexy on his lips and I wanted to hear more. His commutes between the two formidable American cities sounded glamorous beyond my imagination.

Marija and I spent hours every day in cafés and taverns, arguing, spreading antiwar leaflets, rousing heated debates between the arrogant majority of nationalists and the slim but fierce minority of pacifists. One evening Marija was surrounded by a crowd of men who drank every syllable that dripped off her luscious lips whether they agreed with her or not while I was handing out the pamphlets that she and I had worked on the previous night. I had already had a couple of drinks and for some reason in response to Marija's sparkling mini lectures I started elaborating on the connections between patriarchy and nationalism, sexuality and wars of aggression. Something I had once read about nationalistic libido, a new concept for everyone including myself, erupted in my slightly inebriated head and I had to share it with everyone. A tall handsome man who looked American joined the group and I became bolder and offered to buy him a drink. "Vodka on the rocks for the American gentleman here," I said to the bartender and handed the vodka glass to the handsome American with great aplomb. He smiled and asked: "How did you know I was American?" "It's not very hard to guess, you know; your trusting smile I suppose," I said and left the group of students with Marija in the center to join him at a table at the far end of the bar. Behind my back some of the guys in Marija's group called me a traitor and "fraternizer with Western elements." I heard that and

turned back yelling halfway across the bar: "Really? Look
at you boys—what are you wearing? Levi's jeans. What are
you listening to? Michael Jackson. And those of you who are
not drinking vodka, what are you drinking? Is it not whiskey? Who's the fraternizer?" I felt powerful and light, as if
I could take on the world. I looked back at Marija and she
was smiling like a proud mother. The American started talking and before I knew it, we were drinking shots of vodka
together. Even though I was used to having vodka shots from
the practice I had had with Marija during our college years,
for some reason after the third shot in the company of the
American tourist with a penchant for humanitarian activism,
everything became blurry and confused. The sound of an
accordion playing a heated Hora, Marija's eyes moving from
the crowd around her to me with the expression of a wild-
cat ready to pounce, the American brushing his long fingers
against my cheeks and then kissing me on the mouth right
there at the table in the corner of the tavern, antiwar leaflets
spread on the floor and flying in the smoke-filled air, his invitation to join him at the studio apartment he was renting, my
counteroffer that he join me at my studio apartment. It all
ballooned into one never-ending night that stretched out into
another day and another night, which all led to my moving
into his apartment only a week later, which then stretched
across the summer and into the fall when it ended with our
wedding in an Orthodox church and my leaving for America
as his bride.

In his tiny furnished studio apartment in the livelier part of the Dorćol area adorned with Serbian traditional rugs and wall hangings, Mark Lundberg acted shy and reserved on the night of our first encounter. He showed me his collection of Serbian rock and pop albums among which was the popular Ekatarina Velika band and their famous *Ljubav, Love*, and asked me if I wanted him to play them for me. I hated all Serbian rock as I did most traditional Serbian music and asked him if he had any American music instead. He looked slightly taken aback, as he had thought his knowledge and appreciation of the music of my country was going to impress me. But he quickly recovered and pulled out from the collection stacked up on his desk several American CDs—Frank Sinatra, the Doors, Aerosmith, Dire Straits, the music Marija and I listened and danced to during our college years and in particular during our bald-headed fiercely countercultural period. "Take your pick," he said regaining his full confidence, with a smile so alluring that it seemed to combine the best and sexiest of the Marlboro Man, Gary Cooper, and humanitarian principles all in one. I chose the Doors, and he asked me to dance holding out his hand as if we were at a grand ball. He was as smooth a dancer as I had ever imagined someone could be, swirling me around the tiny apartment this way and that way, one minute in a tight embrace the next in savvy swing turns, in perfect control and yet making me feel I was the one leading the dance. His apartment was small but we never bumped into furniture the way my parents always did whenever dancing to the sugary "Somewhere My Love." We danced for what seemed like the whole night, in slow motion, in rapid steps and dizzying turns, his legs knowingly coming between mine for the quick turns, his hands warm and steady on my back. At some point our dance moves morphed into kissing, caressing, undressing, as if it were all part of the same ritual. First we were swinging, and next we were entangled in his bed feeling each other's sweaty bodies, skin-to-skin, like it was the most normal thing in the world. I fell asleep thinking that I had finally had adult sex, all the rest had been just fooling around, even Milko. In Mark's strong knowing arms, everything before seemed childish and inexperienced. This was the real thing, the American thing: rock music, freedom, humanitarianism, Jim Morrison's lyrics, Mark's savvy caresses, the smell of American cologne, all wrapped up in the spring breeze and night sounds that rushed into the room from my Serbian native city. I had entered a foreign country while still on native land. When I first came to consciousness in the morning, I had no idea where I was, and for a split second I wondered whose arm was folded delicately around my breasts. Mark kissed the nape of my neck and asked me what I wanted to have for breakfast. I felt mature and glamorous like an American movie star.

During the following days the minute amount of national pride that must have resided lost and forgotten at the bottom of my psyche was awakened by Mark's genuine interest in my native city. I played the tourist guide, showing him

around quaint alleys unknown by regular tourists, old Orthodox churches with golden icons and infused with the smell
of burning candles and incense, parks, ruins, the Danube,
the Sava, the place where the Danube and the Sava mix with
each other, old districts, new districts, he took it all in stride
with curiosity and a winning smile. During those same days
right at the beginning of the war in April, I continued to meet
Marija in bars and at street corners, at her apartment or even
at my parents' apartment, feeling almost delinquent as if I was
hiding something. Somehow I managed to meet Marija and
Mark at different times of the day and fill every moment with
either playing the tourist guide, American dancing and sex
with Mark, or in political discussions, writing and distributing
antiwar manifestos, and drinking in bars with Marija. My days
seemed endless and demented, sexy, humanitarian, both painful and hopeful, large-winged above Belgrade. After Marija left
for Sarajevo part of me turned numb, while another part of me
was more alive than ever. I had been careful to keep Marija and
Mark separate and distribute myself to each of them in what
seemed like two different lives that barely brushed by each
other and managed to keep them from ever crossing paths.

From that single night when I met Mark in the Belgrade
tavern, events crowded and rushed and tumbled their noisy
clamor into my life with the speed of a derailing train. The
war catapulted everything into a mad series of occurrences
that ironically weren't going to stop until I landed on American soil. It was as if I went to America to calm down and

find peace, to rest and slow down the unstoppable rumble of happenings running me over in my native country. In the middle of that turbulent period of the beginning of the war there was one particular day that kept its clear and painful contours. It was the day when Marija and I said good-bye in her apartment, the same day that she was leaving for Sarajevo and I was moving in with Mark in Belgrade. It had all the weight and slowness of defining days that slice your life through the center and you have to leap across an abyss to be able to start the other half. It was a cruel spring day with blooming chestnut trees and forsythias and news of rampant killings of Bosnians by nationalist Serbs in Sarajevo. It was the day when Marija and I said good-bye on the threshold of her apartment with mascara running down our cheeks and agonizing fears weighing in our hearts. A slow, heavy-laden day carved with all the markings of grief, regrets, and apprehensions. It smelled raw and bloody, and the blooming trees appeared like a huge cosmic mistake. We sat in silence for a while at the table in Marija's minuscule kitchen. There was a spring breeze coming through the window and an eerie light. The world seemed to quiver. The fragrances were painful. Although I hadn't closed an eye all night, I felt light and luminous. I was wearing the blue silk dress I had worn the night I met Mark, and my grandmother's turquoise necklace. Looking at Marija's brooding eyes and exquisitely carved features I impulsively took off the necklace and handed it to her: "Marija, keep this, it would look beautiful on you. I want you to have it." Then I took out the antique edition of Plato's *Dialogues* that we had studied so often during our college years and handed it to her, too. "And this, I want you to have this, too," I said feeling my eyes overflow with tears.

"Why are you giving me all this?" Marija asked almost teasing me. "You are not dying or anything, you are just moving in with a goddamn American."

"I know, isn't that sort of like dying?" I said.

Something shifted and quivered again in the room, the city, the world.

"You can have Milko, too," I said wickedly and we both laughed hard, until our laughter turned to tears. We held hands for what seemed like a long time. I had a feeling of heartbreak, like literally something inside me was cracking in two.

"What are you going to do in Sarajevo?" I asked.

"I don't know, what are you going to do in Belgrade? Maybe I'll become a full-fledged journalist. Journalists are always needed in times of war, you know. Time to do something useful for once," Marija said, brushing away the waves of dark hair falling on her forehead.

"You already are a journalist, Marija, and a brilliant one. And you've always done useful things. They need you in Sarajevo. Who knows how long this war is going to last? Not long I hope. The UN, NATO, America, they've got to do something, they can't just let civilians get shot like that every day by an army of nationalistic fascists," I went on, feeling an uncontrolled agitation rise up inside me.

"Yes, of course they can, my dear, America and NATO and the UN never intervene promptly when it comes to just saving human lives," she said cynically. "Something else has to be at stake, some important resources like oil or nuclear power or huge international interests of power and money." Then Marija shifted to the topic that must have been on her mind more than the war: "Do you think you'll ever go to America with Mark?" I kept quiet and averted my eyes from Marija. I realized that not only was I thinking of it, but I was really wishing for it. What was there for me to do in Belgrade anyway but put myself in danger with revolutionary pacifist ideas preaching to a bunch of fanatic nationalists? "You know, this turquoise necklace doesn't look as good on me as it looks on you, Lara, with your blue eyes. It will clash with my green eyes," Marija said suddenly, as if embarrassed about her question.

"A string of twine would look good on you," I said with conviction, "and blue and green do match, despite what is conventionally thought. Do the sky and the grass ever clash with each other?" I then told Marija that she, too, should try to get to Santa Barbara and work with Sally. As if acquiescing that indeed I was going to go to America with Mark. Marija straightened her back the way she did sometimes when something bothered her and said in an almost harsh tone: "When someone you love is in danger and in pain, that's when you love them the most. There is no way I am staying far from my Sarajevo for any length of time." I knew it all but somehow wanted to justify my own intentions of leaving the country by tempting Marija to do it, too. She assured me that I had her blessings to go to America, and that she hoped I would. We spoke such serious stuff, and also banalities and niceties, heavy painful things and frivolous girlish things, until a deep silence fell between us. We were dried up of words. Words were failing us. Words became irrelevant. We held hands again. We thought of the movie *Casablanca* that she and I had watched so many times. We didn't say it, but I knew we thought of it together, because just when I was about to leave the room Marija asked: "What about us?" We held each other in the doorway for a long time. She asked me to write to her parents' address, and then she asked me to take care of myself. I told her she was the one who needed to take care more than me because she was the one going into a war zone. War sounded almost childish, unreal, like we were just pretending and we could have said rain or snow instead of war. I ran down the stairs of the apartment building and I knew Marija stood in the doorway listening to my steps. I went out into the street and started running and crying. I felt Marija watching me from her window but did not look back at her. If I had looked back I would never have continued on to Mark's place. I disappeared into the crowd and ran all the way to Mark's apartment.

After Marija and I parted I decided to patch the two parts of me into one whole unit and I threw myself into Mark's

arms and charms with a vengeance. Sometimes we talked
and danced until late into the night in his apartment and fell
asleep in our clothes like two roommates. At other times we
made love in the morning before breakfast and just as the
first night I always felt mature and sultry, glamorous and
grown-up, ready to take on the world. Mark made me feel
all those things. I couldn't quite figure out whether it was
because he was American and his ways were so different from
any of the Serbian men I had been with, or whether it was
because I was confused with the beginning of the war, missing Marija and eager to leave Belgrade and start something
new far away from news of war and the atrociously nationalistic atmosphere. Late in the summer, with the war raging in Bosnia, horrifying news of snipers shooting from the
hills surrounding Sarajevo and shell bombings all over my
beloved childhood city, Mark and I had the life of a couple
and were making marriage and immigration plans. I thought
it was time to introduce him to my parents.

On a sweltering late-August afternoon, Mark and I dressed
up for dinner with my parents. Mark was genuinely nervous,
as if worried about the "marriage proposal" he was going to
present to my father. I laughed out loud hearing him talk like
a fiancé in an old-fashioned movie and thought maybe he was
joking. He wore a light-blue shirt and a red-and-yellow paisley
silk tie and despite the heat, he even put on his best navy-blue
blazer. I knew my mother would appreciate his elegance. She
was always one to make snide remarks about the "ghastly"

way my friends dressed, except for Marija, that is, whom she thought was a little too flamboyant but at least had a sense of style. Right before leaving the apartment, as I was trying to impress a semblance of smoothness to my unruly hair that was flying in all directions, knowing that it was going to be the first object of my mother's criticism, Mark held me gently at arm's length as if to steady me and looked me straight in the eyes. He produced a red velvet box from the top pocket of his navy-blue blazer and opened it to reveal a diamond mounted in a circle of pearls. "Lara, will you marry me?" he asked me in the most classic way. I thought it was the funniest thing in the world, almost unreal, like he was truly trying to imitate a hero in an American movie, so I burst out laughing. Besides, we had already been making marriage plans so the official proposal felt amusingly redundant. When his face became red with embarrassment and his eyes filled with sadness I regretted my callous laughter and realized he was as serious as anybody had ever been with me. I said: "Yes, of course, I'd love to marry you, Mark." He gently placed the ring on my finger and it fit to perfection. *Good sign*, I thought, *it must be a good match.* He kissed me on the mouth and I couldn't help thinking to myself with a mischievous smile that it was *just like in the movies.*

The evening with my parents turned out to be a bottomless box of surprises. Mark used every single one of the Serbian words and idiomatic expressions he had acquired from his "learn Serbian in a month" audiotape. My parents couldn't get enough of hearing him talk Serbian, my mother laughed and hugged him incessantly, while my father slapped him on the back with great affection and frequency, and then he tried out his English, mixing it with some French and German. I'm not sure how, but in the mixture of Slavic, Romance, and Germanic languages, exaggerated gestures, and body language, my parents and Mark managed to exchange a stunning amount of information and opinions, ranging from my childhood food aversions and school pranks to Yugoslavia under Tito. "It was good with Tito," my father said in his barely understandable English. They talked about the growing Serbian nationalism, my father's diplomatic missions in Greece, and went on to cover the majesty of the Parthenon, the corruption of Milosevic, and the new war, "this is bad war, more worse than ever before." And the conversation naturally concluded with my mother's reminiscing about scenes from Hollywood movies and, what else, *Doctor Zhivago*. "You know scene when Lara and Zhivago hidden in country house in winter, make love and poetry, so beautiful," I heard my mother say to Mark. "Best film in the world, no?" Then she ran to the record player to play the song "Somewhere My Love."

Sometime during the evening my sister had burst in from one of her dance rehearsals, all flushed, in her workout tights, gauzy clothing and colorful ribbons covering her from head to toes and giggling like a teenager. Mark made his marriage proposal to my father in a ceremonious way in a perfect Serbian sentence he had learned by heart, and my father took out his best aged slivovitz of which they both had several shots. Mark asked my mother to dance to the *Zhivago* tune and swirled with her between our dining room table and the overabundant lacquered furniture with the grace and smoothness I had gotten to know so well throughout that long Belgrade summer. By the end of the evening I was in awe of my future husband, his incredible social skills and savvy, his charm that transcended language and culture barriers. And miracle of all miracles, he even managed to make me feel proud of my family. The cabbage and beef stew that my mother had prepared didn't seem as bad as it used to, the dessert pudding for the first time seemed almost tasty, and my parents' agitated and chaotic way of communicating and mixing languages, politics, cuisine, and issues of national identity seemed almost endearing. By the end of the evening, my mother followed me into the bathroom and radiating with joy told me I was a lucky girl, Mark was the ideal man and husband, "Take good care of him, will you!" She told me also to try to leave for America as soon as I could: "Things are only going to get worse by the minute in this damn country and in this city." She had tears in her eyes and she hugged me with a warmth I hadn't seen since I was a little girl. I hugged her back and the warmth of my mother's embrace filled me with confidence. It took a sexy American to bring a new sense of harmony and understanding in my family.

When we were about to leave my mother took Mark aside

in the hallway and she whispered something in his ear. Mark blushed and smiled a big happy smile as if he had just hit the biggest jackpot of his life. He told my mother he was going to send her a new and better-quality videotape of the *Doctor Zhivago* movie from America. He told my father he admired his courageous attitude of resistance toward the war and the growing nationalism, and also added that he was the happiest groom in the world. He told my sister he would send her the tape of the *West Side Story* movie with Natalie Wood. In a moment of dizziness, I stumbled over the threshold of the entrance to the apartment, wishing to find myself in the evening open air. But in the stairwell there was just the same heavy smell as always, of the neighbors cooking their Serbian evening meals, the heavy meats and cabbages, potatoes, sausage.

Mark and I walked down the stairs holding hands, and I was overwhelmed by a profound feeling of loneliness. Memories of my childhood and teenage years swept through me. I saw myself running up the stairs back from school, breathless, eager to share with my father news of a new stupidity that the history teacher had uttered. I saw Marija and me running up those same stairs after school and my mother making us hot chocolate on a cold winter afternoon. And I clearly remembered the last time Marija and I visited my parents, only weeks earlier, the day before the war started, when we had gone down those same stairs together. Marija and I had held hands, just like Mark and I were now. I knew I was leaving to that coveted America for good, and everything around me suddenly seemed more precious and dear. The heavy smells and folkloric sounds suddenly felt familiar and cozy, part of who I was, whether I liked it or not. In the street Mark stopped under a streetlight and kissed me for a long time, slowly and methodically, almost as if we were going to part as well. The air was heavy with a metallic feel of war and separation. The large boulevards lined with chestnut and linden trees, and even the street with Communist buildings in the center where my parents lived, all shone. After the long kiss Mark whispered in my ear that he was kidnapping me to America and grinned mischievously. I said I was a willing hostage and we both laughed in the sweltering night. I felt a tinge of unease like a beautiful shoe that didn't quite fit. *But the ring fits perfectly*, I reminded myself, trying to eliminate any trace of doubt in the warm glow of magical thinking. When I looked up at Mark as we walked late at night to his apartment in the fancy part of the Dorćol neighborhood, his handsome profile stunned me. He looked back at me and smiled his most winning smile. I had no reason to worry, I told myself. I was going to start a new and exciting life at the side of a brilliant sexy humanitarian American.

We chose to get married in Saint Mark's majestic Orthodox church, or rather Mark chose it not just because it carried his name but because he wanted me to experience my own tradition for the wedding. I could not have cared less and a justice of the peace would have been fine, but I thought it was cute and thoughtful of him to want to go through the exhausting ceremony for my sake. While I was standing in my poufy white dress next to Mark all stiff and handsome in his tuxedo, and I was about to faint from the heat, the tight shoes, the nonstop incense that the priest kept throwing around with his incense burner, I had a feeling that there was something overdone, ridiculous, and unattainable about the whole thing. In order not to faint I went through the philosophers' alphabet, finding a name for each letter from A as in Aristotle to Z as in Zeno, passing through Locke, Montaigne, Russell, Wittgenstein, Young. I was happy I could even find one for Q, Quintilian the Latin orator. The priest pronounced us "man and wife" when I reached X for Xenophon, the soldier-philosopher who marched through deserts and over snow-covered mountainous chains until he reached Trebizond by the Black Sea. I felt great relief that the ceremony was over and I had managed to cover each letter of the entire alphabet with a philosopher's name.

The remaining months in Belgrade with the preparations and the paperwork for my departure to America seemed a few steps removed from my own life. I went through everything with precision and attention to detail but with my mind elsewhere. The affection I had experienced for my native home and city the night Mark made his glorious wedding proposal and met my parents in a swirl of languages, sentimental music, and shots of slivovitz wore off and was replaced by a feeling of estrangement and weariness. Belgrade without Marija seemed like a lifeless city and I might as well leave it for good. The news of the war and the siege of Sarajevo, the nationalistic discourse on the radio and television in which it sounded like it was still the Serbian armies and people who were the victims of the war they had waged against their neighbors, gave me a sense of bitter satisfaction about my impending expatriation. Packing for my next life, saying last good-byes, obtaining all the necessary documents from my university as proof I had actually received a degree there, organizing the church wedding ceremony for my parents' sake and Mark's delectation in ethnic traditions, talking to Marija on the phone once a day to find news of the war from her side and just to hear her voice, it all filled my days and months until it was time to embark on my grand adventure, to get on the plane to my new and mythic country. My family accompanied Mark and me to the airport wearing dark-colored clothes as if for a funeral. My mother was wiping tears that she said were for happiness at my good fortune, my father was smoking incessantly saying the country was going to be destroyed and a good thing it was that I was getting the hell out of there, and my sister sobbing with hiccups and asking me to write to her often and not forget them in that big America. As cool as I tried to be when we said our last good-byes I felt hot tears streaming down my cheeks and smearing the mascara I had carefully applied an hour before just to look at my very best when I landed in Washington, DC. I knew once I got on that plane I would forever be a different person, a different category of individual: an immigrant, an expatriate, someone without a country. It felt bitter and satisfying, painful and thrilling. I picked up my carry-on suitcase and walked toward the gate on Mark's arm without looking back.

Washington, DC.
Immigrant Life

1992–1998

During the first months of my American life, Washington, DC, puzzled me in the exact reverse of the ways I had imagined it would. I had moved to America to live in a museum and I was a part of the display. Here is the Museum of Natural History, and here is this girl from Serbia. Here is the modern section of the Art Gallery, and here is the Serbian woman that Mark Lundberg married. Here is the Pentagon, and here is Mark's wife, the Serbian woman who escaped the war, what a tragedy, a European war in this day and age. As I had played the tour guide with Mark during our first weeks together in Belgrade, so did he now proudly guide me through the architectural and cultural gems of Washington, DC. He showed me the great landmarks of his city as if I were a tourist on a short visit and he took me on endless tours to introduce me to all his friends and colleagues. Sometimes he even told me what to wear before meeting them. We had our first fight a month after my arrival in America, on account of what I should wear to visit his department chair in one of the chic residential neighborhoods of the city. I swore at him, which was an extremely rare occurrence for me. "I'm not your fucking mail bride," I said putting on the belt of the floral silk dress that my mother had bought for me before leaving Belgrade, in one of our rare, warm mother–daughter moments: "To have it for a special occasion, out there in America," she said, "and to remember your home," she added, wiping a tear. "I'm wearing whatever the fuck I want." I regretted my language and high-pitched voice the second they emitted from my own puzzled mouth. "You're right, sorry," he said. I brushed that weird exchange off as an anomaly in our otherwise happy and smooth relationship.

At his department chair's party Mark was the very personification of charm just as he had been at the first dinner with my parents and on every social occasion during our Belgrade months. He talked with great pride about me as if I were a newly purchased car or a new mahogany chair: "Lara speaks four languages fluently." "Lara is a political scientist." "Lara was an antiwar activist in her country, very courageous!" "What language did you two speak to each other when you first met?" the chairman's wife asked. She was wearing a pair of baggy black pants and a boxy faded-blue shirt that made her look like a human square. Now I knew why Mark didn't want me to wear the fitted floral dress: I couldn't be too ostentatious and sexy, but not too drab, either, the academic chic was to be understated as if you didn't care and to hide as much of your body as possible under folds of badly fitted material. "First I tried my Serbian on poor Lara," Mark said with self-deprecating modesty, "after which she took pity on me and we switched to her impeccable English." "How romantic," said the department chair's wife. She was "a stay-at-home mom," I was told. I had no idea what that meant, though it was true, I could have given a lecture in any of the four languages Mark was so proud of, about Plato's theory of ideal forms or Aristotle's political and ethical views. I asked her if other moms did not stay home and if so where did they stay when they stayed away from their homes? I was shocked to find out that a stay-at-home mom was a woman who after she had her baby did nothing but just that: stayed home with her baby and waited with a warm meal for her husband to come home. Everybody laughed and thought I was adorable. They asked me what we ate in my country. That touched some wicked chord in me for some reason as I felt again put on display next to the other Washington curiosities and artifacts from foreign countries. I said we ate mostly rat sausages and during Tito's time cat and dog sausages used to be a great delicacy. "Too bad now there's such a shortage of cats after the fall of Communism, and what with the war and all," I said. Everybody laughed profusely and said I was "a riot" and Mark said I was "on a roll." I hated my English teacher in our former Belgrade high school for having skipped American idiomatic expressions while teaching us every useless word denoting literary devices used in a poem or the different parts of a Shakespearean historical play. I knew what a *synecdoche* meant but had no idea what the expressions *to be a riot* or *to be on a roll* meant. I delighted in literal interpretations of American expressions and imagined myself starting a big riot right outside Mark's chairman's house to liven up the dead street. Then I would have been a riot all right. I imagined myself rolling down on the floor as you do in the fire drills to kill the flames that somehow lit up all over me. Then I would have been "on a roll."

Then the most unnerving question of all came from the wife of another colleague of Mark's who taught journalism. The wife was in her last month of pregnancy and proud to have decided she was going to also be a stay-at-home mom: "Why do you think your people started this terrible war in the Balkans? It must be so hard for you." She was a sympathetic woman and cared about my Serbian sentiments. "We started the war because we want to kill our neighbors the Bosnians, take away their land, and erase them from the face of the earth. We are a greedy brutish people. Wait, didn't your ancestors do the same with the Indians? Oh, and then there was slavery, too. Any idea why your people had slaves and decimated the Indians?" I said. There was an awkward silence around the table and I realized I had gone too far. I thought I noticed an angry expression pass on Mark's face like a fleeting shadow. I had a sinking feeling that he would punish me for it. Maybe I had drunk too much; maybe I was still adjusting to the new schedule, climate, culture, and alcohol affected me differently and more dramatically. As we left the chairman's house I thought I detected a mean-spirited look on the face of that chairman's wife, the woman with the boxy shirt. A look that for a very brief second seemed to say: *We'll get you sooner or later, Serbian girl with funny jokes and sarcastic remarks.* I brushed it off again. I was just adjusting to my new surroundings after I had escaped a country at war that had been a Communist country before the war. I was entitled to brief moments of paranoia.

I had imagined streets swarming with people, but instead the streets were empty in the evening. Mark said the downtown area was where most government people worked so when the offices shut down, so did everything else and the people went home. The first day I wanted to go out on the bus, the train, the metro, to try everything in my new hometown. I wanted to go by myself and Mark said I couldn't, I had to be careful. I had no idea what he meant. In Belgrade I went wherever I wanted and there were people in the street near the government buildings, too. Not to speak of Sarajevo that was always swarming with people, street vendors, and open markets. When I wanted to shop at the outdoor market for our weekly groceries, Mark said there was only a farmers market at the other end of town on Saturdays. I walked on the streets in the downtown area during the day to see if there would be more people and was delighted to see that there were, like a child who discovers the way home after thinking she was lost. I had to get used to the rhythm of my American city.

After the first months of incongruous encounters, conversations, and curious evening ramblings on empty boulevards, I was determined I was going to love my new city, and I did. Life seemed to move at just the right pace, not too fast, not too slow. I loved the duplex where we lived. It was right in the heart of the nation's capital, on Connecticut Avenue, and I was enchanted by the large boulevards, parks, and bridges with people jogging and walking their babies, or jogging while walking their babies in funny-looking three-wheeled strollers. During the day the streets in our neighborhood were lively and I tried to stay outside in the street as much as possible. I was happy we lived in a district with people in the streets and outdoor cafés. I sometimes sat on the stoop in front of our duplex just to look at the passersby and I even counted the number of people that walked by our house on some days. The next-door neighbor thought I had locked myself out of the apartment and asked me if I was okay, as if I were ill or had lost a relative. I was thrilled to start a conversation with the neighbor, as in our old Belgrade apartment all the neighbors talked to one another and sometimes knocked on each other's doors to borrow a cup of sugar or chat about daily hardships and politics. But she said "goodbye have a nice afternoon" and shut the door to her side of the house in my face. I continued to sit on the stoop and counted thirty-three people in an hour. That was fewer than the day before and fewer yet than the day before that. The thirty-fourth person that day was Mark who was returning from his day at work. I wanted to come back from work, too, and not spend my time sitting on the stoop like a stay-at-home mom. My initial tourist's naïveté and excitement about America were turning into palpable boredom and I realized I needed to work and to find a clear direction in my life. Sometimes I wished I had been a classic immigrant, the kind that landed by themselves in a big American airport with no money and not a soul to help them and they worked night shifts while going to school in the daytime, or the other way around and they didn't have money for rent at the end of the month and were terrified of becoming homeless. I was slightly ashamed of the easy way in which my immigrant experience was shaping up. *Poor little Serbian immigrant bride,* I thought to myself with a certain amount of self-disdain.

Being an immigrant in America both matured and infantilized me as I stood and looked aghast at formidable constructions, obelisks, giant drinks with cherries and miniature paper umbrellas on top, and as I tried to pull out of my fractured psyche and life experiences enough strength and energy to keep up with some kind of a reckless race for something that everyone around me seemed to be engaged in. I couldn't believe President Clinton's abode was only a few minutes away by car from where we lived. We were practically neighbors. Maybe I could see him or picket the White

House with a sign saying: HELP SARAJEVO! or STOP THE WAR IN BOSNIA! I saw people with all sorts of signs moving or standing in front of the White House and some seemed to have stopped counting the years, as they looked as if they'd been left there since the Vietnam War. I wanted to tell them that particular war was over and others had come and gone and new ones were starting again. And also to suggest that maybe if they washed and changed their clothes, they might have more success with the president that way.

In my second year in America I avoided the nagging feeling of guilt about having left my parents, my sister, and my beloved Marija by drowning myself in graduate studies. With Mark's encouragement and financial help I started a doctoral program in political science that not only filled some of the empty spaces in my time and heart but gave me the self-importance of an immigrant molding her American Dream with a steady step and fierce determination. I was making it in America. Marija's blessing was coming true, the one she had given me when I first called her in the shelter where she now worked as a journalist for Sarajevo's main newspaper: that I find marital bliss and professional fulfillment. I devoured the scholarly studies listed on my endless bibliographies with as much hunger as the ethnic foods that Mark introduced me to with great meticulousness: the Thai and Vietnamese cuisines, Indian, Middle Eastern, and African. My palate made the tour of the world in my first Washington years. Whenever Marija called me, though, and I heard her deep raspy voice move in its various tonalities from excitement to serious engagement, from irony to melancholy resignation, I became jittery and ill at ease for the rest of the day. The building of the main Sarajevo newspaper had been blown to pieces at the very beginning of the war and the director, a passionate journalist and reporter, had set up the headquarters of his paper in a forsaken bomb shelter left from the Cold War era. Marija was utterly thrilled to work there as a war journalist. It sounded movie-like, so perfectly fit for Marija and her adventurous, courageous spirit. When I heard voices of fellow journalists in the shelter where Marija was calling from, I experienced tinges of jealousy. They were living under daily bombings and off humanitarian care packages, yet in the background they sounded so animated, like they were having the time of their lives. For one thing, war must not have been too boring. Sarajevo was crumbling under mortar and shells every single day, my friend was in danger of being shot dead by snipers with every step she took in the street, and I wasn't there to help. I missed Marija's presence to the point of desperation on some days, her voice, spirit, and humor.

During those first two years of the war I received several letters from Marija in which she gave me more details about her life in besieged Sarajevo, the journalistic work in the bomb shelter, and news from her parents and grandparents. They had all moved in with her parents, in their three-room apartment, crowding together as well as they could, as the hills had long become uninhabitable. Farah and Kemal held on to their house for awhile longer until they were forced out by the continuous shootings and bombings. Marija described how she drove her car through intersections at 150 kilometers an hour to escape the snipers, feeling like a plane pilot. One time the team of journalists had a party with sausage, cheese, and whiskey inside the bomb shelter. They even had chocolate and they danced the twist and rock-and-rolled to songs by Elvis Presley, Frank Sinatra, and Elton John. With chocolate and whiskey in an atomic bomb shelter, they produced a truly glorious two-page newspaper every day, Marija said. There were packages of UN humanitarian aid that their editor distributed to them. My life in America seemed so insipid compared with Marija's exciting life under bombs. Something heavy and hollow like a missed heartbeat echoed through my days in the nation's capital, and in my marriage.

My love for Mark went up and down in cycles and stages as if searching for a particular shape or a place to settle. Was it a comfortable domestic kind of love as we chose new furniture for the duplex or decided what food to take out or what to cook for the couple we were having over for dinner on a Saturday evening? Was it a sweeping love that made you hold your breath in excitement like some wild ride, as my first nights and days in Belgrade had been in the atmosphere at the beginning of the war with foreign journalists and loud disgruntled students swarming all around us? Was it a calm tender and intellectual love that would finally settle with us writing joined scholarly articles together? I picked a little from each of these options like I picked a spring roll from the Vietnamese restaurant and a samosa from the Indian one and then gorged on a burrito and was still left wanting, missing.

On some days Mark seemed both too deep and not deep enough. We still talked about all the intellectual and political problems that we used to during our long hot summer in Belgrade. I now missed the premarital honeymoon days with Mark when I was showing him secret walks on the Veliko Ratno Ostrvo magic island where the Danube and Sava poured into each other, took him to five-hundred-year-old Orthodox churches with Cyrillic writing and golden icons of puzzled faces of medieval saints, or showed him the old ornate school building where Marija and I spent much of our preteen and teenage years. Now the roles had changed: He was the guide and I was the tourist, even though I was not supposed to be a tourist but a full-fledged immigrant, soon to become a naturalized US citizen. While in Belgrade, Mark had particularly impressed me and lured me into his world with his relaxed and debonair attitudes, the way he always listened to me and seemed interested in every word I enunciated, a rather rare occurrence with the Serbian men I knew who would tell you that your eyes sparkled like stars while you were heatedly talking about national identity and ethnic hatred. Most of the Serbian men I knew didn't listen to a word you said if you were a woman and happened to have a pair of eyes, relatively decent-looking hair, and two normal legs and arms. Milko might have been an exception, and maybe some of the Goth men that Marija and I hung out with in our proverbial taverns. But Mark seemed genuinely interested in all of me. And he was. Only now, on his own native earth, his debonair and relaxed attitudes, his humanitarian perorations and intellectual musings, could seem pretentious and overbearing. He still listened to my thoughts and opinions, but now it seemed he could hardly wait for me to finish a sentence so he could develop a complicated argument to show me how I was wrong. Unlike Marija, who would fight to the death over a political argument, I would always give in. I just didn't feel the same energy and passion for the intellectual or political arguments that Mark did. Sometimes, particularly if the argument took place while we were walking in the street, or while he was driving, I pretended to be absorbed in the passing landscape, the faces of the people we walked past, the architecture of the gigantic government buildings, or the layered tastes of the Guatemalan cornmeal or Vietnamese soup we might have been eating in one of the myriad ethnic restaurants Mark took me to.

One day I told him I wanted us to start cooking at home and not go out to eat all the time. Even when we ate at home, Mark brought in take-out Indian, Chinese, or Mexican from one of the restaurants in our neighborhood. We sat across from one another at his large mahogany dining room table eating out of cardboard boxes like we were in an airport or railway station. I thought it was the American way: easy, fast, disposable, prepared by someone else, usually an illegal immigrant working in the kitchen. I found myself missing the dinners with my parents. As heavy and greasy as some of my mother's cooking was, at least it was served on beautiful china with rose or sunflower motifs on the edge of the plates. I had no idea why such details would spurt into my head, except that I must have been experiencing some form of immigrant homesickness. *It will pass, just wait to get more settled and adjusted*, I told myself. Mark was ecstatic at my proposal that we cook more at home. He hadn't dared to mention it himself, not wanting me to feel obligated to cook for us. I thought that was another one of Mark's endearing traits of thoughtfulness. I had no idea what to cook, and true enough, I would be the one preparing the meals. In our house my mother most always did the cooking while my father did the grocery shopping and dishwashing. And I had no ideas of recipes or meals that I could have prepared.

I called my mother for a goulash recipe, thinking that I'd tone down the fat and salt and add some fresh vegetables and American spices, and it couldn't be too bad. My mother couldn't believe her ears that I was calling her for a recipe. She asked me how I was doing, and told me again how lucky I was, and updated me on the ever-growing violence of the war. Mark shopped for every ingredient on the grocery list with rigor and enthusiasm, proudly unloading each item like it was an artifact for a museum. We prepared the meal side by side, and for the first time I had a sense of home, and did not feel like a tourist on a limited visa. Mark played a Beatles record and once or twice even twirled me across our blue Italian kitchen tile floors, in between browning the beef and caramelizing the onions. It was a hot humid summer evening in Washington and a fragrance of honeysuckle entered our kitchen merging with the smell of cooking beef and onions. It reminded me of the smell of beef stew on the evening when Mark and I visited my parents for the first time. The Beatles music made me more nostalgic than the stew, reminding me of the high school parties at Marija's house for her birthday. Mark's presence made me feel safe and cozy, yet the mixture of smells and music overlapping onto my memories from a country and family at the other end of the world also gave me a feeling of vertigo. I was hanging above a transcontinental precipice and I could have been anybody, or no one at all. I could have been an opportunistic hairdresser, a greedy Serbian American housewife, a double agent working for the Bosnian Federation and the UN. Mark was the only one to hold on to, to remind me I was Lara Kulicz, a political science graduate from Belgrade University, born and raised in a modest Serbian apartment by intellectual parents in love with Hollywood movies. He alone was the witness to my heritage. He was handsome and kind, a great dancer. He could recite entire sets of Shakespeare sonnets by heart. He even liked to prepare Serbian goulash with me on a humid August evening when all our neighbors were eating Ethiopian or Thai takeout from cardboard boxes. It was a new kind of happiness, but it

was one that obliterated entire portions of myself. This must
be the immigrant experience. There were no roots, just lots
of leafy branches reaching out toward the starless Washington evening, the great American night with twenty-four-hour
supermarkets, millionaires, homeless people, truck drivers,
movie stars, neoclassical granite buildings, high-rises, malls,
and everything else in between. It felt hopeless and exhila-
rating at once. As we sat across from each other at the long
mahogany table like an aristocratic British couple from a
BBC series proudly eating our American version of Serbian
goulash, I looked at Mark and tried to figure out who he was
at his core. I was desperate to find the rawest and crudest part
of him, a burning quivering point of truth and vulnerability
behind the witty conversations, perfect dance moves, Shakespeare sonnets, steady thoughtfulness, and occasional distance he took whenever he prepared for his classes or wrote a
scholarly article. I thought I'd get to that by opening up first.
"Remember our first evening at my parents' apartment in
Belgrade, when you made your marriage proposal?" I asked
Mark, smiling and looking at the diamond and pearl engagement ring on my finger. "How could I forget, it was a lovely
evening," he said. In my mind that translated to, *Why waste
our time reminiscing about the past? Wouldn't you rather talk
about the metaphysical poets or Clinton's foreign policies?* I
tried again, thinking the more I was going to unfold my nostalgic soul, the more he would unravel his. "I wonder how my
parents are faring with this war, I miss them sometimes. The

news from Sarajevo is getting worse every day. I miss Marija, too, I worry about her. Do you think the war will end soon?" "I have no idea, my dear," he said with the accent on *no* in the typical emphatic way Americans uttered that phrase, with a quick raise of the eyebrows and shake of the head. "I'm sure your parents must be okay, they are not in a war zone yet," he said, calmly taking a large spoonful of the successful goulash. For a millisecond I saw myself throwing my bowl of goulash right at Mark's head, and fantasized about it dripping with stew, caramelized onions, and local organic beef sticking to his ears. Instead I politely soaked a piece of the whole-grain bread in the stew and ate it quietly. The record had stopped playing and only Mark's methodical chewing could be heard in the room, which ground more on my nerves. I wanted so badly to love my American savior and know who he was. But he suddenly seemed like a well-mannered stranger. *Why the hell are we eating so far away from each other, at the bloody mahogany table,* I thought. *Whose table is it anyway, maybe he has other wives that bequeathed him expensive mahogany furniture, what do I know of his past? Nothing. What do I know of his soul? Nothing. Why did he come to Serbia? We should be eating at a round table next to each other,* I went on in my head. *We should be touching knees and kissing between bites.*

"Mark, where is this table from?" I heard myself ask. He looked up at me with his eyebrows raised in surprise, then smiled and said: "It was a gift from my mother. When my father passed, she divided some of her most precious furniture between my sister and me. She said she had no use for so much stuff around her." He seemed genuine, and I was desperately searching for genuine. I felt like a policeman investigating a crime, Inspector Columbo looking for the littlest details, a scratch on a mahogany table, maybe a drop of Serbian goulash on the Italian tile. The wine had made me tipsy, Argentinian wine that Mark had spoken very highly of as if describing an important philosophical principle.

That night I cried quietly in my pillow. Mark kissed me good night and he said I would feel better in the morning. I probably drank too much, he said. The future was gaping in the dark like an open crater. I cuddled close to Mark, and his calm breathing and warm body were soothing. Despite everything I was glad he was there sleeping next to me. What would I have done all alone in a bed in a foreign city, in a foreign country, not a soul who cared or knew who I was? Somebody called for Bobby in the street outside our window and laughed heartily. For some reason that felt reassuring. The honeysuckle smell felt reassuring, too, reminding me of another night back home.

Over the course of the next couple of years I threw myself into my graduate studies, spinning the threads of Continental, Eastern, and American political philosophies from Aristotle to Locke to Machiavelli, from Confucianism to *The Federalist Papers*, from Marxist feminism to everything else in between, to the point that any clear idea of goodness, democracy, justice, government, and leadership turned round and round in a murky whirlpool. On many of the days I came back from my classes excited about a new idea or book. I had brilliant discussions with Mark. He became particularly excited about notions of goodness and democracy and in turn shared his love of American poetry and the Transcendentalists like Emerson and Thoreau. He quoted from them by heart, dancing and sliding on our shiny hardwood floors, picking up a leather-bound edition of a metaphysical poet from his long and perfectly organized rows of books in the study and then coming to swirl me around in a spontaneous dance, kissing me on the mouth with breathless agitation. I found myself giggling like a teenager in love with her literature professor.

Still, those moments became rare and what began to set in was more like cohabitation with a stranger than the continuation of the sweeping love affair that had started at the beginning of the war. I still didn't know what had made him come to Belgrade in 1992 and why he continued to be involved in the war, to the point that he had even decided to bring Hassan Rakic, the director of the newspaper where Marija worked as a wartime journalist, to Harvard on a prestigious fellowship. "I promised Marija I would stop the war, remember, Lara?" he said with a cunning smile one evening over a dinner of take-out Indian food. He'd truly meant that, hadn't he? I remembered that one night in Belgrade when we were slightly drunk and I called Marija from his apartment, he had taken the phone from my hand and asked Marija in his most charming tone what he could do for her. Anything that she wished, he would do it. I picked up the receiver in the other room and listened in. "Stop this war for me, will you?" Marija said simply and crisply. Mark said: "No, seriously, what would you like me to do, Marija? I would do anything for Lara's best friend." Marija answered breathlessly: "I couldn't be more serious. Stop the fucking war and you'll be my hero forever." Mark answered confidently: "All right, I'll do that for you, Marija, anything really. As soon as I get to America I'll get on to trying to stop the war." I remembered thinking then for just a quick moment: *What a fool, what a self-important fool. Do I really want to spend the rest of my life with him?* But I never answered that question and the next day we were making wedding preparations. I chose to believe he was truly an idealistic pacifist and fighter for human rights. "Bringing Hassan to America, a Bosnian hero and a first-class journalist who risked his life to produce a newspaper even at the height of the armed conflict, is the perfect way to bring this war to the attention of American politicians, even President Clinton, can't you see that, my dear?" When he saw I was looking at him in utter puzzlement, Mark corrected himself without batting an eyelash: "All right, not stop the war, help stop the armed conflict, contribute to the peace process, something of that nature. It's something, all right, better than nothing." The more he tried the less I believed him.

"Why didn't you talk to me first, Mark?" I finally asked.

"You know of Hassan from me and I know of him from Marija and she is my best friend in the world. How is your getting a Harvard fellowship for Hassan helping the peace efforts? Why aren't both of them coming over? That would have made more sense both politically and personally, for me," I told him. Mark looked as puzzled as I had ever seen him. "And it's not a goddamn armed conflict but a war of aggression and ethnic cleansing. Besides, Marija is the one running the newspaper now in Hassan's absence, and she is the one out there in the street every day sneaking her way through sniper bullets to get news and stories for the newspaper. She is at least as much of a hero," I flared up at Mark. "In fact she *is* the real hero."

He looked straight at me with his deep-blue eyes the way he had the night when I was imparting antiwar lectures and vodka. He dismissed my anger as one would an annoying mosquito buzzing around one's head or the antics of an unruly child. "I did what I had to do," he said with his usual calm. The glacial expanses of self-composure and calculated behavior that Mark served me in our hardest confrontations left me confused and lonely. *Who is this man posing as my husband?* I thought in quick flashes that left me spent and panting.

Mark wanted to make love in the different places in the house and at odd hours, at times when I was either writing a paper or getting ready to go for a run, in the laundry room or on a chair in his study, and I always went along, whether I felt like it or not. Then there were also the times when I genuinely desired Mark and found him charming and irresistible and felt lucky to be his wife in his apartment on Connecticut Avenue, amid his dark-colored velvet and mahogany furniture like an exotic princess in a Westerner's palace. But those times became scarce as time went by and the only safe place from my marital conundrums was the crystal realm of abstract ideas and theories. And the short stolen telephone conversations with Marija when she sometimes called me from the bomb shelter where she did her journalistic work. The background noise of journalists, always talking, arguing, laughing, gave me a rush of pleasure mixed with jealousy. I held on to each conversation for as long as I could, and asked Marija to tell me more. She gave me abbreviated news about mortars and shells and market bombings or a rock concert held in a basement as if it was no big deal and just as ordinary as a walk in the park in times of peace. Sometimes she sounded extremely upbeat and almost happy, pouring on awful and wonderful information all together, in indiscriminate order, snipers killing children as they crossed the street holding their mothers' hands, getting a pound of fresh coffee and five eggs on the black market, a poetry club in times of war, her grandparents having to leave their house on the hill because that area was being taken over by Serbian snipers altogether. I wanted to hold on to one image alone and process it and talk more about it but Marija went on at a dizzying velocity and then she would stop and say: "But tell me about you, how's life with Mark? How's life in graduate school? Are you learning anything?" I would hear her light up a cigarette and drag from it at the other end and I felt a fierce desire to smoke with her and be in her presence, my heart beating, my mind racing, all of my senses alive as I always was in her proximity. There was nothing for me to say about Mark. "It's great, my courses are fabulous, and life with Mark is exciting." I mumbled banalities that sounded so important in English, but so hollow in Serbian.

One day after a similar exchange she said: "And Hassan, how is he doing in America, is he at least drawing the attention of that president of yours?" Then came a silence, filled only with the sound of Marija puffing her cigarette. I felt ashamed, yet I didn't want to trash Mark's name to her. But I wasn't going to insult her and our friendship with some worn-out cliché. "I know, it sort of sucks," I said. "You should have come instead."

"Well, at least I got his job, you know there is a big shortage of jobs out here what with the war and all," she said, slicing our conversation with her unforgiving irony. Then she corrected herself: "Never mind, I wouldn't have come anyway. How could I have possibly left my parents alone in the middle of this raging war?" Then she said: "I am wearing your turquoise necklace, Lara, you were right, it looks good on me, green and blue go well together." She laughed, and I felt like walking out the door of Mark's and my mahogany furniture-filled home on Connecticut Avenue, joining Marija under the rain of bombs and sniper bullets the next morning. Instead, during the second summer of the war, I became pregnant.

I knew exactly when it had happened. I had come home earlier all elated about my classes that day, happy that my professor of political philosophy had found my defense of Machiavelli's notions of virtue and leadership intriguing. It was a cool and brilliant early-summer day in DC, a rare one of its kind, as summers in Washington were usually miserably hot and humid. I was wearing a light gauzy white dress with red and blue flowers. I felt airy and everything in my life seemed in its right place. Even the news of the war in Bosnia seemed pale and quiet for a short while. When I walked into the house, I was surprised to see that Mark was already home, sitting at the computer in his study, probably working on one of his articles. I didn't want to disturb him so I started making myself some tea in the kitchen. Suddenly I felt him next to me, watching me as I filled the kettle. He was smiling one of his rare happy smiles. It must have been the article he was working on, I thought. Wallace Stevens sent him into ecstasy every time he worked on one of his poems. But he said: "You look really hot in that dress, Lara!" I had a sudden urge to hold and kiss him, the way I had the first time I met him in the Belgrade café. I liked it so much more when he called me by my name than by the clichéd "babe" and "honey." I felt bold and sexy and in that moment in our fancy kitchen it felt so right to be in Mark's arms, pressed against his strong chest. I indulged in my naive immigrant state of mind, the Eastern European girl who got her Marlboro Man, rugged but also intellectual and poetry loving, an American dream come true. Mark actually picked me up and carried me to the sofa in his study. I undressed him with fidgety and eager hands, forgetting about political theories and the war and even Marija. After some time Mark got up from the sofa and brought me my cup of jasmine tea. He was tender and graceful. We sat for a while naked and in silence: me drinking from my tea, him holding me with all the affection he was capable of expressing. There was something to be said about flying to America: "the pursuit of happiness."

Then Mark told me that he had begun to help bring Hassan's wife and children over from Bosnia the following month and could I go with him to Boston to offer company and translation skills to Hassan's family as they tried to settle into their new life. "It would be nice for Hassan's wife to have the presence of a woman from her part of the world, wouldn't it?" I stared at Mark and only said: "Yes, it would be nice for Hassan's wife to have the presence of a woman who speaks her language." Mark blushed, quietly put on his pants and buttoned up his shirt and left the room. I looked at my dress negligently thrown on the floor and realized it had the colors of the American flag and for some reason that seemed funny. How could something feel so right one moment and yet be so wrong the next? Mark was both right and wrong for me and that realization seemed like too hard of a nut to crack on that clear summer day when I had just acquired a new ontological status in the large book of lives: I had become a mother.

On April 5, 1995, I gave birth to an ethereal and perfectly

shaped girl whom we called Natalia. It was the third anniversary of the Bosnian war. Marija called me the next day and said she had a feeling I was giving birth and that it was a girl. I was stunned, but then remembered Marija's craft at feeling events, people, situations as if she had magical powers. Her friend Ferida had also given birth to a girl that same night. She called her Mira, which derived from the word for "peace." "That should be a good omen, shouldn't it?" Marija said. "Two girls born on the third anniversary of this hellish war. And by two beloved friends of mine. Maybe there is some hope. These girls will make the world a better place."

Her voice quivered with emotion, as if she was on the verge of tears. She told me that she helped deliver Ferida's baby in her basement during a concert and art exhibit. She gave a huge sigh. Natalia was sleeping blissfully next to me after her morning feeding and I suddenly felt afraid for all of us, for Marija and me, for Natalia and Ferida and her newborn baby girl with the identical birth date as my own daughter, for our worlds, our bodies, and our lives. I didn't understand a thing from the description of Marija delivering Ferida's baby in the basement of their house during a concert and art exhibit. "Everything is possible in times of war, Lara, you know. Don't worry, it was actually fun. And it's not all that bad. I'm getting a lot of sleep." She was lying of course. I knew that it was just that bad.

In the end, my primitive maternal side won over the rest of me and my daughter took complete possession of my life.

I stopped worrying about Marija and took her for her word that all was not "that bad" and she was doing all right. Mark surrounded us with a pleasant and comforting protectiveness without being too intrusive. What with the constant nursing, changing, putting to sleep, waking up three or four times a night, my mind became wrapped in a gooey numbness that rejected with stubbornness any input from Plato, Aristotle, Locke, Machiavelli, Marx, Hegel, the whole lot of them. I postponed my comprehensive exams for the following year and moved through my beloved Washington with panache, proudly strolling my porcelain-skinned green-eyed baby daughter up and down those busy streets. I was now a full-fledged stay-at-home mom myself and didn't mind it too much, except for when I caught a glimpse of a sassy woman in pumps rushing to work, alive and excited about her day. Some days I felt like a mail bride, prize wife, something that Mark got on a trip to the Balkans. On other days, I almost enjoyed my lazy days filled with parenting and household duties, beautiful things and ethnic foods. And still there were occasional other days, when I wanted to get on a plane and flee to where the war was.

Toward the beginning of that summer there was news that President Clinton was going to order an intervention to stop the war in Bosnia. The region of Srebrenica had been a site of indiscriminate mass killings, and other parts of the country were seething with mass rapes of women. The last time I had heard from Marija was July 4. She had called to jokingly wish me happy birthday for America. She told me that her father's family had gone back to the region near Srebrenica in Semizovac, where they had a farm, and that she and her parents, Farah and Kemal, were all going to join them the next day. She said the UN declared the region a safe area and they needed to see the rest of their family and help them out. "I'm sick of living under the snipers' rule. And it's safe...or safer," she said tentatively. "Didn't you hear about it? So I'm packing up and off I go," she laughed. "Be careful Marija, please, promise?" "I promise. Here, I promise on your turquoise necklace, I'm wearing it right now." She laughed and hung up. Something felt awfully wrong and unfinished. But I felt helpless. I knew something new and dark had entered my life and it would change me forever.

After that last phone conversation an intolerable silence spread between Marija and me. Whenever I talked to my parents I got mixed messages: One day they were telling me that things were calming down, the next that something terrifying was going on in Srebrenica, Potocari, and Banja Luka. Every time I asked about Marija they said there was no news from her or her parents. "They are probably fine," they said with hesitation. But I knew better. It was a silence that smelled like death and blood. Nobody was answering at the newspaper offices, either.

I went back to studying for my doctorate, took my comprehensive exams, and wrote my doctoral dissertation on the role of women leaders in the "newly freed" Eastern European states. My professor wanted me to refer to these states as the "new democracies" but knowing too well what went on in my native "newly freed Eastern European states," the word *democracy* seemed like a cruel joke. Even the words *newly freed* seemed altogether sadistic and ludicrous. But my professor insisted that I choose one comprehensive term to refer to all of them, even as I kept explaining that just the fact we had all been crammed out there in what Western Europe had conveniently relegated to the realm of the "Eastern Bloc" and the "Iron Curtain" did not mean we were all the same, it certainly did not mean that all those states had achieved equal levels of democratic governance, nor did it mean they were all "freed." Some got freed only to start chaining and massacring others. "I know, I know," the professor would say, nodding his graying head at me with a bemused smile as if I were telling him the joke of the year. "But just for simplicity's sake, go with that title," he said. "You can explain all that in the body of your dissertation."

Whenever he said "body" he would look at me with a prolonged stare measuring me from head to toes as if he was going to grade me for *that* "examination." I always had a queasy feeling I tried to ignore when I left his office. Surprisingly, he went along with my new topic, the role of women in the Eastern European governments. He was apparently a feminist when it came to ideas and theories, even though I'd heard stories of times when he'd sexually harassed his female

students, maybe to make up for the boredom of being a feminist in theory, I thought.

In my dreams I saw Marija running ahead of me in a
tunnel filled with water like the one she had described that
Bosnians had built as an escape route and that was leading
to the Sarajevo airport. She always melted in the darkness
at the end of the tunnel. There was no light there, only raw-
smelling blood. Another dream was of Marija in front of a
mirror fixing her hair. I could not see her actual face but only
its reflection in the mirror. She was going through an elabo-
rate hair combing and fixing, braiding, teasing, the works.
Her hair was shiny black and stunning as always. Then she
turned around and her face was ashen and filled with holes, a
terrifying vision of death and decay. I would wake up screaming from my dreams and with a great desire to get on a plane
and visit the Balkans and see everything with my own eyes.
The last time I called the newspaper I waited for five minutes
until the ringing stopped by itself and a metallic tone took its
place. I called her parents' number, her grandparents' number. I even called Ferida's number and there was only ringing
with no answer at the other end of the line.

Washington, DC, and Belgrade. Revelations

1998–2000

I missed my parents and my sister, Biljana, and the heavy smells in our Belgrade apartment. The feeling that Marija had been swallowed up inside a dark hole paralyzed me. But Natalia and her incredibly clear greenish eyes telling me that she needed me gave me a center and a hold on reality during those months and years. By the time Natalia was three and talking in full sentences, more than three years had passed since the end of the war in Bosnia and I decided that Marija was dead. The letters from Sarajevo no longer came. None of her friends, the ones whose numbers I still had, ever answered the phone. After hearing what had happened in Srebrenica, Tuzla, Banja Luka, and other places throughout Bosnia, I wished for her to have died a quick death in a red explosion like the ones in my dreams or by a sniper bullet in the street as she was running to her newspaper reporting job.

I was now teaching political philosophy to college students, carrying a full load of mothering duties, and entertaining our friends on weekends. Yet there was a constant and painful ringing in my head, ears, soul like the sound made by wind through an empty hallway. I had heard from Mark that Hassan was running a newspaper in a suburb of DC in northern Virginia and that he never went back to Bosnia. At first he reported or wrote articles about the situation in Sarajevo, but soon it seemed that his sources weakened, or even more likely, news about a civil war in a tiny faraway country in the Balkans wasn't hugely popular among the rich people and politicians living in the vicinity of the capital and eventually the news about the war disappeared altogether. It became clear to me that Mark had used the Bosnian war and his so-called activist work only to advance his career in America, his aura of the politically conscious academic who not only wrote brilliant articles and enchanted his students with his charismatic lectures but was also involved in what everybody called "the real world." He wrote powerful political letters to the *New York Times* and cared about the suffering of people in remote Balkan countries. How desperately Marija must have wanted to escape the nightmare of her "real world," I thought. How painful it must have been for her to see her newspaper director being swooped up across the Atlantic directly into the world's most prestigious university by none other than my own husband.

I was talking to Biljana more often now and the sound of her voice, always upbeat, optimistic, and positive no matter what misery was lurking around her, would give me an invigorating shot of hope. Biljana was specializing in art and dance at the University of Belgrade and got parts in all the musicals and shows at the university and in professional companies around the city. She was becoming restless and talked more often about wanting to come to the States. At first I pretended I didn't get what she was alluding to, until one day when she actually said it bluntly: "Lara, what the hell is wrong with you that you are not getting it? Can't you just bring me over? I want to come to America, I'm sick of this fucking country and this fucking city." I burst out laughing and said: "Well, if you put it that way, I'll see what I can do. Why don't you start by trying to get a visa for the States? I'll do all the necessary formalities at my end. How is that?" "You mean it?" she screamed with joy. "No, I was just teasing you to see how you'd react. Of course I mean it. Just get your dancing butt into motion then! Only one thing: How about Mama and Papa?" "How about them?" she asked, pretending not to get it. "You know what I mean, how will they take it, having both their daughters gone?" "They'll be just fine, Larichka, they've even told me to try leaving if I could, that they didn't see much hope for my career and future in this country. And you know how tied to each other they are, they'll be fine without us, as long as they have each other." Biljana's words, both wise and blunt, made me realize that what I had been waiting for was precisely that: someone with whom I could be as deliciously enraptured as my parents had always been with each other. That someone was not Mark.

I promised Biljana I would help her come to the States, to Washington, to Connecticut Avenue duplex heaven. What a boon after all to have my own flesh and blood, my beautiful red-haired nymph sister next to me and be able to talk my mother tongue and reminisce about our messy native part of the world. Whenever Biljana kept saying "my country" or "this country" or "our country" I would have an initial reaction of wondering: *What country? Whose country? Oh, that country, the one that has been decimating, massacring, raping its neighbors, Sarajevo, my best friend, and her family? That country?* That was certainly not my country. In that quick second I experienced a surge of joy for having immigrated to America, and Mark seemed like a pretty great deal despite his cold and even duplicitous nature. He seemed like a godsend actually. I had no birth country as far as I was concerned, only an adoptive utopian, idealized country. As for my native country, I wouldn't even know what to call it. Was it Serbia, was it Yugoslavia, or was it Republika Srpska? None of that touched an affectionate chord and the third one actually sent shivers of terror throughout my body anytime I heard it pronounced. Whenever people asked me where I was from, I would tell them I was from Sarajevo. I lied about my birth country with impunity and named the city, not the country. Sarajevo was city and country in one and I preferred siding with the victims than with the genocidal Serbs at any moment of my waking or sleeping hours.

Mark went along with my idea of bringing my sister over with no resistance. That was what confused and threw me off balance about Mark: Whenever I took it for granted that he would go along with something without a blink, we ended up in a huge argument that lasted for days and poisoned my life to the point where I cursed my white bridal gown and those nuptial vows in the Orthodox church in the center of Belgrade. It could be anything, a one-hundred-dollar difference in the monthly fees for one day-care center for Natalia versus another one, or whether we should invite the McElroys or the Bryans for dinner on Saturday night. And then there were those times like now when he acted like the most generous and easygoing guy in the universe: just like the sexy American I remembered in the Belgrade tavern when we first met.

Biljana arrived at Dulles airport a week before Christmas in 1998. The six years since our separation had molded her into a stunning, voluptuous young woman. She treaded the ground with such steadiness, precision, and grace, as if expecting that at every second the world would be her audience, her adoring public. Which it often was. As soon as she emerged from the gate at international arrivals people stared at her, turned their heads and twisted their necks to catch a glimpse of her as if she were a celebrity who had just landed from a Caribbean trip. Some failed to see their own relatives coming out, so enthralled were they by the apparition of my younger sister and her flaming curls bouncing on her back, the cavalcade of scarves and ribbons around her neck and hanging from her hair, and the colored layers of sweaters. As for me, our childhood and teenage years rushed into my head like a torrent, sweeping away everything in its path. For a few moments I even forgot Natalia who, almost four and a stunning apparition herself, was jumping up and down and asking every second when Aunt Biljana was going to come. Our reunion was every bit as dramatic and colorful as Biljana's appearance. Tears flooded our faces, screams emerged spontaneously from our throats, sighs and moans from our heaving chests. Natalia was confused when she saw us crying and started howling and pulling at my coat, thinking that something awful had just happened. But Biljana immediately recovered, picked up Natalia with one arm, and started talking to her in Serbian and telling her what a beauty she was. Natalia was transfixed and although she did not understand one syllable of Serbian, she stared and smiled at Biljana as if she had just met her fairy godmother who happened to speak an incomprehensible magical language. Biljana breathed in the American air, took in the dreary sight in front of the airport where buses, shuttles, and taxis moved in a continuous flow poisoning every metric cube of atmosphere, and said: "Hm, rather ugly but exciting, I can live here!"

Biljana's presence in our house made everything harder and easier at once, sweeter and more raucous, more interesting and more painful. The air quivered, the atmosphere brightened up, but the constant swinging between Serbian and English, between stories of "home" and the realities of my new "home," marriage, child care, and work routines, between Mark's increasing passive-aggressive moodiness and Biljana's intensely manic personality, placed a huge strain on my psyche and made me feel like a paragon of calm and sanity by comparison with either of the two adults around me. The feeling of something out of balance seeped through me at all hours of the day. I had secretly thought that Biljana's presence would soothe Marija's absence instead of sharpening it. But it became clear that Marija was not replaceable by anyone even if that someone was my diva sister, and in fact her presence incited torrents of memories from Sarajevo, Belgrade, our childhood and youth that had stayed somewhat dormant before her boisterous arrival. I now yearned for our trio of girlish exuberance and mischief as we flashed across the streets of Sarajevo in our mad runs, or as we sat and talked about everything under the stars in my parents' apartment in Belgrade. And in that trio of our youth, the three musketeers that we thought we were, it was Marija who had always brought the clamor of magical adventure. Without her, a gaping void of loneliness opened on all sides and gave a hollow ring to our voices. *Hello, hello, is anybody there, there, there?* I kept hearing in my head, in the hallways of my memory. *Marija, are you there?* I wanted to say out loud sometimes. Her absence was steely and I was cold all the time.

At the end of the first week in our house, which felt like

a month, Biljana came into my study and curled up on the bed breathing hard. Enormous tears were streaming down her freckled cheeks and before I could say anything she was pouring out sentences and news that were to leave me in wrenching pain for a long time. Through tears and sobs, Biljana blurted out the news that Marija's family had all been killed. Just like that, shot to death, all murdered under a blue July sky. Everybody? Her parents, Farah, and Kemal, too? I kept asking. Everybody, all of them, she kept answering. "How do you know, Biljana, who told you, maybe it's a mistake. Sometimes faulty information gets transmitted in times of war." "I know because I talked to Ferida and Marija's old friend, the sculptor Mirza. But no one would reveal Marija's whereabouts. In the summer of '95 when the big massacres happened I couldn't get ahold of anybody. But then a year later when I actually ran into Mirza at the university, I asked him about Marija. At first he wouldn't say anything. He just stood in the hallway and stared at me. Then I pressured him and he told me. Marija's family made the huge mistake of going to Semizovac after the UN declared the region of Srebrenica and its vicinities a 'safe zone.'"

I remembered the Fourth of July conversation I'd had with Marija, the one when she told me they were all moving into the countryside near Srebrenica. "We'll just be there on the farm with my grandparents," she had told me with an almost hopeful tone. "Until things get better and more tolerable in Sarajevo."

"Is Marija dead?" I asked with my heart pumping out of my chest. "No," was all that Biljana said. She stopped crying and just stared at me. "No?" I asked. "Where is she then, how is she?" Then Biljana stayed quiet, she simply could not talk. Her face was momentarily racked with grief, her beautiful features all out of whack. I got it perfectly. I had read the reports about what happened to Bosnian women, always hoping Marija was not one of them. Marija herself had told me about how the snipers and bombings were easier to understand than the rape camps. I hadn't wanted to imagine anything, when she'd mentioned that on the phone, but now my imagination was finding the darkest corners, and the most hideous images bombarded me. I wanted to know at least if the Marija that I knew still existed, that she was still sane, or at least recovering. "Where is she?" was all I could ask. "In Sarajevo," said Biljana in a whisper. "At least that's what Ferida told me. But Marija doesn't want to be seen or found by anyone. Even Ferida hadn't actually seen her, only heard from her by phone and once in a letter. She was secretive but at least she gave me that bit of news about Marija. She told me there is a chance Marija might be brought over to the States. There were lots of American psychologists, human rights activists, artists, lawyers, and archaeologists who went to Bosnia in the years after the war, particularly after that big-time American lawyer won the huge lawsuit against Karadzic for the Bosnian women." For a moment I had no idea why archaeologists would be on that list of professions. But then I understood in horror that the archaeologists must be unearthing the corpses hidden in the mass graves. The hills and mountains in the Srebrenica region were packed with mass graves made in a hurry by the Serbian armies. Instead of searching for Etruscan amphorae those brave archeologists had gone to Bosnia to use their digging skills in unearthing the corpses of Muslim Bosnians. Biljana told me an American therapist worked with Marija. What did she mean "worked with"? I wondered. Then she said the therapist was trying to bring Marija to America. Someone finally was working to bring Marija to the States and it wasn't me. I now understood why Biljana hadn't been able to render all this information before.

Christmas was in two days and it seemed a cruel joke at that juncture. The world was never going to be the same for me or for Biljana. The Marija I knew was forever gone. I understood that although she was not dead, her kind of disappearance might have been worse than death. Natalia bounced into the room, terrified by the darkness, by Biljana and me sobbing, by the grief that hung around us like a palpable laden body, and she immediately left again, howling and calling for her father.

I envisioned Marija in her full Indian goddess majesty, her mesmerizing way of talking, her shiny dangling jewelry, her incomparable dark hair and how fast she ran, like a firebird. I played our phone conversations during the war in my mind, trying to recapture her voice moving between exuberance and despair, her unlikely stories. Biljana and I hugged and sobbed in the utter hopelessness. Biljana said she could only now mourn fully and properly for Marija, that she'd had to wait to be with me. She told me she had kept in touch with Marija during the entire time of the war and sometimes she sent her provisions and foods through people who were going to Sarajevo—journalists, activists, or just random people who were reckless and crazy enough to venture into that hell. I said I wanted to go back to Sarajevo and take Marija back to the States with me. Biljana said it was impossible because Marija hadn't given away her location to anyone. "Nobody knows where she is." She repeated that again and again. Not even Ferida knew. Marija wanted contact with no one. She wanted to remain invisible.

As I looked out from the window in my study, an overpowering feeling of inescapable doom hovered around us. The sky suddenly seemed to be covered in flames and crossed by explosions. *How does she go on?* I kept wondering. My life was sliced in two like a butchered piece of meat: the part before Marija's doom and the part afterward. *How does one go on raising a child, working, eating breakfast?* I kept asking myself, too. Natalia ventured into our room again and this time she cuddled between Biljana and me on the bed. She took turns wiping our tears and asked: "What is wrong, Mami, did a wrong thing happen?" I pulled myself together and tried to explain to Natalia the reason for our grief and tears: "Yes, sweetie, Mami and Aunt Biljana's good friend Marija was very badly hurt by some bad people back in our old country." I was amazed that I could even articulate that much and reduce the whole miserable story to a simple sentence that sounded like a bad fairy tale: *The princess was eaten up by the bad dragon.* "Will she get better, Aunt Biljana?" Natalia asked. "Yes, my love," answered Biljana like a true fairy godmother: "There are some good people who are taking care of Marija and who are trying to make her better."

"Is your country bad, Mama?" Natalia asked. Her question took me by surprise. I hated my country at that point but somehow I didn't want to give Natalia that prejudice against her own roots from the very start in her life. Maybe I could at some point recover the good things about my country of birth and then I wouldn't want her to be already turned against it. I tried to reconcile, negotiate, wasn't I a political scientist after all? "There were some very bad people in our old country that hurt a lot of people from Marija's city and family, but everybody is not bad in our old country. Mami and Aunt Biljana and Grandma Anica and Grandpa Petar and their friends are not bad." "Mami, I don't want to go to your old country," said Natalia after thinking for a while. Not all my infantile-sounding explanations and negotiations could take away the bad feeling that Natalia got from catching that glimpse of our pain and rage at that old country of ours. The language of fairy tales didn't work to articulate the adult pain that Biljana and I had revealed to her. Maybe that's where our society went wrong, providing palatable and sometimes even pleasurable explanations to make violence seem like nothing more than a scary story, some red paint smeared on the body of an actor who pretended to be dead or wounded.

As the three of us lay on my bed in a state of stupor there was a gentle knock on the door and Mark walked in. I was taken by surprise. It had been some time since he'd entered, not since our relations started to be so strained. He asked in a gentle voice if anything was wrong and if there was anything he could do, and for a moment I remembered the beginning of our relationship, and how thoughtful and kind he was. Without hesitation I blurted out the horrible news: "Marija's family have all been killed. Dead. And she is...she is...not well." Mark stood stunned in the doorway. "I'm so sorry, so, so sorry. How terrible," he said, his face pained. And for that moment I felt no anger toward him. I even felt affection and a sense of discovery as if it was now only, on the cusp of unbearable news and when our marriage was estranged, that he revealed a real and raw section of his core that I had once so desperately searched for. Marija's family would have been killed, after all, even if Marija had been here with me. And then how could she have possibly been able to bear the reality of her being gone halfway across the world while her family had been killed? Sometimes evil and tragedy trapped us on all sides and there was no right way to turn. Mark sat down on the bed next to us and stroked Natalia's hair.

It had grown completely dark in the room and all I could hear was the soft snow tapping against the windowpanes and our heavy breathing. Mark had left the room as gently as he had entered it and the three of us were still lying on the bed. It felt as though Marija's spirit had entered the room like a brooding wind. Natalia had fallen asleep between us on the bed, holding each of our hands as if she were going for a walk into a secret land. Then a name struck my memory and made its way almost involuntarily out of my mouth in a whisper: Sally Bryant. The therapist, psychologist Sally Bryant with whom Marija and I spent a night to remember in one of Belgrade's outdoor cafés right before the start of the war. "Biljana, do you know by any chance the name of the therapist who is working with Marija?" Biljana answered sleepily: "A classic American name, someone from California, Susie or something like that." My heart missed a beat and then another: "It wasn't by any chance someone by the name of Sally Bryant, was it?"

Of course it was Sally Bryant who had gone to Bosnia with other psychologists and archaeologists trying to unearth bones and patch up broken spirits. In all the confused pain that had entered my mind with the news about Marija, this new discovery was a single drop of light. At least if she was being pulled out of her hell by Sally Bryant, maybe there was a chance that Marija could somehow prevail over her misery. For Natalia's sake, I held on to that possibility. I heard Marija's voice in my head: "Come on, Lara, run faster, you can do it." She was running ahead of me through the snow on the hilly street that led to Farah and Kemal's house, wearing a black coat with white fur trim around the collar, and her face flushed from the cold. Biljana touched my face and I touched hers and our palms were soaked in each other's tears. Biljana was in that picture, too. She was standing next to Marija in a maroon coat with beige trim and her red curls were falling impertinently down her shoulders. We fell asleep thinking of snow.

The massacres of Srebrenica and the stories of the camps became a taboo subject in our house. Mark had shown a kinder side that winter evening when he found us sobbing in my room and heard about Marija's calamitous predicament. But my persistent recriminating looks and words made him distant again, and I re-became my angry, unforgiving self. It seemed that the only way to compensate for that burdensome silence was for me to revisit accounts of the genocide in Srebrenica, the excruciating day of July 16 when hundreds of men of all ages were executed on the Branjevo farm, when the officer responsible for the killings had been given the witness protection status. Between the thirteenth and the nineteenth seven thousand Muslim Bosnian men had been executed, all done during six sunny days in July.

Biljana couldn't understand why I had married Mark and why I had left everyone to be in what she thought was a "sad" marriage. I explained that I had once liked his American ways, his ease, his grace and smoothness, so different from our Serbian macho guys. "You would have fallen, too, if some kind of Tony reminding you of the hero in your beloved *West Side Story* had walked your way one evening in a Belgrade bar, talking about humanitarian ideals, wouldn't you?" I told her with self-assurance and indignation. Biljana denied it all with vehemence as if she were the only person in the world who was right about important things like love and marriage. I brooded over the conversation and admitted to myself that yes, indeed, it was in part what I perceived as Mark's Americanness, the glow of freedom and ease, that broke down my defenses and made me act in an impulsive way. It was as if I were following some movie heroine's script. Lara, the heroine, believed she had been attracted to Mark's ideas, intellectual savvy, love of poetry, and passion for humanitarian causes. She could still feel the sex appeal on the American's lips in that smoke-filled Belgrade tavern. I couldn't blame that Lara. And perverse as it might seem, I felt that Lara would do it again: marry the American.

And as it happened, my own moralizing sister ended up finding her own American hero not long after our conversation about my "sad" marriage. At one of the schools of dance in DC, she actually did meet her Tony, who was really named Ricky. They fell in love instantaneously and within a month they were making preparations to marry and move to Chicago where they had an opportunity to open their own school of dance together. Right then, Biljana stopped preaching to me about Mark and our marriage and became hugely sympathetic to everybody's love sorrows. She was convinced and determined that her marriage would be successful and happy. "I felt it in my flesh, Lara, the first second we set eyes on each other," she told me. "I felt it in every inch of my flesh that we were meant for each other." I rolled my eyes and let her talk about the intuitions of her flesh, hoping that maybe at least one of us would end up happily married.

As Biljana was dancing her way into the love story of her life, our native city of Belgrade was being bombarded by UN raids and American bombs to stop Serbia's war with Kosovo. Our country never tired of wars. In the middle of wedding and moving preparations, one afternoon Biljana appeared with a face as devastated as when she had told me about Marija. "Who died?" I asked instantly. Nobody had died yet, she said, but Papa was in the hospital for a hernia surgery, and they were bombarding our city. Our mother was a wreck. "Our city sort of deserves to be bombarded, doesn't it?" I said unflinchingly, to which Biljana answered equally unflinchingly that maybe it did, but it was still our city and our parents lived there, and one of us needed to go back. With Biljana involved in her wedding preparations, it was clear that it was me who would be going to Belgrade to be the savior of our family. Maybe it was an opportunity to put some order in my ethnic and linguistic identity, to try to figure out where I actually belonged. And maybe I'd be able to get news about Marija on my own, even try to find her. Against Mark's and all of our friends' advice, I bought a ticket to go back and see Belgrade under bombs. I had run away from war in the first place, and now I was headed straight for the bombs and the explosions, the US air raids and the NATO tanks. At that point in my life I seemed to need war like some people needed peace.

My father died a few hours before I arrived in Belgrade. His surgery, I found out, had been interrupted by bombs. The empty hospital bed where he had died was surrounded by mortar and broken glass. Soldiers removed the debris in the hospital and told me to leave the premises; I was forbidden to be there, they told me.

At the funeral, remorse and nostalgia swept through me like arid winds. The priest droned on about my father going to greener places in a better universe where there would be no sorrow, and waved the incense burner across the grave. I thought about the three years when I was small when we lived in Greece, where my father had been sent on a diplomatic mission to work for the Yugoslav embassy in Athens. My father often repeated that even when we were in Greece, we should live as if we were still living in Belgrade, never getting too greedy or presumptuous. Maybe that was why my memories of Greece were like torn postcards—a corner of the Parthenon, a slice of the Mediterranean against chalky columns, the head of Zeus on top of a megalomaniacal temple—all with Belgrade towering above. I had taken my father's advice to heart, I never forgot Belgrade. I hadn't spent enough time with my father during my last years in Belgrade; I couldn't even remember a warm good-bye when I left Serbia as Mark's bride. I hadn't written or called him enough after I'd gone.

With the slow descent of my father's coffin into the freshly dug grave, I was too frozen to throw the slim bouquet into the ominous hole in the ground. Friends and colleagues from the embassy, neighbors, aunts and uncles whom I barely remembered, all dressed in black attire, tossed their flowers while I watched. Biljana's absence from the scene felt profoundly wrong. My father's death felt profoundly wrong, and utterly irreparable. A corner of sharp Athenian blue sky appeared, a vision from thirty years before, above the fresh grave.

It was from my father that I had gotten my obsession with ideas of goodness and political workings of states and governments. I wished I could have asked him what he really thought of my messy painful life. There was a heavy thud as the coffin hit the bottom of the grave. That, and the sound of my mother's inconsolable sobs. When we got home, my mother broke one by one each of the glass miniatures she had gathered from the glass factory where she worked as a chemist—the black-and-white penguins, the small red shoes, the dolls, the birds—until a shiny pile of colored glass crumbs lay at her feet. She played the *Doctor Zhivago* theme song on the turntable and cried with big howling sounds until night fell.

On the exploded street corners and dirty boulevards, I gathered shreds of my youth and of my college years. I walked by Marija's old studio apartment where we had last seen each other and held each other at the start of the war. There was no possibility of news about Marija in the desolate grayness of the Balkan madness. I walked around her apartment building several times, hoping I would meet someone who knew her. I should have gone back that morning when I'd left her, I should have at least waved back at her. "Doesn't that Mark of yours have a brother or cousin I could marry, too?" she had asked in a playful, self-mocking whisper before we'd parted. "And don't completely forget me, all right? Go to that Mark of yours, don't make this any harder, all right?" She could always joke off all her pain and resentments.

Living with my mother for a few days in our old Belgrade apartment with its decades of bad smells and cracks in the walls, I started calling anyone who knew Marija in search of a lead. I called Ferida, the sculptor Mirza, a cousin of Marija's Sonja, Sabina our old friend from middle school, and people from the list Biljana had given me whom I'd never even met. No one would share anything, let alone tell me about Marija or anything that had to do with the war. Only Ferida lingered with me on the phone in a friendly way, sharing news of her daughter, Mira, and her activities with international organizations of poets working for peace. But when I'd mention Marija, there was a hole of silence as deep as my father's grave. I wanted to go to Sarajevo and see for myself but there was no longer any train there, and the buses were not safe. I went back to the black sadness of my mother, who tearlessly spent her days rummaging through my father's possessions and clothes, talking to herself as she handled each item. The people I loved the most were disappearing one after another.

When I parted with my mother at the airport, it was as if she were looking through me. We waited together for my turn to go through the security check. I wanted to cry in her arms, but her arms barely embraced me. With my father gone, she had lost her will to embrace anyone. My connection to my birth country was almost entirely gone. I hurried to my plane that would take me back to Washington, DC, without any tears.

Provence and Paris, France.
Country of Lies

2001–2003

My trip to southern France soon after the events of September 11 seemed like an inexplicable and unlikely dream. I had gone to Aix-en-Provence in mid-September of that year, for a conference on Rationalism and the French philosopher Descartes. Although French Rationalism and Descartes were not my specialization, I had decided to attend the conference in a fierce desire to take a break from my Washington life, Mark, and even motherhood. Natalia never clung to me when I went away to a conference just as she hadn't clung to me when I decided to visit Belgrade under a rain of bombs. Now America had succumbed under a rain of attacks, the Twin Towers and the Pentagon had just fallen, and I was going to France. I seemed to be drawn to wars and dangers. On the eve of my departure Natalia just looked straight at me without saying a word, gave me a quick kiss on the cheek, then turned around and fled like a bird. I told her I would bring her something warm and sunny from southern France. She said, "Goodbye, Mama, bring me a hat." I left in a swirl and with a tickle in my heart as if I was on the verge of something new: a new country, new city, new climate, and Descartes, the father of thinking rationally.

The colors of Provence burned desires into my soul, and its sharp winds swept over me with inebriating flutters. It was all unexpected, reckless, and impossibly brilliant. At the conference I first felt out of place and slightly awkward among the crowd of Descartes lovers, although I spoke French fluently. In the afternoon of the first day, I felt ravenously hungry after an entire morning of bathing in the French Enlightenment. I stepped outside to get a sandwich at the next-door café. A man brushed by me and said "Bonjour." He was one of the conference participants. I said "Bonjour" right back and before I knew it we were having warm panini and espresso and laughing like teenagers. He was Tunisian and taught at the University of Tunis. He wasn't a Descartes specialist, either, and had also just come to the conference to get away, hear new ideas about old ideas, and see friends he hadn't seen in a while. His name was Karim and he was smoldering in his smoothness, like a mix of Clark Gable and Omar Sharif. Mustache, dark velvety eyes, a way of tilting his head to listen to you, a spontaneous laugh that made you think the whole world was in a state of hilarity. There was a film of melancholy over his dark eyes that made him seem the incarnation of Mediterranean cool. And I was not immune to it. That kind of masculine charm may have been as old as the world itself, but it was new to me. We sat talking and drinking coffee and wine and lemonade and eating small savory snacks and luscious desserts and then more coffee and wine and lemonade until my head was spinning and Descartes and the French Rationalists were as far away as a floating island lost on the horizon. The city of Aix-en-Provence came ablaze at twilight, the wine was flowing in the outdoor cafés, the streets were swarming with people chatting blissfully, the last sun rays graced the multicolored buildings with magical puddles of light. Before I could even understand what was happening, Karim Rachid, the Tunisian professor and scholar of existentialist philosophy and political theory, was removing my clothing in my tiny hotel room with delicate and maddening precision. That night, amid Karim's intoxicating caresses and kisses, with the full moon of Provence shining shamelessly in our window, occasional troubling thoughts darted by like comets: *I have become an adulteress. What will happen with Natalia? I will never be whole again. I am living the adventure of my life, I am on a path of no return.* Karim was sleeping and his body was warm, with a lemony fragrance, in the Provence night. A delicious feeling of irreversible sinfulness flooded every one of my senses and every corner of my conscience. I felt depraved and I loved it. Sleeping with a stranger in a hotel in southern France, I had finally taken a bite out of the fruit of life, the real fruit of life that came with a roller coaster of guilt and thrill and delicious torments. I heard myself giggle in the middle of the night, the fragrant Provence air cooling my heated body. I was greedy for happiness.

For the remaining three days of the conference Karim rented a car and we scorched the roads of Provence at 120 kilometers an hour like a couple on the run. We were on the run from French Rationalism, from our own lives, from the whole world. We stopped by the side of the road and made love in lavender fields. The sun poured its demented scarlet sunset over our heaving bodies. Washington, even Natalia, my university career, my own sister, my father's funeral and my mother's weeping, they were all worlds away. Marija's face glided surreptitiously into my conscience only once, a fleeting reminder of something that I had lost and I was continuing to lose in never-ending lavender fields and lustful whispers. The rhythm of my own perdition was both fast and slow— a fast-forwarding of my life that also moved in slow motion where I saw myself glide into an endless abyss. We returned to the conference only for a few hours so Karim could deliver his paper on existentialism and postcolonial consciousness. It seemed to me he was speaking a cryptic language and yet I absorbed every raspy word that he uttered that morning thinking that his lips had traveled the length and width of my body. It all came to an abrupt halt the evening before my return to the States when I saw my face in the window of a boutique jewelry store. Between sapphires, amber, and turquoise stones glowing in the Provence twilight, I saw a disheveled face with poufy hair and cat eyes. It was Lara Kulicz staring back at me with a look and a face from a different realm. I felt a sickening rift between the real me that was standing transfixed by the luscious jewels and the image that reflected back. I touched my face and the person in the window did the same. I stuck my face to the cool window and prayed to her for wholeness. She blinked, she closed her eyes, she whispered incomprehensible words, she mentioned Natalia, Mark, Biljana, Marija, a list of people and countries that made no sense: Serbia, Bosnia, America, Mexico, France, Tunisia. People were countries and countries went to war with one another. Karim touched my shoulder and asked me if I wanted a piece of jewelry. When your world collapses, buy jewelry. The person in the window with cat eyes laughed at my thought and said that yes, she wanted a piece of jewelry. The next moment I was trying on a silver-and-turquoise necklace. Karim said it looked "*fabuleux*," and it matched my eyes. He told me of the jewelry bazaars in his native city of Tunis and how he'd bring me an emerald necklace the next time we met. Emerald was a popular stone and gold was cheaper than saffron. What was I going to do with saffron? I didn't understand what "next time" meant. I didn't understand what saffron meant. I tried on the necklace and had a snippet of a memory of a morning when I gave my turquoise necklace to Marija. A war was starting nearby and we cried and held hands. The world was a fucking mess and I was trying on a turquoise necklace that was the price of some precious spice in another country. The woman at the counter smiled the most fake smile in the world and said the necklace looked *"fantastique."* She didn't mention any spices, but she asked: "Would you like some earrings to go with the necklace, mademoiselle?" And Karim asked her: "Yes, could we see some?" before I gave my answer. They were both deciding about earrings as if I were absent or a child. I tried on turquoise earrings that were dangling alongside my neck. I had seen women like that before: women who stood in jewelry stores while a rich man bought them expensive jewelry and satisfied their whims. I had never wanted to be a woman like that and now I was one. I didn't know if Karim was a rich man or just trying to impress me. He whispered in my ear that he loved me; he said *"mon amour,"* which sounded as fragrant and light as that expensive saffron must have tasted. I hadn't thought of love one bit through the ride of those reckless days and now he was whispering love words in my ear as I was trying on turquoise earrings. The woman turned her head away discreetly and I thought I deciphered a surreptitious smile back at Karim. Then I turned to look at Karim and a big smile stretched across his face. It seemed fake, too, like a simulacrum, the copy of another smile. Then I had a sharp moment of clarity, edgy, piercing, and swift: *Who is Karim?* He could have been the Tunisian mafia for all I knew, a drug dealer, a saffron dealer, a terrorist, a heartbreaker, a miserable wretch trying to pose as a rich man, a married man. Oh yes, the blade of clarity struck again: He was a married man and I was a married woman. What was I doing in that store? I turned down the earrings and wore the necklace. Somewhere in the world Marija, whose entire family had been killed on one sunny July afternoon, and who had been raped by Serbian soldiers, was wearing a turquoise necklace, too. The evening was limpid and we strolled back to our hotel holding hands. I wore my necklace as we made love. For some reason I cried. For some reason Karim cried, too. I said I didn't know when I would see him again, maybe never. I had a family and a career. It sounded hollow in the tiny hotel room. Yet my body felt full to excess, only my heart felt hollow. I wanted my body to be my heart. I knew Karim and I would meet again. The next day I was on an airplane back to the United States and all of me was an empty crater adorned by silver and turquoise.

Despite the thousands of miles, the marriages and children that separated us, Karim and I continued to plan incognito meetings at conferences over the next two years. We met mostly in France and stayed in small hotels on side streets as if worried someone familiar might see us on one of the main boulevards. I prepared my travels with great precision as if I worked for a spy operation. At home I overcompensated for my delinquent absences by taking on more chores, being kinder to Mark, cooking an abundance of Serbian meals to his great surprise and delight. For a while, the more entangled

I became in my affair, the better I was as a wife. As for Natalia, I spent intense hours with her involved in all her activities, wrecked with guilt for lying to her, hoping that some of her purity and innocence would rub off on me. I taught my courses with more attention and dedication than ever. I did everything with a higher degree of truthfulness and passion in an attempt to melt away the shameful, adulterous slivers of my life.

Between the events of September 11 and the beginning of the Iraq War, Karim and I steadily built a shiny web of lies and a second life of illicit encounters across the tumultuous ocean that separated us. When the bombs started falling over Baghdad, we were making love in a small Parisian hotel room. We had burst into the tiny room furnished with fake antiques all heated up, each arriving from our different corner of the world: me from America, him from Africa. We turned on the news right away because the beginning of the war was imminent—and we needed to know the fate of the world. The ominous lights of the explosions broadcast by the French television flickered on the dark-red flowery wallpaper. Karim's flesh smelled of lemony cologne, a whiff of Parisian spring air entered through the half-open windows, and all of my American problems dissolved in our chaotic embraces and breathless whispers. It seemed to be all there in that moment: fire and ice, burning snows and cool sands.

I had found a new survival strategy for the messiness of my life when I was with Karim: I created pockets of pure oblivion in which all things past melted like a spring snow. I hid inside those pockets in the illusion of safety and happiness and pretended everything was as it should be, floating in a womb-like cavity carved inside memory and history, where nothing and no one could reach or touch me. In those pockets of oblivion I willed my entire past out of my present, even Sarajevo, everything good and bad, beautiful and horrific; the entire mosaic of my life became white and shimmering nothingness. Oblivion was white and merciful.

In the evening of the first night of the war with Iraq, we went out into the streets for a reality check. We wanted to make sure the war had actually started and it wasn't just a trick of the French television. We joined a group of French students demonstrating against the war and against the American president. With the young voices screaming against the bombs over Baghdad in the chilly March evening it all seemed pretty real. I was nervous about my American passport, so I relied on my Serbian identity as a fallback. The French liked me as a Serbian, much more than they did as an American; they didn't seem to care that my country was run by a genocidal makeshift government at that point in history. They were just mesmerized by the idea of the "exotic" Balkans. Karim had his Tunisian passport to rely on, not quite a trust-inspiring identity at that time. We held hands and joined the voices of the students, and once in a while Karim whispered my name and French love words in my ears. The thought that we'd make love in French again later on made me smile proudly. When back in America, caught in the mire of my marital problems, staring at the blue wall of my kitchen in anger and confusion, I could always say to myself—with bitter satisfaction—what Humphrey Bogart told Ingrid Bergman in *Casablanca*: "We'll always have Paris!" That was Marija's favorite movie line, which she uttered with childish delight in difficult situations. I was stealing our movie lines for my affair with Karim, and that wasn't by far the worst thing I was doing. My sense of right and wrong was all sagging at that time in my life and I didn't care much. The layer of oblivion made it better.

I was terrified of those American bombs that kept falling and, selfishly, of what they were going to mean for my clandestine meetings with Karim. I felt strangely exhilarated chanting hand in hand with Karim in the streets of Paris. I was part of a bloody moment in history. I felt cornered by history and somehow that was exciting. After the students' demonstrations, Karim and I strolled through the narrow hilly streets of Montmartre. In Place du Tertre, one of the portrait artists offered me a 50 percent discount to draw my portrait when she heard I was Serbian. I didn't say a word while posing but just smiled my most seductive smile as Karim stood next to the artist, watching her every move and letting me know that my portrait was coming along nicely. I hungrily watched him watch me and I prayed that we would freeze, just like that, in the bustling corner of Montmartre and that my American husband, personal and professional worries would all vanish from my life and memory forever, leaving only my pearly daughter Natalia as the one palpable fruit of my otherwise questionable choices. After the portrait was done Karim took my hands in his, turned them over, touched my life line and kissed it many times, after which he gently closed my palms. *"Pour garder les baisers quand tu seras sans moi."* To keep the kisses for the time you are without me. There was one thing that did make him anxious, though, and that was the new war, the growing hatred toward the Arab world, his passport, the visas, the profiling in airports and embassies where he had to keep asking for visas so we could see each other for a few days.

"It's not going to get easier for us, you know," he said, later that evening. "Americans and the rest of the Western world are going to make it harder for people from my part of the world. What am I saying … it already is harder … this time it was harder than ever to get the French visa. What do you want, look at me! I don't look very Swedish, do I?" And he laughed with a twinge of bitterness. Karim was calm even when he was worried and the shadow of the new war, though looming above us and sneaking all around us in the piano bar in Montmartre, seemed to leave him unfazed. He just pulled at his mustache a lot more when he was nervous. I, on the other hand, fidgeted, bit my nails, grabbed his hands across the table, laughed nervously, and gulped down my oysters like a hungry cat. Karim had one daughter, Arina, and I had my Natalia. The symmetry made us say we were meant for each other and helped us to weave the illusion that our respective divorces would somehow solve themselves miraculously just because of that apparent cosmic synchronicity that balanced the lack of synchronicity of not having met a decade earlier. We were determined to part with a clearer plan for our future than we had at the beginning of our Parisian reunion. We were also determined to make the most of every second and fill it with magic, sex, and wine despite the guilt and the worries about our messy family situations and the bombs blasting over Baghdad. Karim and I left the restaurant dizzy from the wine and strolled around Montmartre tightly enlaced, admiring the view, kissing at street corners, hurrying to our little hotel room in the Latin Quarter. But as I lay awake for much of the night, next to Karim's warm body, scenes from my home life forced themselves into my conscience: the heavy silences at breakfast time, Mark's concentrated or absent look, his hurried rush out of the house to make sure he had enough time to prepare for his class. And then my own Tunisian makeshift Prince Charming would wake and ask me gently: *"Qu'est-ce qu'il y a, Lara mon amour?"* What is it, Lara my love? *"Rien, rien du tout."* Nothing, nothing at all, I would lie with conviction and cuddle in Karim's arms, pulling over me the magic white layer of oblivion.

That night Karim received a phone call from his family in Tunisia with the news that his mother had a stroke. I heard an angry female voice on the phone speaking to him in Arabic, to which he was responding in what sounded like

monosyllabic words. The phone conversation seemed inter-
minable, and when Karim lifted his eyes at me, there were
tears in them. He grabbed my hand and held it till the end of
the call. He had to go back earlier than planned, he said after
he hung up. His mother's life was in danger and his sister
said he needed to be there as soon as possible. His wife was
angry that he'd left in the first place. The room started turning as if I had been hammered on the head. Every force in the
universe was against us being together. I could find no words
for the news. Karim was upset and guilty for being away from
his family. I was heartbroken that our already short trip had
to be cut even shorter. I couldn't gather much sympathy for
Karim's mother or for any of the women in his family calling
him back with such urgency in loud Arabic words. We threw
ourselves in each other's arms, made love until dawn, and fell
asleep glued to each other for a couple of hours before taking
on the new day: March 21, the third day of the war in Iraq and
the last day of our togetherness for who knew how long. We
packed our suitcases in silence and took a taxi to the airport.
We each changed our respective flights from March 25 to that
day. I winced at the thought of Mark's inevitable accusatory
questions about the reason for my early return. My mind was
already circling in a maddening carousel of potential lies that
I would serve Mark upon my unexpectedly early arrival.

My plane was the first one to leave. We had two hours left
to spend together in the Charles de Gaulle airport. I asked
Karim to tell me about his country, about his city of Tunis,

the labyrinthine layout of the streets, the white stone Arab houses, the markets, the dense crowds, the ornate mosques, the ruins of Carthage, his daily schedule at the university. Tunis sounded like Sarajevo only with a big blue sea at its edges, instead of wooded mountains.

As I stood in line to get on the plane, my face streaked with tears, my bag filled with gifts for Natalia, and my carry-on luggage clumsily falling off my shoulders, not little was my surprise to see a colleague from the journalism department of my university standing in line to board the same plane back to Washington, DC. I froze with fear thinking he had seen me kiss and embrace Karim in our tearful farewell. The colleague just smiled and said hello, I answered with fake enthusiasm, dreading the possibility of my seat being next to his. Mercifully the seat beside mine was empty, and I had the full eight hours to think up a credible story about my early return. As the plane took off, and I reviewed every precious moment of my three days in Paris with Karim, I wondered: *What if I told Mark the truth?*

Washington, DC. The Truth

"April is the cruelest month." T. S. Eliot's line from *The Waste Land* had never felt truer. The days after my return, the air in our house was unbreathable, the space suffocating, and the walls too tight around us as we struggled to move from day to day through the mire of our work and family obligations. Mark seemed to punish me for my having been away at the conference. Some days I tried not to think of Karim and see what happened if my mind focused entirely on my family right then and there. I used all my organizational skills and the self-discipline that had helped me become a political scientist to orchestrate our lives in a semblance of contentment and peace. After my classes I went directly to Natalia's school and picked her up instead of letting her go to the after-school day-care program, and we made it into a special afternoon at the zoo or the National Gallery. We walked through the Hirshhorn Sculpture Garden trying to imitate all the postures of the statues in front of us, the contorted Rodins, the enormous group of the burghers of Calais, the emaciated Giacomettis. The feel of the April breeze on my face, or the way a sun ray fell through the blooming trees, would wake a longing in my chest. And carefully I had to hide my tears, so that Natalia wouldn't see them. I sometimes launched into fantasies about my having been born and raised in the Tunisian medina and wearing a white dress with sparkling blue embroidery; Karim would notice me in the crowd out of thousands of people and neither of us would be married but single and available for each other and we would live in bliss in a white Arab house with an inside courtyard invaded by scarlet bougainvillea. Natalia would bring me back to the hard earth of our Washington existence with a crisp tug at my coat or a squeeze of my hand. "Look, Mama, a bird just pooped on the Rodin statue," she shouted and then giggled as we were slowly walking through our favorite sculpture garden. Natalia looked stunning in her Madeleine green coat with the chestnut hair framing her oval face and her shameless laugh at the poop on Rodin's statue. I touched the silver-and-turquoise necklace I now wore all the time and thought of the chain of memories and associations attached to those pieces of blue stone. Karim and Marija, both absent, each on a different tectonic plate of the cracked and damaged earth. I would never be whole again.

On some days Mark was warm and reasonable, the man I had once loved. "He knows that something's going on,

Larinka, he's not dumb, you know. He is probably suspecting you are cheating on him," said Biljana on the phone. Her words made the reality of my relation with Karim sound so wrong: a bored Eastern European wife cheating on her good American husband. Three years after she had left Washington as a happy bride herself, Biljana was now a successful dance teacher in Chicago and had a rowdy, happy family with her Mexican American husband and two Mexican Serbian American daughters that she impatiently conceived one after the other. After my father's death, my mother had moved in with my sister. Biljana was a firm believer in the American principle of "working on your marriage." When she talked to me now she often used words like *cheating*, which sounded like judgment to me. I had no clear justification for my adultery, a word that to me sounded harsh but mythic. Francesca da Rimini and Paolo Malatesta in Dante's *Inferno* were murdered by a jealous husband for the crime of adultery, in flagrante delicto. Cheating sounded cheap and bourgeois, adultery sounded ominous and biblical.

One Sunday afternoon in April, I was admiring the budding maples from my bedroom window on Connecticut Avenue and I thought of my portrait experience in Montmartre with Karim watching me being drawn in charcoal. My ash-blond hair felt luminous; my indefinite blue-gray eyes were filled with sparkles. A deep longing for Karim seized me so I sat down at my computer and wrote him a passionate love letter reminding him of our stolen Parisian encounter and the romantic stroll in Montmartre. Then I took the portrait I had carried with me from Paris from the hiding place inside my wardrobe and stared at it. The moment when I watched Karim watch my face being drawn in charcoal lines became so real I almost felt the chilly March Parisian breeze on my arms. Just then Mark entered my room. I tried to hide the portrait, but he saw me and asked with a smile: "What have you got there?" I put the drawing behind my back and said: "Nothing, it's nothing really." He pretended to play as he was trying to get me to show him what I was hiding behind my back. He embraced me grabbing my arms and laughing. I was holding my arms back trying to save the rolled-up paper from him. Being much taller than me, he stretched his arm behind my back and grabbed it. When he tried to take it from me the paper gave in and tore. I gave a scream as if he had torn into my flesh. I pushed him away and burst into tears. I stretched out what was left of the portrait and the tear went right through the middle of my face, separating it in two. I threw it on the floor and he stared at it.

"I'm sorry. I'm so sorry, Lara, I don't know what got into me," Mark said and he did seem to be genuinely sorry. His face was sad and regretful and I almost felt a new surge of love for him. Then Natalia came in and seeing my torn portrait on the floor she picked up the two pieces and said: "Wow, Mama, this is really cool. Who did this?"

"An artist in France," I said and tried to regain my composure.

"I'll glue this back for you, Mama!" Natalia said and sat down on the floor next to me to hug me. Mark looked ashamed and left for his study with a red face. Natalia did indeed fix my torn portrait. She glued the pieces on the back until only a thin thread was noticeable, starting from the arch of my left eyebrow, going down around my nose and through the middle of my mouth. But even with all of Natalia's meticulous work the portrait wasn't the same. She knew it so she decided to make it more bizarre. She put colored sparkles all along the line to make it more artistically obvious. It looked funny in a beautiful sort of way. "See, Mama, it's better now, it's less boring." Looking at my distorted portrait creatively repaired by Natalia my life seemed in shambles, and impossible to glue back together. Half of the world's population copulated and produced children with partners they either didn't love or stopped loving at some point. Why couldn't people just wait and have children only with someone they were absolutely sure that they loved? The rift caused by the reality of loving your child more than anything in the world and not loving the child's parent or even hating him was irreconcilable, and impossible to live with. How did people do it all over the world?

I had pangs of worry about Natalia, who was going through a hard period. She'd begun stealing Barbie dolls and baseball cards, golf balls, Ping-Pong balls, BB gun pellets, and tiny toy NASCAR race cars from CVS stores as a way of asking for attention. When the CVS manager would approach me, Natalia would produce the stolen things right away and hand them to the manager as if she were the one doing the manager a favor. "Thank you, honey," the manager would say. "Don't do that again, okay?" or "This is not nice for a pretty little girl to do." I just stood and stared at the manager while my face turned bright crimson. I felt sorry for Natalia and instead of scolding her I always held her tight and stroked her hair. The managers all looked at me disapprovingly, as if to say I was a terrible mother. I dreaded that by the time I got home to Connecticut Avenue our house would be surrounded by police cars and a truck full of pink-haired Barbie dolls and Sammy Sosa baseball cards would be pulling out of our driveway: our daughter's CVS spoils for the week.

I climbed in bed and Natalia climbed next to me and leaned her head on my shoulder. We sat like that for a while in silence. Then she asked abruptly: "Mama, is it true that you and Papa are going to split up?" I sat up, startled. I was always truthful to Natalia about everything, but never about how I felt about her father. Well, almost everything, since I never did nor was I ever going to share with her the reality of my double life and of my transnational love affair. She needed my purity even if it was contrived. Or so I thought.

"Who told you this, Talia?"

"Grandma Susie; she said you don't love Papa anymore and that's why you are away at conferences all the time."

"Did you believe her?" I asked, furious at the sneaky mother-in-law of mine, who seemed to perfectly fit the stereotype of a bad mother-in-law. "First, Talia, how many times did I go to a conference this year, hm?" I knew that for a nine-year-old, Natalia had an unshakable respect for logic and pragmatic facts once they were pointed out to her.

"Once, one time, you went last month," she answered, knowing exactly what I was doing.

"Well, see, Grandma Susie was exaggerating, wasn't she, because once since the beginning of the year when we are already in April is not all the time, is it?" She was quiet.

"No, it isn't, but it is," she finally said.

"What do you mean, Talia?" I asked puzzled.

"Because you and Papa are fighting all the time, and you don't do nice things for each other anymore, and we don't go on any trips or walks just the three of us anymore."

You couldn't fool Natalia about anything. I needed to brace myself and tell Mark the truth, like I had told myself I would in those seconds as the plane took off from Charles de Gaulle airport. *The truth, the truth, the truth*, I kept thinking, trying to give a concrete shape to that term so vague, so slippery. The truth was a deep pond, with an unfathomable bottom. I couldn't see the truth in the shape of something I could tell Mark, looking him in the eyes and saying to him: *I am deeply in love with another man. I want us to get a divorce. We've never really been a good match. I thought I was in love with you when I met you in Belgrade as an idealistic journalist and human rights activist. But really, I don't understand you... You are not the person I thought you were when I met you then. Can we be reasonable about Natalia and custody and visitation?* Could I really say those words?

The beginnings of our threesome after Natalia's birth were almost happy. Mark would look at me admiringly and almost in awe as I nursed the squiggly translucent baby that was Natalia. So much of what went on in our marriage was in the indefinite area of "almost." Mark acquired a poetic melancholic humor that motivated him to launch into tirades about the miracle of motherhood. He held the baby for a little while and walked around our apartment humming an old English tune and closing his eyes while he did that. I wanted to scream *Watch out, open your eyes when you walk with the baby.* I was a controlled, rational person who knew where everything was, always prepared for my classes; I was never late for anything and meticulously wrote down my dreams the night after I had them. Yet I was destabilized by irrational impulses and thoughts once Natalia landed in my arms and grabbed my breast with her tiny lips.

That evening lying with Natalia on my bed and holding the rolled-up paper with the torn portrait of myself in Paris under Karim's affectionate eyes, I felt eviscerated. I asked Natalia to go out for a walk with me. She wanted Mark to come, too, and I agreed. Maybe we could rebuild, restart, and make that thing called marriage more tolerable. Maybe Karim would dissolve in oblivion and I would stop that emotional outflow once and for all. Mark was enthusiastic about the walk and even asked Natalia if she wanted to go to a movie, it was Saturday after all, and then he turned toward me and winked. For Mark to wink at me, something special must have occurred in his professional life, such as a prestigious journal accepting an article of his, or a conference inviting him to give a keynote address. It was when his work went really well that part of his happiness also spilled into our family life.

The April evening was fresh and fragrant. We went out on our beloved Connecticut Avenue like a happy family. I loved our street so much that I sometimes thought I had sedated myself and feigned contentment in my marriage just so that I could always go out on a spring night like that one or on a clear fall morning, or on a sweltering summer night and walk to the corner of M Street and Dupont Circle, or eat at a Mexican restaurant at the corner, then sit at one of the cafés on the sidewalk sipping a latte for an hour while correcting a pile of exams for Politics 101. We decided to see *Frida* at the cinema near our house. I never cared much for surrealist art and Frida's images of miscarried fetuses, or her self-portraits with eviscerated hearts didn't particularly touch a chord with me. I didn't understand why Frida put up with so much crap from that lecherous Diego Rivera, with all his demented infidelities, and then when she herself had an affair the best she could find was Trotsky, a Stalinist fugitive.

After the film and before we went home, we stopped to have an ice cream. We walked back licking our ice creams, and Natalia dropped hers in the street. "It's nothing, no big deal, I'll get another one," I said, licking my own lemon sorbet. "You have no parenting principles, Lara," Mark said, throwing his own half-eaten Oreo cookie ice cream in the trash can. "That's right, I don't want to develop any clear principles about ice cream consumption in our family," I said, throwing my own sorbet into the trash can. The way Mark would give such importance to a trivial issue that to me didn't deserve a minute's attention irritated me now more than ever. I always thought there must have been other rationales behind Mark's overblown arguments over tiny domestic issues, something deep and mysterious, like a childhood trauma or a burning concern for world peace. The little idiosyncrasies of our daily life, I thought, must offer a pretext for a greater drama. I cursed the Oreo ice cream in my mind, as well as Mark's impenetrable self-righteousness. Yet when I looked up at him I was still stunned by his beautiful and manly profile, as much as I had been in our daily ramblings through Belgrade that summer ten years before, and even in my first years in America. Only now his high forehead, beautifully carved cheekbones, and dreamy blue eyes all seemed shadowed by a cloud of worry—or maybe it was sadness? I felt sudden pity for him, for his trusting me during the two years of my reckless multicultural love affair, and now in his delicate gloom Mark appeared to me more real than ever before. Right then on our way back from the *Frida* movie and the failed ice cream experience, I decided I was not going to tell him of my love affair and that I would slowly let my relationship with Karim fade out of existence. He seemed to want to make peace, too. "Lara, what do you say we take a weekend vacation, just the two of us, to New York or maybe to the beach somewhere? We can leave Natalia with my mother, she's always happy to babysit, you know. We haven't been together just the two of us on a trip since before she was born, do you realize that?" His proposal sliced painfully right through my heart. He was the Mark I had fallen in love with, plus an added warmth, something quivering and raw without the movie-like image. It was as though he had just then decided to crack the icy wall that always seemed to be protecting his heart. Maybe the knowledge of Marija's tragedy, maybe an intuition that I was unhappy and unfaithful, maybe a renewed sense of mortality and growing old. Why had he waited so long? I wondered with tears in my eyes. "What a great idea, Mark. Let's go to New York, I've never been...all right," I heard myself say. My voice seemed foreign and wobbly, insecure and untruthful. I didn't recognize it. It was the voice of a deceitful and confused woman.

I was only grateful that Natalia was happily sauntering ahead of us. And then the spring evening breeze lifted my dress gently and a fragrance of fresh leaves and spring swept over me. Paris came alive. It all came back again: the longing for Karim, his melancholy smile, and his delicate sexy gestures that transported me away from everything banal, conventional, and American. I imagined Karim walking next to me instead of Mark and next to Natalia, talking and giggling, his twelve-year-old daughter Arina. Mark's and Karim's names were almost palindromes, almost. Mark was not Karim just as Victor Laszlo was no Rick. At least if Mark had been an alcoholic, or an abuser, it would have been easy to divorce him, and I wouldn't have been torn apart by guilt for being a reckless adulteress. But he was perfect, what reasons did I have? He hardly ever raised his voice. Even when he reprimanded me like just then about the Oreo ice cream, or when he cursed, he still used a leveled tone, he had a respectable tenured professor's job and earned a good salary, he was a faithful husband, he was concerned about human rights violations, he loved all my cooking and was a caring father.

He must have had his reasons to bring Hassan over instead of Marija, and indeed he had tried to help stop the war with his actions of consciousness raising about what went on in the Balkans. Maybe I was just as much to blame for not pushing harder and not being more active in trying to bring her to America. My mother loved Mark like her own son. Sometimes she would call me from my sister's apartment in Chicago, just to tell me for the millionth time how lucky I was to have a husband like Mark. If only she knew... I was worse than Frida, who had a pathological cheater for a husband. What were my reasons? The answer was Paris. I could never have Paris with Mark. He made love as correctly and levelheadedly as he talked. The sultriness and charm of our Belgrade nights and mornings had long ago faded away in our Washington duplex. Was I okay, he always asked during the sexual act, like I was having a root canal done. Until Karim I had thought that was the best one could have in love. But with Karim I was unhinged and explosive, whimsical and impatient, everything that I had never been before. The metamorphosis I'd been going through was both terrifying and irresistible. Swimming in guilty fantasies, a clear thought lit up in my mind. Mark was romantic without being passionate, while I was passionate without particularly caring about what people, especially American people, referred to as romantic. As for Karim, none of the American romantic categories applied to him—passion, melancholy, tenderness, sex appeal all radiated from him organically in an overall smoldering presence. Mark and Karim canceled each other out, I concluded, and I was caught in the middle unable to make a choice.

Back in our apartment, I went to the kitchen to make myself some tea, and Natalia went to her room to build a puzzle I had brought her from Paris. I sat at the kitchen counter with my elbows on the blue Italian tile and experienced an actual moment of contentment looking out the window at the maple tree swaying in the evening breeze and listening to the street noises, sipping from my jasmine tea.

Just then Mark came in with an unusually abrupt step and asked: "Who is Karim Rashid?" Because he said his first and last names in one breath, for a second it sounded like an unknown name and I thought Mark was asking me about someone else. Then I realized I must have left my laptop open in my study with Karim's email on it. I could see a grin of satisfaction on Mark's face, but combined with a grimace of pain around his mouth, his usually smooth face with his piercing blue eyes now looked distorted. At that pivotal moment, I felt no fear or remorse, or anxiety, or sadness. He asked again: "Who is Karim Rashid?" I looked at him in silence for one long second, and then I said in an even, unshaken voice: "He's my lover!"

On May 1, our divorce litigation started, with Mark as the plaintiff and me as the defendant. I had nothing to defend. I took care of Natalia, I taught my courses, I started preparing my tenure file. Mark had filed on grounds of adultery the Monday after he found Karim's amorous email to me on my open laptop. He asked for full physical and legal custody of Natalia, with "all reasonable visitation rights" for me. "It's illegal to use adultery in the custody litigation because it's strictly tied into the divorce and not the parenting component," my lawyer kept saying. "There is evidence that the mother has an immoral influence on the child," the prosecuting lawyer kept saying. "Mr. Lundberg is concerned about his daughter's moral upbringing," Mark's attorney kept saying.

Natalia wasn't taking it well. In school, her homeroom teacher complained that she used "four-letter words" a few times when she got angry at a boy called Tanyu, and that she read from *The Catcher in the Rye* in class instead of doing her work. Maybe she was bored, I told the teacher. Maybe Tanyu was a bully, and maybe the class wasn't exciting enough. The teacher pursed her lips, and then said that maybe I wasn't giving my daughter "the proper values and manners." What were "the proper values"? I wondered. Natalia exceeded everybody in her class in reading and math, she had lots of friends, she stood up for other kids whenever she thought they had been treated unfairly, and never told on anyone who had been mean to her.

I started calling Karim on my cell phone from my car, sometimes sitting in the parking lot of my university, at other times just pulling over and parking on a side street on my way home. I didn't feel safe talking now, fearing both my husband and the Patriot Act. Karim had started his divorce proceedings, too. For him, custody wasn't a problem, but money. *"Elle veut tout mon argent."* She wants all my money, he would say referring to his wife, then he would laugh, and then change the subject and say *"Enfin, qu'est-ce que tu veux..."* Well, what do you want... There was no poetry or romance in any of that. The double adultery pattern was inscribed somewhere in Dante's *Inferno*, right there with walking on burning sands or having your head switched backward so that it faced your ass. I wished I could laugh about that image now as I used to with Marija when we were reading from her luscious leather-bound edition. But only a bitter grin moved over my anxious face.

Washington, DC.
The Truth and Everything
but the Truth

Summer 2003

I found out from Mark that Hassan was now overseeing the newspapers all over northern Virginia. "What news of interest could there be in northern Virginia?" I asked Mark. I held on to my Serbian sarcasm, I was on a roll as he had once said at the beginning of my life in America at the chairman's party: "Rich senator living in Alexandria slips on ice, litigation lawyer from Herndon runs into a pole at a stoplight, news like that, Mark? This is the news that Hassan was brought over from war-ridden Bosnia to report on?" Mark was walking next to me on the National Mall with the debonair air that had so charmed me at the beginning of the Bosnian war. It had been his idea to walk and talk about the next steps of our litigation instead of arguing at home where Natalia could hear us. He kept his calm; only his jaws moved imperceptibly as a sign he was reining in his anger. I had no desire to talk about the litigation, it seemed like the most boring subject in the world to me. Only Natalia's custody worried me. I listened to him talk in legalistic terms about our child and our future in a language that was as foreign to me as Karim's Arabic, which nevertheless sounded sultry and sexy during our illicit encounters. "Mark, please tell me if you have heard anything about Marija from Hassan," I begged him. An African American vendor behind one of the food carts on the side of the Mall winked at us as if we were young lovers and offered us discounted pretzels. I stared back at him as he reminded me of Karim. "Hassan must know something for sure; he is from the same city, after all, and the same Bosnian community. He knows everyone," I went on feeling more and more distracted by the foods, sights, smells bombarding my psyche. An Indian vendor offered us tandoori chicken, then a Mexican one lemonade and churros. The smells and sight of foods fogged up my thinking and made everything seem trivial and frivolous. In my Serbian family we didn't mix eating junk food with tragic stories. In America, everything was covered up in greasy foods, ethnic foods, fast foods, junk foods, advertisements for panty hose and detergent and then life was made to look easy, clean and sweet, *a piece of cake*, the saying went. I was a foreigner amid foreigners.

"Go and speak to Hassan yourself," he said, walking

ahead of me on the endless grass strip. Why hadn't I thought of that myself?

When I went to Hassan's office the following afternoon, for some reason I put on a nice dress as if going on a date. In the old Yugoslavia, Serbia, Bosnia, people dressed up for even a casual meeting. Even in times of war they dressed up. As if to defy the ugliness of the siege and bombardments, they crossed the streets under the rain of sniper bullets in their Sunday best, women wearing lipstick and nail polish they had gotten on the black market or through daily acts of barter. My heart was beating like mad when I knocked on Hassan's door, expecting a harsh self-confident man who had stepped over Marija's chances of coming to America without a second's hesitation. Instead, Hassan reminded me of Kemal, Marija's grandfather: He was on the short side, with a white beard, a red round face, and a heavy limp. He hugged me like he had known me for a lifetime and asked me to sit down, and I felt sorry that I had never met him until now. He spoke softly and looked straight into my eyes. He lit a pipe that smelled just like Kemal's pipes, and wiped his forehead with a chiffon handkerchief. All those old country habits and objects, men with white handkerchiefs with embroidered initials in the pockets of their coats. I missed that.

I didn't ask him about Sarajevo, Belgrade, or Alexandria. All I wanted to know about was Marija. Did he know anything about her, was she alive, where was she? I grew more agitated as he took his time to answer. First I learned that Hassan initially didn't want to come to the States, and even suggested that Marija go in his stead; he had other occasions to leave, he could have been aided by UN organizations that knew of his work, and he had a family, wife and children, whereas Marija had no husband or children and it would have been easier for her to emigrate to America with Mark's help. In 1993, in 1994, and in early 1995 she could have come, before the sunny July of genocidal murders and rapes. "What wasted opportunities!" I said and realized that Hassan was becoming uncomfortable. I spoke not in Serbian but in angry simplistic English. "Where the hell is she, Hassan? Where is she?" He couldn't tell me where Marija was, he didn't know, it was something of a mystery, he said.

"How bad was it, Hassan, did Marija suffer a lot? Can she ever recover? Will I ever see her again? How bad was it really?" "Unimaginable," he said. "And yet for those who went through it and survived, nothing is unimaginable any longer." I saw that his eyes were heavy with tears. Hassan's laugh was warm and enveloping and again it reminded me of Kemal and everything that had once been warm and joyous in my life: Marija's brilliance and love, Sarajevo in times of peace, the smell of cinnamon and the taste of Farah's apricot jams. We spoke Serbian again and the many consonants of my native language soothed my burning mouth, my parched throat, my devastated soul. I needed a break from English, from America, from idiomatic expressions and mannerisms.

Hassan had gone back to Bosnia several times during the war and saw Marija. Apparently he was in awe of the tremendous job she was doing running the newspaper in the darkest times, without a single day's break. "She did a better job than I ever did," Hassan said. "She had humor and poetic flair and she was afraid of nothing. She was a stunning woman." I noted he said "she was" as if she were dead. My dearest Marija, of course she awed him, of course she did a better job than anyone else. She wrote like she spoke and she spoke like she lived: with unforgiving energy and intelligence, with dizzying flair and reckless humor. As I had always thought, she could have been the president of the country, if only our people hadn't been so stupid to elect a vicious president, the new Hitler and Stalin together, only more pathetic. Who in the world actually cared about little Bosnia and tiny Albania with no oil fields for any Western countries to dig in? The politics became even more confused in my mind as I was sitting in Hassan's office reeling from what I had found out about Marija.

Just as I was about to leave and Hassan got up from his chair to walk toward me and give me a good-bye hug, I couldn't contain myself and asked him looking at his limping leg: "What happened?" He was quick to answer as if waiting for the question: His leg had been torn by a blast while driving his car from the newspaper office in one of the 140-kilometer-an-hour races to elude the Serbian snipers. He got to the hospital too late, and had to wait for hours with pieces of flesh hanging from the bones of his calves and his femur crushed until a doctor was available. He was lucky his leg wasn't completely amputated, just the steel rod, half an amputation, he said and laughed. A man in the bed next to him had shared his vodka bottle with him, and that had helped. Now a metal rod was replacing his femur bone. "It's all right," he concluded, laughing as if he had just told a funny story. "I survived, that's what matters."

I left Hassan's office staggering and drove aimlessly around northern Virginia until I remembered I had a home to go to. I had a family that waited for me, disjointed as it might have been. The thought of Natalia, so fragile, so torn between Mark and me, made me weep in the car as I drove through atrociously ugly new developments and malls and waited at the red light in a state of utter alienation. It all looked like the new inferno, a place with no shape and no soul. The light changed to green and I rushed home to hold my dear Natalia.

After the meeting with Hassan I strangely felt less angry at Mark. Maybe because now I knew more of the truth about Marija, and hard as that truth was, it was better than the fogginess of ignorance. Maybe also because Hassan reminded me so much of Kemal, warm, thoughtful, and straightforward. I kept trying to find my own big truth pulsing underneath the messiness of my life. Some nights, falling asleep with Natalia next to me, I yearned for the quiet times before Karim. "Haven't we been a happy family?" I was asking myself in the private litigation with my soul. "Yes, we sort of have, for periods of time at least," said my soul. "Have you really given Mark a chance, all the chances he deserved?" My soul answered: "No, not really, I haven't given Mark and our marriage all the chances they deserved." Some mornings, when I woke up and took full consciousness of the new day of misery that lay ahead of me, I was determined to meet Mark in our beautifully tiled kitchen as he was drinking his coffee, take his hand, and tell him: *Let's forget that this ever happened, let's start a new day and stop the madness that is tearing us and Natalia apart!* But each morning brought only a new legal notice from Mark, a severe statement about our next court date, or about Natalia's schedule over the weekend, which now was divided equally between the two of us.

Natalia always seemed to find the split second when Mark and I crossed paths in the kitchen to make her morning appearance and acted as if we were the same family as before. "Can we all go to a movie tonight?" she would ask. "*Pirates of the Caribbean* is playing." Mark and I pretended we hadn't heard her and went on doing whatever we were in the process of doing. But then she got angry. "Hey, guys, are you deaf or something? I asked a question." Then Mark would lecture her about the "inappropriate" tone of her voice or I would tell her she needed to finish her homework. Sometimes she ignored our answers and would return to the kitchen ten minutes later dressed in an old Halloween costume as a ladybug, or as a biker rock star, which was her most recent costume and involved a pink wig. When I told her she needed to get dressed for school, she said that she was dressed for school. One day when I did take her to school dressed as a biker rock star, her homeroom teacher looked at me angrily and with disgust when she greeted us at the school entrance. I watched Natalia as she walked into the school with her huge backpack, her back slightly bent, her pink biker's wig perched on her head. I regretted everything.

That day I arrived at my office with my eyes red from crying. On the way up the stairs to my office, my cell phone rang and I answered without looking at the number calling. It was Karim with his sweetest and most loving voice telling me he missed me like crazy, his divorce was coming along, he had reached an agreement with his wife, and he was coming to see me this summer because he couldn't stand being away from me any longer. Stupefied and confused by the unexpected news I asked where he planned to come see me. He said Washington of course, wasn't I happy? Then he said "*Lara, mon amour*," and my knees became weak. A student of mine was waiting at the top of the stairs to talk to me about his paper on Plato's *Republic*. How did people carry on with their lives under bombs? I wondered again, reaching the top of the stairs, while at the same time smiling at the student and speaking to him in French by mistake. Karim asked me if I was okay, wasn't I glad? The student was staring at me in puzzlement as to why I addressed him in French. I reached the door to my office and tried to unlock it while dropping my purse on the floor with everything falling out of it, including a couple of menstrual tampons. The entire material world was against me. I told Karim in my sweetest voice that I was ecstatic about his visit, could I call him a bit later, after my class. He said *"Je t'aime,"* and I said *"Moi aussi"* while smiling at the student with the Plato paper. I dropped everything I had in my hands on my desk and sat down facing my father's eyes in the photograph on my desk, smiling his ravishing smile in the picture I had taken of him in the spring of 1989, the year that Communism fell. When the student left my office I felt a big hole in my heart. There was no perfect city, no perfect human relation, the hell with Plato's perfect forms and cities. What really worked?

For the several nights preceding Karim's arrival, I couldn't sleep. I took sleeping pills. And combined with the anti-anxiety pills, I was brought into a state of bipolarity that some people had naturally and were given medication to combat. I woke up groggy and barely able to articulate a coherent sentence, and then the anxiety would kick in. Once I took the anti-anxiety pills I felt ready to walk on all the tin roofs of my beloved Washington and chant the American anthem at the top of my Serbian lungs. In mid-July the air in Washington was a hot gooey soup in which we were all drowning and Karim's arrival was in two days at Dulles airport. How was it going to be with Karim here, in my "hometown"? How were we going to re-create Paris in Washington? But most important, what kind of lies was I going to find to excuse my absences from home, and how was I going to hide Karim so we didn't run into anyone I knew? *Make love not war,* as a favorite seventies movie of my parents advised the entire world? I was inescapably caught between the two. I decided I would tell Mark I needed a few days off to collect myself and that I would be driving to Virginia to consult some of the university libraries for my new research project on war and civic consciousness. I was going to get together with some colleagues in political sciences at a summer NEH seminar, I lied with a wide smile. He was happy to have the time alone with Natalia, he said, they would take a trip to the beach.

We weren't having another court hearing until the end of August, even judges were resting from litigations. Having a husband and a lover wasn't the worst thing in the world, I kept telling myself in those liquefying moments of moral confusion. The heat was getting worse and the massive neoclassical government buildings seemed to sway in a veil of liquid air during the day. Karim asked me to write a letter of invitation for the US embassy. I wrote a letter saying we would be working on a common research project on practical applications of Plato's theories in modern democracies, wondering in whose hands that letter was going to fall and under what section of the Patriot Act it was going to be judged. I even found a small Plato colloquium at a university in Virginia and called the political science department for more information. The delinquency of my personal life pushed me toward professional virtue and an illusion of moral virtue. I wanted things to actually match, the letter of invitation with the reality it referred to, what I told Mark about my whereabouts with the actual places I would cross or find myself in. The romance part of my relation with Karim had to take place in a virtual space between DC and Virginia, somewhere secret and inaccessible, or somewhere entirely obvious and under everybody's eyes.

It made sense to love Karim. Paris, Montmartre, Aix-en-Provence, sultry hotel rooms, and student antiwar demonstrations flashed through me in a moving collage of images and emotions when I saw his freshly shaven face at the airport. Our joyride went along the bluish misty chains of the Virginian Appalachians, driving into orangey flaming sunsets or immersed to total oblivion in our delinquent caresses in tiny motels by the side of rural roads. A crisp sense of existential symmetry seemed to have taken over my destiny. In the glassy sphere of my own lies, I felt protected. Our love was transnational, the open mountain ranges of my dreams. *"C'est beau, l'Amérique..."* It's beautiful, America... Karim said at some point during one of our shameless Virginia nights. I was filled with patriotic pride for my adoptive country; as it turned out our love wasn't just Paris-bound.

The litigation started again at the end of August, and Mark produced for the court an array of pictures of me and Karim during our five-day joyride from the moment of our encounter to the second of our separation and the last good-byes: Karim and Lara kissing at Dulles airport, Karim and Lara kissing in the rented Kia in a parking lot or on the side of the road, Karim and Lara entering a small motel in the Appalachians, Karim and Lara crying and kissing at Dulles airport on the day of his departure. Karim wiping a tear off my face seconds before he disappeared through the security gate. My lawyer showed them to me when we entered the courtroom for the hearing. He said I should deny everything, photos could be doctored up and manufactured, everyone knew that. He didn't want to know whether they were truthful or not. The pictures were part of exhibit A, evidence to show that I was unfit as a mother, an immoral influence on our daughter. Exhibit B displayed photographs of Mark and Natalia by the Atlantic beaches in Virginia and North Carolina: Natalia splashing with Mark in the waves, Mark and Natalia playing mini golf in a park filled with wooden dinosaurs, Natalia collecting seashells on the beach.

Belgrade and Sarajevo

THANKSGIVING 2003

Over Thanksgiving break I went to Belgrade in search of
Marija. And then to Sarajevo for the search of my life. This
time I took Natalia with me, despite fervent pleas from my
entire Serbian family to curb my patriotic urges. I didn't care
about patriotism or my native country, but I gave the excuse
that the vacation was as good a moment as any to reconnect
with my roots and for Natalia to connect with them in the first
place. "To help her understand her ancestry," I told Mark. In
truth, all I was dying to do was find traces, threads, clues
that would lead me to Marija. Ironically enough, only Mark
supported my decision. When it came to things like "Natalia needs to know and understand her roots" Mark was all
understanding and support. His respect for ethnic diversity
and his political correctness were actually as embedded in
his person as his stubbornness about the divorce and custody
litigation. If nothing else Mark lived by those principles, and

strangely enough it had been both what had attracted me to him in the first place and what in the end bored and dissatisfied me. When I asked him in our kitchen before he was leaving for work if he could trade his time with Natalia over Thanksgiving break so she could travel with me to Serbia for a whole week, his face relaxed and he said simply: "Yes, sure, that's a good idea, it's important for her to discover where her mother comes from." I thought his voice mellowed with affection. Referring to me as "her mother" was distancing, yet those two words also carried a world of meaning and so much of our history. They carried the memory of us conceiving Natalia on a breezy summer afternoon when I was wearing a fluffy dress in the colors of the American flag, hundreds of hours of us caring for Natalia, worrying about her, making decisions about her life, everything big and small, trivial and exceptional, deciding on a birthday gift or the school she was going to. But it also carried the singed afternoon of my torn-up portrait, the sour smell of the glue Natalia used trying to put it back together, the dreary discovery of my relationship with Karim and everything else after that. I was that mother, "her mother," with a deep gash cutting through my portrait and through our lives and marriage, a crack poorly covered up in sparkling glue and lies. When Mark caught himself looking at me for a second longer, his kindness and his half smile turned to a grimace; he brushed by me and left the room. His gait seemed heavier and less assured. I knew that he, too, had suddenly been touched by that wicked flutter of our history. And then he shook it off his shoulders like a fleck of dust.

Natalia and I descended upon the Skadarljia neighborhood of Belgrade the first evening looking for our hotel, in the midst of loud and cheerful accordion music, rivers of wine and vodka pouring in all the little cafés and restaurants, and pungent smells of grilled sausages as if we had just entered God's paradise on earth. I had decided to stay at a boutique hotel in the most colorful part of Belgrade, and guide Natalia first through the touristy parts, not the dark, broken, and gray city that I had encountered when I had come for my father's funeral. At least for the first few days, so she would have something pleasant to remember my native city by. A nostalgia as pungent as the smells coming out of the different restaurants pinched at my heart along with the images of Marija and me drinking, joking through the early-morning hours, indulging in the wildest mind games and fantasies, in these same cafés a decade earlier. It made perfect sense that now I was there in that same spot with my beloved Natalia, who took everything in with fierce curiosity.

The November air was crisp and the last chestnut leaves were trailing down the cobblestone sidewalks like lost souls. Some inexplicable ancestral feeling grabbed at my guts and I ordered straight vodka, which for the same unknown reason quenched a deep thirst inside me for something strong and destructive. Natalia watched me with curious eyes as if she was fascinated with this new mother, who spoke Serbian and joked with the mustached waiters, drank shots of vodka without blinking, and laughed loudly at obscene jokes from the neighboring tables. She knew why I had gone to Belgrade. She and I had planned a secret trip within our trip, the Bosnian portion of the journey that not even my own sister, mother, or husband knew anything about. She asked me to let her put the tip of her tongue in my shot of vodka and I was happy to oblige as she scrunched her nose in disgust: "How can you drink this awful stuff, Mama?" "I guess because it's in the blood, as they say," I laughed. The accordionist stopped at our table and played Serbian tunes for us. Tears sprang to my eyes as I remembered Marija singing one of their songs on the morning of our separation. Natalia took my hand. We made a glorious team on that chilly autumn night filled with such unbearable regrets, desires, and sugary accordion music that ripped through my heart like a reckless hurricane.

After a couple of days of being a tourist with Natalia in Belgrade, I started making phone calls and meeting people at street corners or in the hallways of drab gray buildings. I knew Marija knew people in Belgrade who had been against the war, and knowing her as well as I did, she probably reconnected with them after the war for some humanitarian purpose. Natalia held my hand tight throughout all of our ramblings as if afraid to lose me among the rows of shabby blocks left from the socialist era. We walked fast without looking behind us even when we heard steps following us too closely. After the excitement, vodka, sausages, and accordion music of the Skadarljia neighborhood wore off I started feeling strange vibrations pulsate through my native city as we went on our various walks. Pro-nationalist Serbian graffiti on walls and gates such as MLADIC HERO gave me shivers of unpleasantness every time I saw them, and the ones that said things like MUSLIM PIGS froze the blood in my veins. The thought of Marija and her family having been the target of that hatred firsthand turned me alternately into a block of ice and a volcano of sorrow. Hot tears were falling down my face with a will of their own. One afternoon when we stopped in a café to warm up and replenish our energies with coffee, pastries, and hot chocolate, Natalia said looking straight at me: "Mama, I think you are going around in circles. The woman in the offices on the top floor in the ugly building knew something about your friend." "Which ugly building, Natalia? All the buildings we've been to so far are ugly. And which woman?" Then I remembered. It was the office of the human rights organization where we visited Sonja, the director who was working on a huge project of annual reports about Serbia's nationalist orientation and unwillingness to capture the war criminals and recognize the role of the Republika Srpska in the genocide. "How do you know that Sonja knew about Marija?" "Because when you asked her she sipped from her coffee first and then she said she didn't know and she didn't look you straight in the eyes when she said that. Why would she sip her coffee at such an important question? She was buying time, Mama, first she wanted to tell you something, and then she changed her mind." Apparently I had raised a little Sherlock Holmes who read character and psychology better than I was able to. The coffee warmed my insides and the sugary creamy pastry gave me a slight rush like I used to get in my childhood whenever my father took me to the pastry shop on our street for hot chocolate and a cake on cold afternoons like that one. "We'll go back to her then. What do you think, Natalia?" Natalia kept silent and sipped from her hot chocolate. Natalia was both genius and fairy, the one thing in my life I had done perfectly by giving birth to. "Let's go," I said impatiently once she took the last sip from the drink. "Wait, Mama, let me finish my cocoa, okay?" And she stuck her finger at the bottom of the cup to take all the sugary froth.

We went back to the gray ugly building in the far end of the Dorćol neighborhood, near where my parents' apartment used to be, then walked to the nicer part, where Marija's parents used to live, with turn-of-the-century houses and apartment buildings and friendly little parks where children swayed on the creaky swings. Natalia remembered the street and hopped a step ahead of me while still holding my hand. Then she turned around looking at me and with a huge smile said, "Mama, did you use to walk on these streets to go to school when you and your friend were little?" Of course we had, Marija and I running back from school and taking the most roundabout ways in order to prolong our togetherness,

Marija and I pretending we got lost and ending up at the opposite side of town where neither of us lived, Marija walking me to my apartment building and then me walking her back to hers and then having to walk back home alone and wishing it were tomorrow when we would see each other again. And sometimes stopping in a little pastry shop such as the one Natalia and I had just been in, and sharing one fluffy cake and one hot cocoa from the money we had both saved from the change our parents had given us. This new Belgrade was cold and unfriendly, but the ghosts of my childhood and of the fiery little girl that Marija once was, and of the flamboyant and revolutionary young woman she became, ripped my heart into bloody slivers.

Sonja at the Helsinki human rights organization was not in the least surprised to see us back. All the staff had left for the day when we got there and she was all by herself in the office with the large windows looking out onto the Danube River with its lazy nonchalant flow cutting through the city. Seen from up there the neighborhood didn't seem ugly, but rather majestic. I was liking and hating my city in alternate transports even within a single hour of the day. Before I finished my sentence asking again about Marija and whether she had been in touch with her in the last decade after the war, Sonja handed me a piece of paper with some sentences scribbled on it. She didn't want to say it out loud but instead she repeated that she had no idea where Marija was, or what she had been up to, no she hadn't seen or heard from her.

"No, absolutely not," she said adamantly. I was shocked by such caution and mostly by what it implied: that offices and buildings where antiwar, anti-nationalistic, and human rights activities and projects went on were actually bugged just as in the eighties, following Tito's death and even before. The note Sonja handed me said that Marija had been coming to Belgrade regularly to give information to the human rights commission and mostly to get in touch with the group called Women in Black. I had heard of Women in Black from Biljana, a group of mostly Serbian women who were against the war and who every year on the anniversary of the Srebrenica massacres stood in public places in Belgrade dressed in black and wrapped in silence. Not a word, just silent resistance. Marija had stopped coming about two years ago, the note said. Sonja listed some names and a couple of cell phone numbers all scribbled on the same piece of paper that she had torn from her lined notebook. Natalia leaned over to read the note and her eyes lit up as if to say: *I told you, Mama*. I kissed Sonja good-bye and thanked her profusely. She whispered to me to be careful; it was still not safe, she said. As soon as I got to the hotel I bought our bus tickets to Sarajevo for the next morning, the day of the American Thanksgiving holiday. Natalia was jumping up and down with excitement. I needed to find Marija.

As Natalia sat next to me on the bus to Sarajevo swallowing the landscapes that unfolded in front of her, images of Marija, Biljana, and me traveling the same route almost thirty years earlier ran through my head at dizzying velocity: Marija and I holding hands and closing our eyes at the sharpest curves in the road, Biljana waving and grimacing out the window at people standing on the side of the road or in front of their houses, Marija's mother sitting in the seat across from us lost in reverie and sometimes embroidering or knitting an item of clothing for Marija. Pine forests on one side, naked sharp rocks on another, high drops that made your heart swoon, winding turns that left you breathless, and then suddenly in front of you the charmed city where I had spent the happiest days of my life: wooded, hidden among firs and pines, white houses with red tiles emerging like a surprise from behind the dark-green areas, the gleaming rounded cupolas of mosques with the crescent moons greeting you like shining smiles. Natalia looked at me smiling. For a brief second I was ten-year-old Lara and Natalia was ten-year-old Marija. The darkest waters of the last decades had washed over us and left us grieving and begging for wholeness. Clusters of red flowers were hanging on the white houses even in November, though the non-coniferous trees were barren. I realized I had never been to Sarajevo in late fall. I had not been to Sarajevo since I was in college. The hills around us were sprinkled with hundreds of fresh white tombs of Sarajevans killed in the siege. I was in for the time travel of my life, and thank goodness Natalia was right next to me with her glorious smile and warm hand in mine, always reminding me that life mattered, that what we were up to on our secret crazy trip really mattered.

We settled in Sarajevo like it was our home and within hours I refamiliarized myself with the streets, the alleys, the buildings, the views of the river, even though much of it was so changed: Some parts were uncannily smooth and fresh as if just emerged from the ground, which they were, some were crooked and slashed in a toothless grin from the war damage. We stopped at a little café called Pod Lipom, "under the lime tree," and the owner, a beautiful sultry dark-haired woman, laughed at us sweetly as we entered. The evening was light and laughter was quivering in the air as if no suffering of any kind had ever touched the city. We drank hot lemonade and ate warm polenta and felt heavenly from the golden repast. "It's good to be in Sarajevo tonight," I said and her laugh widened and she said back to me: "Yes, it is." This new Sarajevo emerging from the rubble had even more warmth than I remembered, the quivering beauty and sweetness of a creature that had come out at the other end of a long dark tunnel of death and was stretching languorously as it rediscovered life and its balminess. The next day we would start our search—or, as Natalia liked to refer to it, "our investigation."

The golden Sarajevo of our first day was morphing into a harsh and scary one. I was going down many stone steps, down, down between stone walls with the sound of the Miljacka River gurgling nearby. Natalia's firm and relentless grasp of my hand told me it was not a dream. I wondered what devil possessed me to put myself and Natalia on this path. The first number that Sonja had given me seemed wrong. After many tries someone finally answered: a raspy woman's voice, unfriendly and almost hostile. She said she didn't know anyone by that name. I knew she lied. I stood in the street shivering, holding my cell phone like a useless object. Natalia said to be patient, we should try the other number. A woman with a soft voice who sounded almost asleep answered and said to wait. Then she gave us an address and said to go to it.

In the city center, we met Ferida in a small café. She did her best to appear warm and hospitable, but she seemed remote. She had brought along her nine-year-old daughter, Mira, born on the same day as Natalia. Mira, who spoke English better than her mother, asked Natalia about American bands and singers my daughter had never heard of. Mira laughed at Natalia's ignorance and asked her if she really lived in America. Natalia held her own and asked Mira if she really lived in Sarajevo and if she knew of an American artist that she had seen in the Hirshhorn Museum with me. The girlish confrontation between our daughters made Ferida and me smile. Ferida said she hadn't seen Marija in over five years. I didn't believe her, either, but I was learning to live with half-truths. Ferida didn't want to talk about the war, what it had been like living among sniper bullets and shells, with no water, no electricity or gas for three years. "We made do," was all she said. Then with an almost angry tone she also said: "People here want to move on, we all want to move on." I understood, she didn't want American tourist Lara Kulicz who had spent the Sarajevo siege years safely cuddled in her American husband's lush Washington apartment to come now, almost ten years after the war, to gather information and shower compassion. We drank our dark Bosnian coffees and ate our baklavas in silence. After thirty minutes, Ferida excused herself and said she had to go somewhere, and that she was working on an international poets for peace event. She reminded me my country was at war with Iraq, and there were apparently American poets as well who participated in this huge poetry for peace project. I felt guilty, and told her no, I was not engaged in any poetic antiwar activities. As we were saying our good-byes, I grabbed Ferida's hand, begging her to tell me more about Marija. I saw a warm flicker in her eyes for a brief second but then it disappeared. "There is nothing to tell," Ferida said. "She survived, that's what matters. I haven't seen her in years." She and Mira said good-bye, leaving Natalia and me in the café.

Like a descent into some kind of hell we continued on to the next address, below the river down the many stone steps. We crossed the Vrbana Bridge, now also called the Romeo and Juliet Bridge because during the war two young lovers were killed there as they were trying to flee and lay dead in each other's arms for days. Nobody ventured out to retrieve their bodies because of the relentless snipers. I had just found out that bit of information as I was rushing to the address given by the soft-spoken woman on the phone. A small plaque noted the deaths of the first two casualties of war, two women crossing the bridge on April 5, 1992. April 5, Natalia's and Mira's birthdays. As I looked at the plaque a woman stopped to tell us the Romeo and Juliet story. Natalia stared with huge eyes that shone with tears as the woman told us how the girl had crawled on her lover's dead body after she was shot. The Sarajevo of the lower level was a place of small narrow streets, some still broken down or in reconstruction, closer to the hills where entire neighborhoods had been obliterated by shells and snipers. Farah and Kemal's house had been farther up the river on one of the hills. But we were going farther and farther down. "Mama, why are we going on this chase, really?" asked Natalia just as I was about to ring the bell to the apartment. "What are you hoping to find?" "Marija, of course," I said to my little Sherlock Holmes. "Yes, but why do we have to see all these weird people? It's clear she doesn't want to be found. I don't think she is anywhere near here, that's what I think." I had a sinking feeling of hopelessness because I knew Natalia was right. It was her traces, not Marija herself that I was following, hoping to understand some of her terrifying journey. I wanted desperately to understand her disappearance into a dark zone of forgetfulness.

The woman who answered the door looked just as sleepy as she sounded on the phone. She had dark circles around her eyes like she never slept. The sound from another room of a small child whining seemed incongruous with the aged worn-out look of the woman, the cigarette she was smoking as if in a dream, the unkempt aspect of her surroundings. She said my friend had long gone. She didn't know where, but maybe she was out of the country. I wanted to make sure we were talking about the same person and I asked: "Marija Kurtovic? Beautiful dark-haired woman, right?" "Maybe she was beautiful once," the woman answered ruthlessly. "Nobody is beautiful anymore, no one who went where she went. But she survived." That was what Ferida had said, that at least Marija had survived. There was a high price on survival. I knew I couldn't quite appreciate what that meant. Then she said: "Wait here, I have something." The sound of the whining child continued, and the apartment seemed to be getting darker. It smelled of burnt meat and something else that reminded me of Farah and Kemal's house, a sweeter, more merciful smell that was comforting. The overlapping of heavy smells and the cigarette smoke made me feel dizzy, and Natalia started coughing. Natalia was right. This search seemed without purpose. And it was as the result of all the phone calls and visits and stubborn searches that it was happening. I wondered why Sonja had given me this woman's contact. How was she related to Marija's life? The woman came back wiping her hands on the yellow apron she wore and was holding a folder with papers in it. Something that looked like a manuscript. "Here, have this. She said if somebody came looking for her, to give this." "Somebody? Just anybody?" I asked in disbelief. "Yes, anybody, a woman of course, how many people do you think would come looking for her? You must be the one she meant," the woman said. "She'll come back someday, that's what she told me," she added matter-of-factly. "Who knows if she will, but that's what she said! When she stopped here last month and left this, she said she'll be back again. But I won't be here then. I'm moving away." I was incredulous. "Do you mean Marija was here a few weeks ago? What exactly did she say?" The woman looked at me blankly. She stood in silence staring at me and smoking in an unearthly calmness. How could it be that Marija was leaving packages and was in correspondence with this woman? Another awkward silence stretched between the strange woman and me, the whining of the child growing louder in the other room. "Good-bye," she said abruptly, as if she was throwing us out. I held tightly to the folder with the typed pages, the treasure I had yet to discover.

Natalia and I walked for a long time, lost on the narrow winding streets bordered by dark forests on the side of the hill or opening in little plazas with parks or yards where children played on the sidewalks or in the narrow alleys. The streets started to become familiar, a corner house that seemed to emerge from a dream, a tiny bridge that needed repair; some of the houses were rebuilt or new, built to look like the old ones, others were still dismantled or under construction, or studded with bullet marks and abandoned. Gardens were overgrown with bare leafless branches coiling around the wrought-iron fences or on the front porches that looked like unkempt hair and gave the neighborhood the face of a place in mourning. Occasionally a rebuilt, fresh-looking house with its stucco walls and perky orange chrysanthemums looked to the autumn sky with an almost spiteful contrast. A corner of my memory opened up like a window to the image of two little girls running around and gorging on fruit, a grandmother with a babushka picking up weeds and fallen apricots in the violet dusk of a summer afternoon.

I realized I was on Farah and Kemal's old street. Natalia complained that I squeezed her hand too hard, the mysterious folder with the heavy bunch of papers seemed to weigh a ton, and I felt like a possessed creature on a mission. Babica basca, the Babic's garden neighborhood. The layout of the streets was in my blood and in my flesh, every cobblestone and every fence, every garden and every pine or chestnut tree. There was the same peachy color of the roof, part of it had been blown off, and the windows were smashed, like a mutilated person that was still uncannily attractive, like a person you wanted to repair and care for and hold in your arms despite the broken limbs and the bleeding wounds. That was Farah and Kemal's house. Natalia felt my memories and began to cry. In fact she was the only one that cried because I couldn't. I doubted again the wisdom of dragging my angelic daughter, already traumatized by the separation of her parents, through the ghastly ruins of my past and the gory realities of Marija's tormented paths. Everyone here had been killed. I held Natalia for a long time as she cried, releasing all the tension and worries she had held in check for my sake, or just to prove how tough and grown-up she was. We walked around the back of the house and sat on the stone bench where Marija and Biljana and I had sat hundreds of times. Everything was overgrown with weeds and ivy, dark red from the cold autumn, the yard covered in yellow and magenta leaves, giving the place a surreal mix of beauty and unbearable sadness.

Back in our hotel room, we sat in silence, exhausted from the day. Night had sneaked into the room and a distant bell rang like an ominous announcement of something more to come. "It's Thanksgiving, Mama," Natalia announced. Yes, back home, I kept saying back home, even though I was in my birth country now, another home that was no longer mine. When I turned to look at Natalia's face, it was white and glowing in the semi-darkness of the room and staring with terrified eyes. She was reading the package of letters, which I snatched from her hands. I started to read for myself and my blood froze. It was too late, I couldn't delete from Natalia's mind whatever she had read from the manuscript. Why was I always a minute too slow to react? Small notes in Marija's handwriting revealed the stories of the Bosnian women survivors she had gathered to deliver to the Women in Black organization, and also for human rights organizations in the States. The rape camps, hotels, and gymnasiums. The events were depicted right there, directly and explicitly, describing a basement, a dark room, a steel bed in a grungy hotel room, on the floor of a gymnasium. One told the story of a woman who had not been raped, but who had sung day and night all the Serbian songs she knew. The soldiers thought she was crazy and they let her be. Craziness was a safety net. There were other accounts, counting blessings of survival, almost in unanimity. Some sounded almost hopeful. One mother whose daughter had been raped and killed begged for death after having tried to end her life by hanging on a bedsheet turned into a rope, refusing food, and trying to slice her wrists with her own nails. "How much of this did you read, Natalia?" I asked in a barely audible voice, as my own voice was eluding me. "Not much." I knew she lied. "Just the first couple of pages or so." We sat in silence again. We fell asleep in each other's arms. I woke up in the middle of the night, put the covers over Natalia's sweet sleeping body, and went on reading until dawn. At the end of the Bosnian women's stories, I found Marija's notes, which reminded me of the first letters and diary pages she had sent me during the war, only these had a radically different rhythm and tone to them. They were not typed like all the rest, but handwritten in different pens, some clear, others barely legible, and others almost calligraphic. There was no mention of the days or the events in that horrific July, the war, or her family. It was later, while she was recovering, that Marija had written the notes. Her words, I now understood, were not for the Helsinki committee, nor were they for Hassan or the Women in Black. They were for me. In the shuffle of pages that were sometimes out of order and out of chronology, I figured out that Marija was in America, in California, namely in Santa Barbara and later in Los Angeles. She had hurriedly visited Sarajevo a couple of times, to look for something, for someone it seemed, maybe to build new bridges and unearth old ghosts. Just like the woman had said, Marija had visited her a month before. Marija had chosen not to mail me the envelope in Washington. It was as if she knew I would find her pages in the mysterious woman's house. But how in the world could she have known? How could she have possibly decided to leave that precious package in a forgotten neighborhood of Sarajevo? Maybe she was planning to return and pick them up herself. A big secret was hidden in these pages. Marija was like a bird circling around a nest in mysterious ways.

I am writing poems of Lara. In the present. It can only be in the present because the past doesn't exist and neither does the future. The present is a sliver of land between two abysses: the abyss on the right and the abyss on the left. I am in the middle. Lara is with me on this shard of land floating like an aimless island in the universe. Lara has a slender agile body that runs and dances on narrow streets and alleys filled with red flowers hanging from baskets at windowsills. There are always the damn red flowers. I will them into being yellow or beige but they keep coming back to me as red. There are no beige flowers hanging from baskets anywhere, because people think red flowers are so lively and sexy, but for me beige flowers would be rather soothing. When I get out of here I am going to grow a garden of beige azaleas through a process of genetic engineering. Genetic engineering turns something into something else by changing their DNA structure, for instance a pear into a plum pear, a tomato into a cherry tomato, and a Bosnian into a Serb.

I don't have a body any longer, it was stolen some time ago. It could be interesting moving around without a body if it wasn't so boring and if the women taking care of me in this place didn't keep nagging me to keep eating and drinking and walking for my circulation. There was a time when dying would have been easier, if it hadn't been for the woman from Semizovac. The woman from Sarajevo. The woman from Potocari. The woman from Banja Luka. One and the same woman kept moving around and moving me around with her from place to place. Then it would have been easy to die, I could have just told her to let me be in one of those houses, rooms she kept moving me to. It takes some effort to die when you really want to and I was too lazy to make myself die, so I lived. And I kept writing poems about Lara to bring some color to my dreary survival.

Sometimes there were blank pages in Marija's notes with just stains on them that could have been anything from tears, to coffee, to blood. The blank pages made me squirm with discomfort. From time to time I looked over at Natalia sleeping next to me, in the calm of sleep, and despite her innocent breathing I knew the two of us would never be the same after that journey.

I am wearing a turquoise necklace and am reading Plato. They are the two things I have from Lara and these are the only things I have other than the gown they put on me. I can no longer remember how I saved these two things from the incident that brought me to this place. I must have been wearing the necklace and maybe reading Plato at the time. Maybe I was reading the passage about the cave and the people in the cave seeing the shadows of things on the walls of the cave in the light of the fire and taking them for real. One is so often mistaken about what is real and what is not real. But a boot kicking you in your stomach is always real and you can't mistake it for not real. And you can't mistake the dead bodies strewn next to you for the images flickering on the walls of a cave.

The nurse Sonja asks me where I want to walk and I always tell her I want to walk where the copper vendors are. She says there are no more copper vendors since the war, but I insist that there must be at least one copper vendor who's come back and survived the war. And I am right. Tarik, the copper vendor that

Lara and I used to watch in awe as he carved his tea-pots, tiny bowls, and spoons with the precision of a surgeon and the tenderness of a lover, is still alive.

At some point toward morning Natalia woke up and stared at me. There was worry and sorrow in Natalia's eyes but not tears. She had grown up in a few days more than she had in an entire year, she had leaped from childish inno-cence to sudden adult understanding of the world's horrors, a transformation too abrupt for her nine-year-old mind and body. But Natalia always surprised and awed me. "Mama, you should really go to sleep, you are going to be a wreck on the plane back tomorrow," she said, touching my arm. I took her in my arms and followed her advice. We both fell into a deep sleep with no dreams. Both relieved and melancholic to leave Sarajevo, we found ourselves on the plane back home. I returned to Marija's notes and Natalia read *Through the Look-ing Glass*, turning back into the child she had been before the trip. Or maybe she just clung to those bits of childhood before they were all going to be swallowed up in the trials that were awaiting us at home.

It was not therapy, it was the yellow dress that saved my life. It was Sally Bryant and her yellow dress that made me aware that I had a body and that I had once loved my body. One day during one of our meetings she made me laugh without even intending to. She said: "Marija, you might want to comb your hair today and put on a new dress. Here, I brought you this headband and this dress, they made me think of you." For some reason that sounded so fucking funny, that she would worry about my hair and my dress. And I thought that the war hadn't been her fault, that I had no reason to hate her. She had brought me a yellow dress like a huge lemon and that made me laugh even more. She said yellow was proven to be an uplifting color, a warm color that lifted the spirits. Sally combed my hair herself and I stopped her from combing it off my face and my eyes but she gently won that fight. She had been right, the yellow dress lifted my spirits, and for the first time I felt that maybe I did want to survive.

Maybe I would follow Sally's urging and move to the United States, to Santa Barbara, California, like she'd said. I considered her proposal seriously, as you would consider a marriage or a business proposal. "What will I do in America, Sally?" "Whatever you want," she answered. That felt as refreshing and ridiculous as the yellow dress.

When I leave Sarajevo with Sally I know very well I am forgetting something important and that I would come back for it one day. I cannot remember entire blocks of life. I found out from Sally that I suffer from a very unusual kind of post-traumatic stress disorder: the kind that instead of removing me from the present and pushing me into the hellhole of the traumas or shocks that had happened to my system, lets me live in a frozen present and I have cut out the past. Some psychologists call that state emotional blunting, Sally told me it's a kind of freezing of emotions both good and bad so that you don't experience the really awful ones. I didn't understand her psychological jargon, nor did I care. But she was right: I had found a niche in a dark bath of forgetfulness. I wanted to go to the country of forgetfulness and large billboards, to Sally's land of yellow dresses and California oranges. The most desperate wretches of the world had gone to America over the centuries to escape from something, from someone, to find something or someone they thought they could never find in their own miserable native places. It made sense for me to be like all those other wretched forgetful individuals.

As we were suspended in the clouds between two continents, and I turned Marija's pages, with Natalia in the seat beside me, in a temporary state of calm and contentment, we laughed at the idea that we were born an ocean away from each other on different continents. "Thank you, Mama, for moving to America to make me. That was a good move," Natalia said.

Washington, DC.
Attempting Peace

The litigation and trials went on and on and settled in our lives together with the news of war and of American soldiers being blown up in car explosions at various roadblocks in Iraq. Because I couldn't have either of them, I now loved both Mark and Karim. Or I did my best to do so. It seemed to me now that love was also partly built up by our own volition, deliberate accumulation of fantasies, choosing to think more of the good sides than the bad sides of the person who was the object of our affection. I idealized each of the two men in my life differently and longed one moment for the family solidity and togetherness I had once had with Mark and the next for the heated whispers and passion I had with Karim during our transnational stolen encounters. I clung to the husband with whom I had once had an American family and kept the illusion of the Tunisian romantic lover with whom I had once experienced thrilling passion.

I still talked with Karim at least twice a week on my cell phone, in a parking lot or at a street corner on M Street or in Dupont Circle while anxiously looking around me and scouting the area for possible detectives who might be following me. Our conversations always left me spent, as Karim seemed distant and less loving, though not distant enough for me to completely give up the thrill I got from hearing my name pronounced in his soft raspy voice with a French Arabic accent. If he still called me *"mon amour"* he must have meant it. The occasional distant echo of a female voice speaking in Arabic at the other end of the phone made me queasy with a sense of the absurdity of the entire situation, adultery, divorce, custody litigation, family disintegration, the mess that had become my life.

Sometimes Natalia came into my room to talk about our travels to Belgrade and Sarajevo and to look at the pictures we had taken. Everything was still fresh and weighed on her conscience and imagination: Here we were in front of the old fortress where the Danube and the Sava Rivers joined, smiling in the November sun. A kind young couple who wanted to practice their English had taken the photo. Here we were in front of the Romeo and Juliet Bridge in Sarajevo, trying to smile despite the dark drizzly day. There was the woman with the grocery bags who told us the story of the two lovers that had died in each other's arms.

My mother and sister were planning to visit us for Christmas with the entire family, which meant also my brother-in-law and their two daughters. At first I thought it would be crazy for us all to cram inside our duplex over the holidays and wanted to ask them to restrain their familial enthusiasm. But both my mother and sister convinced me that it was good for Natalia to have her "maternal Serbian family around her," "to take her mind off her parents' troubles and the divorce" and to allow her to better know her two cousins. "It's good for her, Larinka, trust me," my sister insisted in her aggressively life-affirming way. "The best medicine for a child torn between two parents in the midst of a bloody divorce is total immersion in family life, playing with kids her age, in other words being normal and spending the holidays surrounded by a lot of cheerfulness. I know it because I have it in my blood, I know what makes kids tick and what makes families work," she said confidently and started to count to three while on the phone for her younger daughter, Amanda, to get into her pajamas and get ready for bedtime. "Maybe if I hadn't helped you come to the States, you wouldn't have found your Prince Charming and you would be cheating on some motherfucking Serbian husband with an American tourist right now and calling *me* for moral support all the way from Belgrade, have you ever thought of that, dear sister?" I joked with Biljana. It was a bitter joke and I felt the tension left by my words quiver in the airtime. There was a long silence on the phone, and I regretted my words.

But then she burst out laughing: "It's funny to hear you swear like that, Larichka. But the man you married *was* your Prince Charming, remember? And remember the great fanfare and pride of your wedding? Look, shit happens and people can be wrong about the mate they choose, but you have that priceless Natalia. How about that?"

"Our mama is a different story, she just wrings her hands all day long, talking about 'the daughter who has taken the wrong path and what did I do to deserve it?'" Biljana told me. "But you know damn well I'm not like that. I have my own set of problems with Rick, too, don't you know it! I'm just making some choices here that are different from your choices. Come on, it will be good to spend the holidays together, to spend some time just the two of us, talking late into the night like in the old days. You might find me useful after all."

My sister had chosen a career in dancing and I had chosen political science and she was better at the politics of everyday life than I had ever been. I hung up and went looking for Natalia downstairs to take her to her cello lessons. She had recently developed a love of the cello and I tried to channel her artistic drives, feeling as confident about my parenting choices lately as my superconfident sister seemed to be about hers. Our journey to my birth country and everything we had seen, experienced, and heard there had solidified our indestructible bond, even if I still agonized over allowing her to step into the dark world of the war with its sickening degrees of violence and Marija's layers of suffering. I even believed that Mark, in his support of Natalia and me traveling and her "getting to know her roots," had become a gentler and more reasonable human being.

One Sunday afternoon in December, I went straight to Mark in his study as he was working on his lectures for the coming week, as if everything were the same as before. I stood in front of him and asked if we could talk. Without raising his head from the computer, he nodded, and pointed to me to sit down as if I was one of his students coming in for an appointment. I remembered the early years of our marriage, when we used to actually play this game, where we acted as if one was the professor and the other a nervous student asking advice for his or her paper on Plato's *Republic* or a Wallace Stevens poem. After which we would tell each other to get undressed and said that having sex first was the only way we could solve the conundrums of Plato or Wallace Stevens.

I sat down at the desk in front of him and started to talk. "Mark, what if we rewound everything and started over?" I said in one breath with the crispiest voice I had used in a long time. To my surprise he lifted his eyes and looked straight at me with almost a shine, something on the cusp of tears. "I would if I could, Lara, honestly, I would. But I just can't. And I just can't see how I can live with you and love you again after all this." Although I had thought I was immune to any feelings toward or from Mark, his words and the sincerity with which he uttered them gave me an instantaneous heartache.

I looked out the window and saw the snow falling, first

snow of the year. The world outside looked so beautiful. I had once had it all. The room with the dark rustic oak and mahogany furniture that we had decorated together, the Indian tapestries on the walls, the Tiffany lamp, the gauzy vermillion curtains, the bare dogwoods and maples in front of the window and the snow gently covering them. I beheld the inanimate objects, and they seemed to scold me for my recklessness, for the arrogance of thinking I could have everything: a brilliant academic career, a model family, an angel of a daughter, an enviable house on Connecticut Avenue in the country's capital, and an exotic lover for occasional flings in Paris. The world I dared to imagine didn't exist even in the corniest Hollywood movies. I wanted to beg Mark to take me back, to forgive me, to please start over.

"Mark, can we please stop the battle over Natalia?" I asked in nearly inaudible words. "It's destroying her. Let's make peace, for her sake...for the sake of our daughter. I made a mistake, I admit it. Why make her pay for it?" The words came out softly and smoothly like the snow. He looked at me with a soulful expression that gave me a moment of hope. But then I heard his words. "Fine, Lara, just give me full physical custody of Natalia and it will all be settled, not one more petition or trial or hearing. Just agree to it, and we'll make peace. Nothing short of that will do."

In the days that followed I tried to fortify myself by working my way backward through the world's worst historical catastrophes. I went back to my textbooks and reread accounts

of the start of the two world wars, Napoleon's Russian cam-
paign, the massacre of Protestants on Saint Bartholomew's
Day under Catherine de Medicis, the massacre of the Mame-
lukes in thirteenth-century Egypt, the Sack of Troy, and even
the prehistoric cave dwellers who seemed peaceful by comparison. Civilization came with wars and destruction, I told
myself. I could choose to study politics, but still I had to live
"the real life." I decided right then to re-study Machiavelli
and Cicero, to find answers to the grave political errors that
rolled through history. But then the image of a mother holding her child to her chest emerged in my mind and prevailed
over Machiavelli and Cicero: She was rushing through fields
and villages and cities at war, through bullets, explosions,
fires, UN and NATO bombs, Iraqi suicide bombs, American
smart bombs. Her eyes were lighting up the violent nights of
history as she kept running and holding her child, trying to
make it somewhere, to a certain spot that only she knew of.
And she did. With her body covered in bloody rags, her feet
covered in blisters, her face darkened from ashes and fires,
she reached a quiet spot by a gurgling river, under the shade
of willows and pine trees. The water was sparkling clean
and she leaned to drink some and to give some to her child.
They were finally safe and they would quench their thirst by
this cool river in a secret place in the Moravian mountains.
That image was in the end the only one that mattered from
my abridged imaginary version of world history, and it wasn't
written in any of the history books.

In the real, domestic part of my life I spent every moment I could with Natalia. I had never felt as creative as a mother as I did in those days and weeks following the conversation with Mark on the December snowy evening. Mark's parenting challenge woke in me the ambition to excel at that job. I took her with me to my office and made a game of preparing my tenure file. I let her choose the colors of stickers for each one of the entries to my file. I had to go on with whatever needed to be done as my life unfolded.

I had been re-reading *The Prince*, and I set myself a utopian plan and challenge for what was happening in the litigation room of my life. I would be both the cunning fox and the strong wolf, as Machiavelli advised. Five days before my family was due to arrive from Chicago for Christmas I fired my arrogant lawyer who cost me three hundred dollars for every hour of lousy advice and insults to my intelligence, and I hired Diana Coman, a young Romanian woman lawyer with a law degree from the University of Chicago. I thought our common Eastern European heritage might finally cut a clear path through the mire of lies and complications created by Mark's lawyers. Maybe I was bolstered by Biljana's upcoming visit.

My family emerged from their red Subaru station wagon in front of our house, like the Serbian Gypsies used to come out of their carts to descend upon the village in the Morava Valley where my parents, my sister, and I used to spend part of our summer vacations. Biljana looked better than ever, her freckled skin glowing in the December dusk and her green eyes shining with mischief as always. Then came her two daughters, Melissa and Amanda, one dark-haired and swarthy and the other a miniature of Biljana, yawning and pushing each other around. My mother was moving slowly, a little hunched and looking older and smaller than the last time, holding her old Serbian fur coat. Finally, Ricky appeared, six feet tall with thick black hair and a matching mustache, his smile irrepressible. Just as when the Gypsy caravan showed up in our Serbian village, my heart beat with joy and curiosity, while my head told me there was about to be trouble, disruption of my attempt at a neatly ordered existence.

Biljana hugged me tightly and kissed me on both cheeks. How was I holding up? she asked. My mother began to cry and took my head in her two hands, as always, to ascertain my state of catastrophe. Melissa and Amanda smelling of cinnamon rolls gave me sticky kisses. Ricky gave me a hearty hug. "Looking good, sister, not easy to get around in this fancy capital of yours." Natalia, who had been waiting with great feverishness for their arrival for two days, stayed upstairs in her bedroom despite the honking car horn. I saw her staring from the window. *She is like me*, I thought as I picked up my sister's orange duffel bag in which she must have packed her entire dance studio and half of the city of Chicago. *That's what will save us both in this custody trial*, I thought as I opened the door to our house. *That Natalia is like me: She*

broods and she makes up theories, solves problems, and likes
quiet white spaces.

As I followed everybody upstairs, an inexplicable hilarity
possessed me. How were we all going to fit in the three rooms
that were available for this wild pack of my Chicago family,
"And Natalia and me?" I said. "We'll be fine," said Biljana.
"In most parts of the world you would have four or five families living in a mansion like yours." "We ran away from such a
part of the world, remember, sister?" I said. When I reached
the landing on the second floor, Biljana asked me in whispers about Mark, where was he? In his office, I gestured. She
rolled her eyes as if to say: *That's all he ever does, how boring, no wonder you cheated on him.* I didn't care how we were
going to all fit in or what our sleeping arrangements were
going to be. I suddenly experienced an overpowering sense
of well-being that I hadn't felt in a long time. My life suddenly
felt rich and complicated, stressful as it might have been.
Natalia came out of her room with a smile and offered each of
the girls one of her Beanie Babies: a toucan for Melissa who
was four, and a flamingo for Amanda, three. They followed
Natalia to her room and the three of them disappeared inside,
enveloped in a conversation about her stuffed animals.

When I had first proposed to Mark that we celebrate
Christmas as we always had, for Natalia's sake, he mumbled a
reluctant agreement to my proposal. It was all part of my new
strategy, of killing him with kindness. "Great, Natalia will
be so happy," I said. And it was true. Natalia was dancing a

gracious social ballet in those days before Christmas, leading her cousins in games and activities that spread all over the house. From puzzle competitions to Ping-Pong games in her room on the new table she had gotten for her birthday. She even invented a game called "refugees on the run," much to everybody's amusement. Biljana's girls followed Natalia everywhere and did everything she asked them to with wide eyed admiration. Even my mother got caught up in the girls' rendition of the Eurydice myth, performed with much fanfare in the living room. Natalia was Orpheus, Melissa played Eurydice, and Amanda wanted to be Hades, the god of the dead who gave Orpheus another chance and allowed him to take back his beloved Eurydice on the condition that he never look back for her. Even though they had no idea or understanding who those characters were, they followed all of Natalia's directions during the rehearsals and mixed them up with fairy tale characters they were familiar with. The evening of the performance, Mark stopped in the doorway to watch. The lights were dim, and the Ravel music that Natalia had chosen vibrated in the air. She looked like an angelic apparition in her gauzy blue Orpheus costume, and at the last minute she changed the story's ending by not looking back at Eurydice and thus saving him/herself from the fierce maenads, to Amanda's great frustration whose favorite part was precisely the gory one of the dismemberment of Orpheus. Natalia was sick of dismemberments, real or metaphorical, so she changed the myth altogether. At the end Rick clapped and the rest of us joined him. "Bravo, great job, girls!" Mark didn't say a word. I watched as he left the room and went into the kitchen with his expression blank. Blankness was his way of fighting me, I thought. But I didn't care. For the first time in months I was not thinking about the future, but just about that messy colorful moment with touches of sparkling white. Mark had been overpowered by the sum total powers of our Serbian Mexican family.

On Christmas Eve Day, I asked Mark to please join us for the evening party. "It would be great if you and Natalia decorated the tree together. In the morning, so it can be done before the party, and the gifts, you know, the girls..." I was sort of stumbling over my words. I was trying hard to follow my new female lawyer's advice to talk in neutral language that did not focus on me and my wishes. I would be Machiavelli's fox. He lost his cool and stared angrily at me. "What's with you pushing me to do all this stuff with Natalia? I do my own stuff with Natalia, I know what to do. I know how to parent. And I don't go around fucking other women. Don't you see, you're trying too hard! It's fake, we are a broken family, can't you get it?" At that point Natalia popped her head in the doorway. *Divorce brings out the worst in us*, I thought. "No we aren't," said Natalia. "We are not a broken family, Dad."

Mark did end up decorating the tree with Natalia. Biljana's girls joined in and the four of them made a beautiful family picture that showed no fissures, no fractures, and no rough edges. My mother and Biljana and I were wrapping gifts together on my bed and having a disjointed conversation half in Serbian, half in English, about my life situation, while Rick was talking to his Mexican family on his cell phone on the landing outside my room: "*Sí, Mami, entiendo, no te preocupes por favor. Sí, Mami, Feliz Navidad.*" Biljana's body always straightened up in some sort of voluptuous move whenever she heard Rick speak Spanish, or speak anything at all. *I will never have anything like that*, I thought as I curled ribbon edges on the red and green presents. *It's all luck, it's all bloody luck of the draw*, I sighed. Just then my cell phone rang. I looked down to see Karim's number. "Aren't you going to answer, Larinka?" asked my mother. "No, it's okay, it's no one!" I said. My mother crossed herself as she did when things weren't right. I was transparent like an empty jar. The raw truth in me ached. I wanted a solid real partner next to me like Biljana had. I wanted a different father for Natalia. I wanted another chance at starting over.

"Is he a good man, at least, Larinka?" my mother asked. "Can you marry him after you are divorced?" She crossed herself again. Biljana told my mother to stop it. We finished the gift wrapping in silence. I thought of my father who would have added great charm and wit to our Christmas celebrations if he weren't buried deep inside a lonely tomb in Belgrade. And what about Marija? I wondered what mysterious circles she was rambling right now.

The girls stood in front of the sparkling tree. Mark, who was sitting next to the tree holding his knees, looked up and smiled. "They did a good job, didn't they?" he said. He sat in the middle of what looked like a happy family picture with no cracks, a blissful holiday moment. It struck me that Mark seemed to have aged and his hair had gotten grayer. He looked even more handsome. His eyes met mine and he seemed genuinely content to be in the center of that glowing family picture. For a moment I thought he moved his hand in my direction as if wanting me to sit down next to them. He also regretted everything, I thought, but was too proud to ever go back. He withdrew his hand and stood up in a quick graceful move, his face turning back to impenetrable stone. Natalia ran to the hall closet. "Wait," she said. "I forgot the ornament for the top." As she rummaged through the top shelves for the treetop ornament, something shifted and a cascade of Ping-Pong balls, golf balls, BB gun pellets, NASCAR mini race cars, and white feathers came rushing down. Natalia stood in the center of a mount of balls and feathers, a touch of blush to her cheeks. Rick clapped his hands in wonderment. "¡Ay chica, qué bonito! What treasures have you got there?" To which Natalia replied simply: "I stole these," as the girls laughed and asked Biljana if they could have some, too. Biljana looked at me puzzled. "What's going on, Lari?" I just shrugged and pictured in my head a news headline: "Broken family reconciles amid stolen sporting goods." I would allow myself to float in the illusion of celebration for now. I knew the days and months to come would bring nothing close to reconciliation.

Washington, DC. War and Negotiations

Winter 2004

The New Year brought frigid cold and snow flurries, new court petitions from Mark, and US soldiers torturing Iraqi prisoners of war. On my first day of the semester, while news of American soldiers beating wounded Iraqi prisoners filled the headlines, my department chair told me that my tenure file was still incomplete. Without the noisy colorful caravan that was my family, Natalia returned to her moodier self and our duplex felt icy and deserted.

I walked into my classroom for Politics 101 and explained the rule of law to my wide-eyed freshmen. In my Advanced Politics class on Eastern European post-Communist governments, the only advanced class that my chair still allowed me to teach, on account of my being Eastern European, I indulged in fleeting comparisons between the American invasion of

Iraq and recent wars of aggression like the Bosnian war. There was no moral basis for the new model of American preemptive war; neither was there a moral basis for the Kosovo and Bosnian wars. Without the rule of law, almost anybody with a gun and a few soldiers under their command could become General Ratko Mladic, I told them. My voice carried through the amphitheater, even though my insides were twisting and thirst scorched my throat.

The trial was only a few weeks away, and I called Diana Coman as soon as my classes were over to strategize before leaving the office. She was hopeful that all was going to turn out all right and told me not to worry, to trust her and mostly, she said, to trust myself. As I shot out into the parking lot, I skidded on a patch of ice. I reminded myself to stay careful and strong. I got into my car with my ankle hurting from the fall and sat for a while looking out the window at the winter dusk and the whimsical snowflakes that were starting to fall. A childhood memory surfaced of the winter when my parents sent Biljana and me to our paternal grandparents, so we could experience country life for a few days, to make "real people of us" as my father said. Our grandparents lived in an old village near Dubrovnik. My father took us there by train during our winter vacation when Biljana and I were eight and ten years old, Natalia's age now. The winter was bitter and thick icicles were hanging from all the village roofs. Biljana and I went sledding on a little hill at the other end of the village.

She was crazy about sledding but this time it was special, she said, because this was an ice hill we were going to go sledding on. I didn't want to go at first, but Biljana coerced me and told me it was like ice skating only downhill, plus you were sitting on the sled, so what was the worst that could happen? We soon found out exactly that, because on our first run she flew off the sled and a sharp piece of ice sticking out pierced her leg through her leggings. Blood gushed and I thought Biljana was going to die from all the blood coming out of her. The ice on the hill was becoming red and shiny in the cold sun. I remembered that hard trip down the icy hill. I must have let go of the sled and glided on my butt because the sled was not part of my memory when I saw myself sitting next to bleeding Biljana. I wanted to cry so badly that my throat hurt. But Biljana looked at me fiercely. "Don't cry, do something!" she said. Even though Biljana produced a vigorous scream at her bleeding leg, nobody came out of their house to help us. I remembered thinking *These are not good people who don't come out to help a wounded child.* I remembered the village looking beautiful and eerie under the heavy snow with no people anywhere in sight. Then Biljana yelled: "What if I can't dance anymore? I'll kill myself!" I took my scarf and wrapped it tight around Biljana's calf in a tourniquet above the gash that squirted blood like a fountain, without saying a word. I tore my checkered shirt and wrapped it around her wound. "What if it gets gangrened and I die?" she screamed.

I told her she deserved it because she had been the idiot who wanted to go sledding on ice. As I was wrapping my shirt around her leg trying to make the blood stop Biljana told me she loved me more than anything. I couldn't say a word, I kept wrapping her leg, the blood kept soaking up the shirt, we had two kilometers to walk home and I would have given my life for my sister right there on the stupid ice hill. We walked the two kilometers back home with me holding Biljana like her crutch.

On the way back from the ice hill, I told Biljana stories of war I had heard from my father, how soldiers were coming home during World War II without a leg or an arm, or with wounds in their stomachs or in their heads, bleeding all over the place, and they made it home somehow: "What if we were at war, sister," I said, "we would have to make it, think of that, what would we do if we were at war and you and I were wounded soldiers?" Despite all the pain she was going through, my sister still found the strength to say I was stupid because girls didn't go to war. "Yes they do," I said, "you and I would."

When she saw the two of us in the doorway, our baba yelled at us that we were idiot girls to go sledding on ice, only cretins did that, and it served us right. Dede gave us each a shot of slivovitz, the awful alcohol that Serbians drank and that burned your insides like hell's fire. Then he called the village doctor. The doctor told me I had done a good job wrapping up my sister's wound; otherwise she would have lost too much blood. Maybe even died, he said. After the doctor left and our baba put us to bed and made the cross sign over us for protection, Biljana and I cuddled and held each other under the thick down coverlet. Then we cried. We had survived. I glowed at the fullness of our childhood, which now seemed so close. I drove home slowly, somehow renewed with hope that the strength I had found that winter of Biljana's bandaged leg would always sustain me. Maybe I could again rise unscathed above disaster and still keep some of my wholeness intact.

On Monday night of the week of the trial, I came home from work, and was surprised to find Mark at home with Natalia, since it was his day with her and he always took her out even if it was a school night. I came in quietly through the back door because I had groceries to deposit. I heard their overlapping voices in an excited, joyous conversation. I felt a jolt of jealousy for which I immediately reprimanded myself and tucked it right back under my new tight blue woolen suit. I walked in on tiptoes, respecting our understanding that on our nights with Natalia, we would each stay out of each other's way. Mark and Natalia were reading together and talking about Wallace Stevens's "Thirteen Ways of Looking at a Blackbird." "A man and a woman and a blackbird are one," Natalia recited in laughter. The joyous relaxed scene between Mark and Natalia made me equally happy and jealous. Mark wasn't just fighting for custody of Natalia to get back at me but because he genuinely wanted to spend more time with her. He really had learned to be a better parent because of our divorce. Maybe he was finally making the transition from teaching poetry to living it, even if it took a family cataclysm for that to happen. Even if it was too late for Mark and me, he could find that happiness with our daughter.

"You and Mommy and I are one and we are a blackbird," said Natalia shaking with laughter at her own inventiveness. Mark was laughing, too, like I hadn't seen him laugh in years. I was sad, too, for all we had missed in each other. I badly wanted to cry, like the time Biljana gashed her leg on the ice, but I pumped myself up, filled with all the sadness I felt, and didn't let one tear fall. We were lonely blackbirds perched on snowy fences, we could have all been one blackbird at one time. "He rode over Connecticut / In a glass coach," continued Natalia. Connecticut Avenue had once been my dream come true, my Cinderella palace. I had flown over it in a glass coach once, landed in it on the arm of my husband who rescued me from a genocidal and war-ridden country, I had made a colorful palace here until the glass shattered all around us. "The river is moving / The blackbird must be flying." Now I was only a spectator, an outsider to the blackbird moment between Natalia and Mark. He looked particularly handsome that night with his delicate yet manly profile, his gray hair shining around the temples. There was a time I wanted him more than anything else in the world. Him and America. In two days we would face each other in court, fighting for the custody rights to the quivering daughter we had created. There was no poetry in that.

For the trial, I found my new survival mode. I disengaged from my own litigation and remembered that whatever battle Mark and I were playing out, there was a world outside filled with war and genocide. The lawyers wanted Natalia to come to the stand and I asked her if she would be willing to make a brief appearance at the trial, just to answer a few questions. She wanted to know only if they would ask her about the baseball cards and golf balls and feathers she had stolen from CVS and Walmart and then arrest her. I promised her that no, nobody was going to arrest her or even ask her about the stolen things, only about the relations she had with each of her parents. And maybe whether she had a preference about living more with one of us than the other. She might have a say in what was going to happen to her living arrangements. She became pensive for a moment and wanted to know if Aunt Biljana was going to be there in court. Once she knew this, she answered that yes, it would be cool to come to court, and was the judge going to wear a long black robe like she'd seen on TV?

The first day when I would take the stand, I left the house early to meet Diana Coman at her office. She told me she would accompany me to the imposing courthouse. Natalia would come later with Biljana and Rick. The die was cast, as Caesar had said when crossing the Rubicon, there was no turning back. When I reached the steps of the courthouse with Diana, I just about collapsed at the sight of the chair of the Politics Department, and beside him the journalism colleague who had been on my plane home from Paris in my truncated escapade with Karim a year ago. His wife, Sarah, was there, too. I had to remember my approach, to detach myself from what was happening. But were Sarah and Brian getting a divorce, too? I actually wondered for a moment in confusion. Everybody was getting a divorce, apparently it was the thing to do that frigid winter. Their presence in the courtroom made no sense. Then I saw Mark talking and laughing with them and his lawyers, glowing with confidence and good humor. I suddenly understood why Brian from journalism had recently stopped greeting me when we crossed each other on campus; why Sarah, his wife, had turned her head the other way when I ran into her at Natalia's school before Christmas; why my department chair acted so strangely, even peevishly, when I ran into him with Natalia. They were all there to testify on Mark's behalf.

Mark's two lawyers extolled his virtues as a father and downgraded me as a mother. He was careful, I was reckless, he was stable, I was unpredictable, he was caring, I was careless. He offered a good role model, I offered the model of a depraved woman, a bad role model for a girl. He had taken Natalia to the beach, I had taken a self-indulgent joyride on the Blue Ridge Parkway with my lover. There were pictures of Mark and Natalia at the beach, on a school bench, on a visit with his mother. And there were me and Karim always kissing. I exposed my child to danger in times of enhanced national security, the lawyers charged.

I nudged Diana Coman and she wrote to me on a piece of paper that the judge didn't like for parents to denigrate each other that way. But the judge seemed to be listening carefully. How did Diana know? I wondered. I stared at the murals on the wall and was struck by the irony of a larger-than-life representation of Lady Justice draped in the folds of a tunic that left one of her breasts exposed as she held the scales of justice. I couldn't help smiling to myself and wondering why even the incarnation of Justice had to be a sex object in a world of men. Images of Gregory Peck or Spencer Tracy, the passionate lawyer defending an unjustly accused woman, a poor man, or a person of color, passed through my mind. But Gregory Peck and Spencer Tracy were nowhere in sight to defend my virtue and my maternal rights under the glaring lights of that American courtroom.

Like a bad dream, Brian the journalism professor recounted how he saw me in Charles de Gaulle airport engaging in lewd acts with an Arab man. He stressed "Arab man" and then repeated that I was kissing an Arab man in public when he saw me. To that he added that after he and his wife had lent us their children's old crib when Natalia was born, I returned it years later, damaged, with several of the crib's nails missing. I had stolen nails from their crib, he said, and from this Mark's lawyer concluded I was teaching Natalia to steal. Mark testified at length about our marriage, our arguments, our parenting disagreements, his shock and pain at discovering my love affair. He sounded convincing, and I even was able to believe his argument. His lawyer produced copies of emails between me and Karim, and more photos from Dulles airport, and I was mortified by the exposure, like a Hollywood star followed by paparazzi for the *National Enquirer.*

Of all the testimonies, I loved Rick's the most. "Ms. Kulicz understands her daughter better than anyone else," he said. "Better than even Natalia knows herself. It's all smooth between them, no edges." Rick looked stately and manly and his Mexican accent gave his speech a special weight of warmth and truthfulness. I understood why Biljana was so crazy about him. Between my sister and me at least one of us had been lucky that way, and had a happy marriage to a good man, without any necessary foreverafterness. It was all in the here and now. "A man and a woman and a blackbird are one."

When Diana Coman started her line of questioning of the witnesses, she was my own Lady Justice holding the scales, my Gregory Peck. Mark, the witnesses, the judge, the lawyers, and everybody in the room opened their eyes wide and seemed to wake up from a long sleep. "Have you, Mr. Brian McAlister, observed Ms. Kulicz interact with her daughter for any length of time, yes or no?" She spoke without gibberish or extraneous talk. "No, I haven't," he said. "Have you,

Mr. Lopez, watched Ms. Kulicz interact with her daughter for any length of time, yes or no?" "Yes, I have." When my turn came to testify her confidence in me was unflappable, like she had waved her wand to make me a sparkling new person. I spoke clearly and coolheadedly about every aspect of Natalia's upbringing, how I'd packed sandwiches with her favorite cheese, and how I'd read her Norwegian fairy tales before bedtime. I described our epic escapades to the zoo and to the sculpture garden, our visits to the doctor and the time we stayed up all night together when she had bronchitis, even before a long day of lectures. And there were the cello lessons and the practicing. Every time Mark's lawyers asked about Karim, I took the Fifth and stared at them silently, just as Diana had instructed. "It is irrelevant for custody, Your Honor," she would say to the judge. And then the judge asked me himself: "Did you have an extramarital affair? Answer the question, Ms. Kulicz, or I'll hold you in contempt." But before I could speak, Diana Coman stood up and approached the bench. Diana asked the judge to wait until Natalia was heard. The judge conceded.

When Natalia spoke, her voice was crystalline, and the room was silent. You had to listen to her, and listen carefully. The judge asked all the questions himself, not the lawyers. His voice became almost tender. He was a tough guy with a kind heart, I thought. He asked Natalia if she had any prefer-ence about who she wanted to spend more time with. She said no, she loved us both the same. He asked her about her cello lessons. She told him about her classes and the pieces she was working on. What would her ideal living arrangement be given that her parents were going to live separately now, the judge asked her. "You mean like my dream living situation?" I watched her face unblinkingly and noticed a quick expression of pain spread over her. She looked so delicate, I thought she might break into a thousand small pieces. At that moment, I was cracking, too. If she broke I would turn to dust. The judge smiled and said that yes, that was what he meant. "It would be fun to live with Aunt Biljana and my cousins Amanda and Melissa and Uncle Rick and see my parents on weekends for now. For a while, until they both calm down, that would be my dream living situation, Your Honor. I still love both my parents but right now things are sort of crazy in the house with the divorce and all." The judge released Natalia from the stand and wished her good luck with her cello playing. He thanked her for her help. "It wasn't to help, it was to tell the truth or something." She smiled and stepped out of the room in her pretty sunflower-yellow dress.

"You should try to settle, Lara," said Diana in low whispers after the judge ordered a recess. "I think neither of you is going to get full custody so it's better at least to attempt to come to an agreement, this way for whatever is left unresolved at least the judge has seen you are both reasonable people and are thinking of what's best for Natalia. Then he will most likely rule in favor of who is showing most reason." "But she said she wants to live with Biljana," I said naively.

"This is not a wish-granting institution, Lara, and you know it. It's a court of law, the judge has to rule according to the way he thinks will best serve the child." Diana told me I should settle for split physical and legal custody. "Lots of parents settle with these kinds of arrangements these days, you could go for one week each, split vacation time and alternate holidays. She's tough, your Natalia, she might take this better than being yanked unevenly in one direction, and the novelty of the living situation might offer her some excitement, too." I told Diana that was fine, I'd go with that, if Mark accepted. But what if he didn't? "Let's see what happens, and we'll deal then," said Diana and hurried to the other end of the room where Mark and his lawyers were deliberating.

Mark did not accept my proposal. He stuck to his initial claim. The judge looked disappointed, and even angry. Then he ordered equally split legal and physical custody between the parents with reasonable visitation rights for both my sister and mother. I had underestimated that owl-faced judge who stared at all the witnesses with a mad fixity. America was not like Serbia after all, Justice was sometimes possible, and as in the painting, Justice meant keeping things in balance, bare-breasted or not. Then the judge spoke to each of us, addressing Mark first. He told Mark he needed to cool off from his anger and hurt, it was human to feel that way, but it was hurting Natalia, too. He couldn't be the best parent he could be if he did not deal with his anger and stop tearing the child in two in order to punish the mother. What had happened between us was solely between the two of us and should not affect the child. He waited to hear Mark say that he understood and he would act accordingly. Mark was shocked, and began to speak in a whisper. But then the judge raised his voice and asked Mark to speak up. That was when I experienced a sharp sense of satisfaction. Mark said meekly: "Yes, Your Honor, I get it, I understand."

But then when the judge turned to me he changed his tone and spoke to me harshly and disdainfully. He told me I should be ashamed for having caused such havoc in my family. Didn't I know that marriage was forever? I had taken vows and I had caused great pain to many people with my reckless behavior. He had scolded Mark but it was a man-to-man scolding, like two guys wrestling and then shaking hands after the match. But he talked to me like I was the fallen woman that all the lawyers had tried to portray in their statements and questioning. I now could understand that "liberty and justice for all" meant that if you were a man, and the judge was a man, you most likely got the thicker slice of that frosted cake called Justice. What irked me most in his statement was the marriage foreverness bit. It sounded like next he would order me to believe in the afterlife or in God. When he asked me if I understood, I said loudly: "Yes, sir, Your Honor, I understand." I wanted to sound militaristic, not to give him the satisfaction to think he had crushed me under his heavy and Just step. I cast one last look at the space in which I had spent the most excruciating eight hours of my life. Lady Justice seemed to wink at me as I left the courtroom. Her exposed boob even seemed to be shining, and I finally allowed myself to laugh.

When I arrived home that evening, depleted of all energy and willpower, a large envelope from Hassan was waiting in the mail. At first I thought it was for Mark, but it was my name that was clearly spelled out in capital letters on the envelope. I breathed deeply as I opened the package, which contained another envelope on which my name was written in Marija's handwriting. Inside the second envelope was a new wad of letters addressed to me and more notes from her diary. Almost forgetting about the day in court, I sat down in my study and began to devour the pages from Marija until Natalia walked in, and I closed them. She of course knew exactly what they were and climbed into bed next to me. I would continue after she fell asleep.

With another spring gliding in after a winter that looked just like the spring, I had to leave the oppressive blues of Santa Barbara and move to Los Angeles. I had to find a place to live and contact Sally's connections, in case I wanted to work. Los Angeles's maze of highways was almost uplifting. I found an apartment near the university with no view of the sea, just trees. I had a craving for trees and dirt as if they lacked from my diet. I craved for copper and snow. I was yearning for tree roots and sidewalks. The Los

Angeles residential street provided some of those. Sally's connections found me work on one of the Hollywood sets. I did freelance writing and reporting for one of the local newspapers. A few times I even reported on a local TV station. I was supposed to bring in my Eastern European perspective to the happenings on the Hollywood set. They loved my accent and my demeanor, they said, I should just be myself. That made me laugh since there was no longer such a being as "myself," but only a palimpsest of bits of myself carefully arranged in a colorful simulacrum. I was light and fake like everybody else in Hollywood and it felt good for a little while. Nobody would have really wanted me to be myself, the hard-core unadorned me, if they had any idea who I really was.

Then the woman from Sarajevo called and asked if I was thinking of going back anytime soon. She was getting tired of doing the work in my place. I told her we had an understanding and it wasn't time yet. Just a little bit longer and I would call her back. She said she needed more money, she had to move to a new place and had no money and it wasn't safe anymore. I told her I would send her more money, if only she could be patient for a little while longer. It wouldn't be long before I would go back to Sarajevo and take care of everything. She agreed and said she would wait for me but might still move. As I was talking to her on the phone in the living room of my new LA duplex apartment I saw that there was a tree with azaleas right in front of my window. They weren't red but white, what a relief. For once, the azaleas that followed me everywhere had lost their color. A group of children were playing outside my window, a rare occurrence on LA streets. They spoke Spanish and sounded joyous.

Suddenly the huge hole in my womb felt full and the Spanish of the children playing in front of my window sounded Bosnian, which really was Serbo-Croatian. Languages morphed into one another and so did the azaleas and the snow and the children and Los Angeles and Sarajevo. Lara and Marija and Biljana were all playing amid scaffolding and chasing each other to see who got first to the highest point on the scaffolding of the National Library reconstruction. Everybody was building something in the world and the crew on the Hollywood set that I was working on three days a week was building a version of Sarajevo during the siege for a movie with Angelina Jolie. They were building shelled, mortar-hit, and blown-up Sarajevo out of Hollywood materials. The woman from Sarajevo kept talking on the phone in a language I could no longer understand, maybe it was Albanian or Turkish. It could have been anything. As I was looking outside my window and watching Lara jump hula hoops on Angelina

Jolie's set imitating wartime Sarajevo and as the
red in the azaleas was quickly withdrawing leaving
snowy-white fleshy petals behind, the hole in my
womb grew to the size of a basketball, to the size of
a grown baby. I knew the time had come to get in
touch with Lara and go back and finish what I had
started as the woman had said. It was time to take
possession of my child. The one I had given birth
to in a state of semi-coma somewhere in one of the
houses where the woman kept hiding me that year.
It was time for me to come to terms with that reality
and embrace it. It was time to keep my promise to
the woman. Remember everything and own it like
it was actually happening in my own life. Enough
of the emotional blunting and all the psychoanalytic
crap. I called Lara. A man who was probably Mark
and had a stern voice answered and said, "Hello,
hello, who is it?" I hung up and I called Biljana in
Chicago. "Hello, Biljana, this is Marija. Remember
me? I'm back from the dead and I'd like to speak to
Lara. I wonder if you could give me Lara's cell phone
number." Just like that. It wasn't hard at all.

I sat on the bed and stared at the wall in a state of stupor. Marija had a child. The news seemed unreal. Bizarre
questions were swarming in my head with a deafening
clamor: Whose child was it? Why in the world did she have a

child? Were her notes really meant for me? Was this her way of letting me know this formidable news? Natalia had woken up and was looking at me. "Mama, what's wrong?" But I couldn't answer, my mouth stayed clenched. Natalia took the letter from my hand and began to read. What difference would another bit of traumatic news make now to my daughter who had already glimpsed a world that most American children her age had no idea existed? I remembered Marija's collected stories of all of the women when Natalia and I sat in the Sarajevo hotel room. The women who became pregnant in the camps, or were made to become pregnant, some miscarried, others aborted gruesomely, many dying in the process. Others gave birth to dead babies that they threw in the trash, others gave birth to live babies and gave them away. There were other women still who carried their babies to term, gave birth to live babies, and then wanted to keep them. Apparently Marija was part of this last group, even though it seemed she had at first given her baby away. Marija was her own group. "A child is a child, Mama," Natalia said quietly. But I possessed neither Natalia's innocence nor her luminous wisdom. For me a child was not always just a child, particularly in Marija's case. I was terrified.

We had to divide everything in half, not just Natalia's custody. We were to sell the duplex and split the profits, savings, and assets, and divide the furniture. We each kept our own cars, me my blue Chevy (I had always dreamed of owning an American car while in Serbia) and Mark his black Honda (he boycotted American cars). The scales of justice were balanced to a T, even if I wasn't. I had thought I would calm down and settle into my new divorced life, with everything in it split in half. But it turned out that until we found a buyer for the house the three of us still had to live under the same roof. With everything now final, and without even a tiny crumb of hope that everything would be the same as before, life was still hard under our roof. This is how it was when wars were started, I thought to myself.

When the phone would sometimes ring, I'd startle thinking maybe it was Marija. But it was never her. Once there had been a call and a cavernous silence at the other end. I now blamed myself for not having felt it, known it, and just said: *I know it's you, Marija, where are you? Let's meet!* Something direct and simple like that. I must have been gathering papers for my divorce trial or correcting Politics 101 exams or doing homework with Natalia. There had been other unanswered calls, too, wrong numbers, weird soliciting. I'd never paid attention to them, I just hung up. Once in the evening when the phone rang, Mark and I both ran to the living room to pick it up. I got there first and said a loud "hello." But there was no answer, just a long silence, the sound of breathing and maybe the sound of soft cries. Or maybe I imagined that. "Hello, hello, is anybody there?" I kept saying, just like in the dreams and visions I had. I was certain that it was only a matter of weeks before Marija and I would see each other. Her notes seemed pretty clear on that. I called Hassan and asked him when he got the package of Marija's notes, in what form had they arrived, were there any other letters with it, and why him? "We've been in communication for quite some time," he said. His voice was warm, just like it had been in his office in northern Virginia. "I sent you the notes because they came to me sealed, inside a larger envelope, with a note from Marija saying they were for you. All the other papers she sends are postwar materials and human rights stuff. If you want to come by the office and talk, you know you're always welcome." I thanked Hassan but I knew I wouldn't go. Any attempts to find her in any phone book in Santa Barbara or Los Angeles were fruitless. And though I knew I could find Sally Bryant, I didn't want to get to Marija in that way. I wanted to leave it to Marija's own orchestrations. Some more time had to pass for me to be ready, and Marija, too. Our trajectories had to match, to come into perfect accord across the American skies.

I started calling Karim again, to fill the void of post-divorce. His voice still sounded melodic and sexy, streaming into my ear in raspy rivulets of French vowels. He asked me to come to Paris for the same conference we had been at a year before, just when the war was starting. The divorce had been finalized and I would think about coming, I told him, although I was nervous about my tenure. He said he really missed me, to please come, that he was scheduled to speak at the conference anyway. It would be mad on our part to miss the occasion to see each other, he said, *"une vraie folie,"* true madness. One April morning as I watched the delicate petals of the dogwoods in front of our house, I decided I would go to the conference. I didn't need to have a paper to present, I was free. I booked my ticket to Paris. I needed to close accounts in all the areas of my life, tidy up all the compartments that composed it like a wobbly house of cards.

We Won't Always Have Paris

April 2004

I made all the arrangements for my trip to Paris. The political science conference was to take place the weekend at the end of one of Mark's weeks with Natalia, so I planned to leave earlier and spend a few extra days with Karim in Paris before it began. My fantasy continued where it left off the year before. Karim and Natalia and Arina and I one day would become some kind of elegant family that people would watch with interest, wondering whether we were the parents of both children or which child was whose. It was my Hollywood way of repairing the cosmic lack of synchronicity of having met too late, too married, and with children of our own.

When I told Mark I was going to be gone at a conference the third week in April, he smirked just a little. We still lived under the same roof, and I wished our new living arrangement could finally start, our fifty–fifty of everything, our lives of halves and new freedoms, when I wouldn't feel as though

I had to ask for Mark's permission to see my lover. But house sales were slow, and our real estate agent said we might have to wait until the summer to have a good offer. Natalia didn't say anything when I told her I was going to Paris for the conference. She put on her impenetrable look and stared at the wall. When were we going to go to Chicago to see Aunt Biljana, she wanted to know. I changed the subject back and asked her what I should bring her from Paris. She thought for a few minutes, her face changing from impenetrable to dreamy, and her green clear eyes became softer and more watery. Then she said she wanted a painting: "A painting like the one from the artist who did your portrait in Paris before, Mama, remember?" Everything was well stored in her mind.

"A painting of what, Natalia?" I asked.

"I don't care," she answered lightly, "just a painting made by one of those street artists, could they make one of me if you showed them a picture of me, Mama?"

Natalia told me she was going to the beach with Mark for spring break and I tried not to show my pain.

"Why don't you and Dad go to Chicago for spring break?" I said cheerfully. "That way you'd get to also see Biljana and Melissa and Amanda and you'd have the beaches all along the lakeshore. Wouldn't that be fun?"

Her face brightened up and her eyes opened. "Do you think Dad will really want this, Mama? With the divorce and stuff, you know…"

"Just ask him, Talia, and see what he says." Maybe there *was* a way to live our new lives of halves.

To both my surprise and Natalia's, Mark liked the idea. He went ahead and reserved plane tickets to Chicago during the same days that I was going to Paris. Maybe he was recomposing himself just like I was. But still, I chose to keep him in my mystery box for now. He seemed safer that way.

Two days before my flight to Paris, Karim called to tell me he wasn't sure he would be able to come after all, because his mother was sick again, and his daughter was going through a difficult period. Besides, he thought he was coming down with the flu. I was walking on M Street in Georgetown as I listened to his slow, raspy words, out shopping for a smashing dress for my Paris trip. I lost my balance and leaned against the wall of a building. Someone asked if I was okay. Did I need help? I heard Karim's voice: *"Lara, tu es toujours là?"* Lara, are you still there? "Are you kidding me?" I finally said. I had already bought the ticket, arranged my family schedule around the trip, I just couldn't believe it. He said he was really sorry. I hung up. The brick wall I was holding was actually the Sephora store. Women inside were trying on makeup, mascara to lengthen and darken their eyelashes, lipstick to add lusciousness to their smiles, foundation to cover up imperfections on their cheeks. What a sham it all was. The only thing I could think to do was go in and look for a deep, dark lipstick.

I was ashamed even to call my sister, but I did, after I
bought the darkest-red lipstick I could find in the store. Biljana sounded troubled, not her usual upbeat cheerful and
unconditionally supportive self. "Just attend the conference,
Larinka, enjoy Paris, make a vacation of it, maybe hang out
with other interesting men at the conference and forget the
motherfucker!" she said breathlessly. But something was
wrong with Biljana. She was quiet for a moment. And then
she told me that Marija had called her. In a tired voice she
continued to tell me that Marija was in Los Angeles, that she
sounded strange and incoherent, something about a child,
a boy back in Bosnia. I felt sick again. Marija's callings and
writings about a child must be true. "Did you know about
it, Lara? Did you know she had a child from the rape?" I
wished Biljana had not named it. Now it was truly real and
truly unbearable. "Sort of, yes, I guess I knew it but didn't
want to believe it. She's been sending me notes, letters, and
I'm pretty sure she called here a few times, but Mark always
answered and she must have hung up. I guess she's preparing me for, you know...for when we finally see each other
again." Biljana said, "There was something so ominous and
cavernous in the way she talked. She scared me. She said she
wanted to come to Washington and try to get the boy out
of Bosnia with your help, Lara. It's awful, Larinka. I would
have killed myself, that's all." I had never heard defeat like
that in Biljana's voice. "Of course her voice sounded ominous
and cavernous, what did you expect after all that she's been

through?" I said in Marija's defense. Though it terrified me, I felt I could deal with Marija's war child.

I did go to Paris after all, and I did meet with Karim, but under circumstances so dire and so wrenching that I wished Paris had never been invented. After my troubling talk with Biljana, Karim called again and poured his sweetest, most loving, most heartbreakingly romantic voice and words into my cell phone. He had been under so much pressure, under such turmoil seeing his family disintegrate. *Tell me about it!* He was torn between seeing his family fall to pieces and his impossible love for me, but I was the love of his life, no doubt about it, he had married his wife out of duty, but I was the one he loved. More than he had ever loved a woman. In my vulnerable state, I believed his words, which felt like soothing medication in a moment of extreme pain. I would both renew my affair with Karim and attend the political science conference, too.

The day before I left for Paris, Marija did reach me on my home phone finally and my heart stopped for a little while. Some people's hearts would have started beating faster and more sonorously in their chests; mine went quiet. Marija's voice sounded far away, speaking in a language I couldn't penetrate. "I'm going to need your help, Lara," she said with a quick laugh. Marija had never asked me for help before. "I want to get the hell out of this perfect blue-sky California crap. You know what I mean, right?" I had no idea what she meant but just said, "Aha, of course." "And another thing"—she hesitated—"I need to go back to Bosnia and get back my kid, you know." She said it like the most normal thing in the world. "He's eight, and I'd like to have him here with me." She sounded lucid and clear, the old Marija I knew, not the cavernous one Biljana had told me about. Still I needed time before I could really believe what she was saying, before I could join her. I would find her as soon as I returned from Paris. She could come and live with me, if she wanted, I said, and we could make a plan of action. I had no idea how those clear and reasonable words emerged from my mouth, but they did easily and smoothly. She said with a laugh to watch out what I was signing up for, but that it sounded like a good plan. "Take my cell phone number, call me when you're ready. And of course if you need me for anything." She laughed. I didn't want us to end the conversation and I asked her in a rush: "Marija, how did you know I was going to go to Sarajevo last fall? . . . Or did you know? Those notes, the ones at the woman's house, they were for me, right, you had left them for me?" "We'll talk about all that when we see each other, all right?" she said firmly and hung up. I felt taken aback by her abrupt end to the conversation, but then I remembered. The cruelty of the war had brushed off on her. At least now Marija was no longer in a thick cloak of darkness and unknown. She was speaking, laughing, thinking and planning. After I returned from Paris, I would find Marija, no matter how hard it might be to get wrapped up in her story. And how like Marija to think I was going to need her! My life's troubles, in comparison with hers, seemed like mosquito bites. And as my plane took off, I was filled with the richness of life, with color and complexity, despite all the wounds and confusion. I was on my way to Paris again.

Karim and I met in the same hotel as the previous year and the first couple of hours together brought back all the delights and passion I remembered. He seemed even more attentive and passionate than he used to; he called me all the endearing French words in the history of French romance plus the added Arabic ones for special spice. It was evening, and we were still lying next to each other in the small Parisian bed, when Karim started crying. I thought it was from happiness to be with me again, that we had finally sort of made it despite such unlikely obstacles. I stroked his face and felt tears welling in my eyes as well. I didn't remember ever crying for happiness before, though I had heard many people's stories of happy sobbing. I was proud I could have that experience, too. Karim then confessed to me that he had slept with another woman since our last encounter, or he had tried to though it appeared he wasn't very successful at it, because all he thought of when he was with this other woman was me and his love of me, was what he said. He could only be a man when he was with me, he told me, and more tears flowed on his face, as though this would give me some kind of pleasure. It appeared that Karim's big problem at that juncture in our lives was that he loved me so much that he couldn't fuck other women because of the love he experienced for me. The woman had called him good for nothing, because he couldn't satisfy her. She had shamed him. No words came out of my mouth. It was impossible for me to produce any intelligible sounds. But I found that my arms and legs could still move. My single persistent thought was that I needed to get out of that hotel room as quickly as my limbs could carry me, out of that street, out of that arrondissement and out of that city and never return until a new geological era started and Paris was nothing but a huge expanse of black sand. Paris had been a huge mistake. Karim had been a huge mistake. Why had I not flown to Marija the moment she called? If Marija asked for help it meant she had thought it over a million times before saying it. I was on the completely wrong side of the world and I was paying for it.

I don't know how, but I managed to get dressed, gather all my things, leave the room, and ask the hotel concierge to get me a taxi to the airport. I found the Air France ticket counter at Charles de Gaulle. There were no more flights to Washington, DC, that evening, so I asked for one to anywhere in the United States. I was desperate to leave the city on the first plane that would take me across the ocean. The next one left for Los Angeles at six the next morning, and that was the one I would take. I changed my ticket to the flight to Los Angeles. I spent the rest of the evening and the night in Charles de Gaulle airport, gorging on sushi, seaweed salads, marzipan candy, and red wine from the various cafés and duty-free food stores strewn along the shiny hallways. I talked indiscriminately to strangers of various nationalities. I befriended the airport custodians from Poland, La Réunion, and Algeria who listened to my sob story in the neon night of the airport and advised me to "forget Karim, bad man, and get good American man instead." I slept the few hours before the departure of the plane on one of the hard benches at the gate, waking up with a horrendous headache.

As I boarded the plane I wondered what LA would be like. I would use the remaining days of my wrecked vacation to discover a new city, Hollywood, the place that produced fake dreams of happiness and heroism and adventure and forever love for millions of gullible men and women, just like me. And most important I would find Marija. A lucky thing that she had given me her cell phone number. As the plane glided above Paris, I sobbed hopelessly. I was crying for Paris, I told the doctor the flight attendant had brought over to me. I cried over the sweet hilly picturesque streets of Montmartre, the shady groves and the blue pond filled with children's boats in the Jardin du Luxembourg, the dizzying views from each bridge across the Seine, and all the kitsch portrait artists that filled the city from one corner to the other. I'll never have Paris, I said, gulping through my own cascades of tears. The doctor gave me a pill to swallow, and soon my tears dried and the dense fog clenched around my brain started to slowly dissipate. I was soon dreaming of the final scenes in the hotel room, arguing with Karim, throwing his cell phone out the window, calling him names in English, French, and Serbian and, as I fled from the room, slamming the door so hard that pieces of molding fell from the ceiling with a crumbling sound like an earthquake.

As the plane was descending, bringing me back to the American soil, I had a vision of Mark and Karim both walking on the runway. They were walking away from me at a steady pace both wearing fancy dark suits. They waved good-bye to me. I felt only a cold sadness, like the passage of an autumn wind. I imagined Mark and Karim walking toward each other at the end of the runway, shaking hands, and then embracing just as my plane hit the hard earth of the City of Angels.

Los Angeles. We'll Always Have Hollywood!

April 2004

Marija was not answering the phone. I stood confused in front of the Los Angeles airport not knowing what my next move should be. Tanned, slender, and overconfident Californians passed me. By some stroke of luck the taxi driver I flagged down was a kind man from Uzbekistan who decided to give me an hour-and-a-half tour of a dizzying conglomerate of highways punctuated by short tours of LA neighborhoods. He then dropped me in front of a lovely white hotel with blazing azaleas on the porch on a sunny street, all for the price of an airplane ticket back to Washington. It didn't matter where he took me, since I had no idea where any part of my life was going.

The hotel room was white and plain. Specks of darkness

and redness like splintered body parts from a recent bombardment were encroaching themselves onto the wall of my room like miniature paintings, the visual art abridged version of my life. I had done bad things and was all alone in a hotel room in Los Angeles. Whiteness and purity were a fraud. Only specks of blood and darkness were real. And then suddenly out of those crowds of black specks that were all the bad things in my life, Marija walked toward me like a goddess of fire, more beautiful than I had ever seen or remembered her. She wore dangling sparkling jewelry all over her body, even on her ankles and in her nose, and her eyes were blazing, but not with hatred, with love. With golden shining love like a benevolent sun. She asked me to go with her. And I did.

At that same moment, my cell phone rang, breaking my reverie, and without even looking at the number on the screen I said: "Marija? I'm in LA." She had the same throaty, warm, somehow ironic voice I remembered. She didn't sound a bit surprised I was there. Her voice matched the image of power and beauty I had just had of her in my vision. There was no whiteness in her voice, but neither was it all speckled with blood and darkness. It was a voice like a flooding river that swept you away and overpowered you. Marija was going to come pick me up at my hotel any minute. When I told her where I was, she said, "Fancy, fancy!" I waited for her sitting on the steps in front of the hotel, framed by enormous pots of azaleas, like a girl in some Mexican painting I once saw.

The street was uncannily quiet as if everybody had died. Yet the sun shone with such warmth and conviction onto everything and enveloped me so lovingly that even if everybody on that street was dead, the warm light made it all right. I dozed off for what seemed to be a fraction of a second and when I opened my eyes a red car appeared from around the corner like a blazing eagle. It sparkled in the sun and for a second it looked like it was all ablaze. Then Marija got out wearing a simple black-and-white dress and a yellow headband. She had none of the colors I had expected, she was a black-and-white movie with a speck of yellow that seemed both amiss and necessary, both attractive and irritating. Marija looked somehow unchanged and yet a completely different person, as if time had not touched her but as if she had gone through a transformation that changed her completely. My greatest shock was that she looked neither devastated, nor broken, nor a pulsing blob of raging anger, as I probably would have been. She laughed when she saw me and her laughter scratched the surface of my brain sharply and deeply all the way to one of the last memories I had of her laughing and talking in the hallway of Belgrade University, surrounded by a group of men and women who all seemed to be mesmerized by every single word flowing out of her mouth. How did one laugh after one had been through what Marija had been through? But laugh she did. War, genocide, mass rapes, NATO bombings, adultery, bloody divorce, and custody battles in between two of Marija's laughs stretched across a full decade and then some.

Marija had a glass eye and a reconstructed nose but you could barely tell. It was all done to perfection by a plastic surgeon in LA who operated on movie stars, on people like Cher and Michael Jackson, she told me. During the attack, the rape, the murder of her family, she "obtained an injury" that crushed her optic nerve and her nose. She used the word *obtained* as if it were something one would ask for. She passed out from the pain and didn't remember the rest, a blessing she said. "Yeah, I was among the lucky ones," she repeated. Marija was frighteningly beautiful while she spoke. There was something detached and unnaturally poised about the way in which she rushed through the telling of those events as if recounting someone else's life. At some point her glass eye produced a tiny sparkle in the sun in the café on Sunset Boulevard where she took me. And at that exact moment something cracked and I started sobbing with uncontrolled rage. My body shook from its core and my chest was heaving in excruciating pain. Marija held my hands without moving and without flinching and without blinking until my sobbing crisis passed; she told the blond tanned waitress who asked if we were all right and whether we needed anything to stay away from our table and not to bother us again until we called her. The people at the surrounding tables cast surreptitious glances and pretended not to hear or see anything. They dug into their salads and sipped their diet drinks. It was only then that I realized Marija and I were speaking English and not Serbian. It felt perfectly normal to speak in English to each other about Serbian atrocities. You saw everything in LA and nobody cared. Marija paid the bill and said, "Let's get the hell out of here. I want to show you something."

I followed Marija into her red convertible. I would have followed her to the moon. She seemed superhuman to me, only her glass eye—the idea of it—hurt me more than the idea of the rape, while to her it was a "blessing" because it reminded her that she didn't remember what had happened. Her own psyche protected her from the memory. She didn't want to talk about the war and that day, only about the future. It wasn't clear to me what future she was talking about. Her son, probably. She asked me about my "adventure" in Paris with a throaty laugh. I poured everything out to her as if she were my personal therapist. She was whizzing across serpentine LA highways at the wheel of her red Corvette with her shock of black hair rising in the wind like a magic bird. She said: "That's awful, Lara, what an awful thing to happen to you, I would have strangled the man." Then she said: "I'm sorry, I'm so sorry." Nothing made sense. How could she be so sorry for me and my little pathetic Paris melodrama, when she survived the unsurvivable? It turned out that I did need Marija as she had suggested when she called me in Washington and a good thing it was she gave me her phone number. It wasn't her who needed saving right now, but mostly me.

She must have guessed my thoughts: "Everybody's

suffering is their own, Lara. We all have our own boulder to bear up that fucking hill. Nobody's pains are traded for someone else's pains."

Because Marija spoke a lot in riddles and aphorisms, I had to construct the puzzle of her full meanings in my mind as we talked while also observing every one of her expressions and gestures. It was exhausting and thrilling, like a carnival of the mind. I felt I was being taken on a spatial journey in Marija's red Corvette and all the questions that were scorching my mind about her past and the last ten years were pulverized into fine dust. At some point she turned toward me smiling lovingly and asked: "How are you doing, girl?" Then she said: "Just because one went through Apocalypse and back doesn't mean one has to wear dowdy clothes and look like shit and be miserable all day long, right?" Soon after that she pulled into a parking lot in Burbank and showed me a sign that said WARNER BROS. STUDIOS. "Come, let's see behind the illusion," she said, smiling again. We got on a small tram and got off at a set that looked French. "We'll always have Paris?" She laughed heartily. "Paris be damned!" I said. But then it clicked and I burst out laughing, too. It was the set where the Paris flashback scenes were shot in *Casablanca*, Ingrid and Humphrey driving in a convertible, drinking Champagne at a piano bar, dancing, swirling, laughing, and kissing, all in a make-believe cardboard reconstruction of Paris. It had all started with Marija: my fixation with *Casablanca*. We were in sixth grade and *Casablanca* was playing one night at the

Kinoteka cinema where they showed old movies in the center of Belgrade and where my parents had first taken me to see the notorious *Doctor Zhivago* under whose fated stars I had been born and raised. I remembered the cans of condensed milk in her pantry that we ate as dessert before going to the cinema. We sat in our chairs at the end of the movie while everybody was leaving the theater, and cried like we had just watched the funeral of our parents or something tragic like that. We stayed up all night talking about the movie and arguing whether Ilsa should have gone with Rick or should have done what she did. We decided we did not like Ilsa as a character either way but we still wanted to be like her—sort of like her—only I would have gone with Rick, and Marija would have left both of them and gotten on the plane alone. I didn't get that about Marija at the time. Why was she going to dump them both? "To increase my chances at happiness and adventure," she had said then, and I remembered admiring her so much for the courage of her freedom. I laughed, imagining the perplexed faces of both men as their beautiful Ilsa/Marija got on that ugly warplane with neither of them. Then we opened and gulped down another can of condensed milk from Marija's pantry and fell asleep holding hands and drowning in sugar overdose. From then on all throughout high school and sometimes even when we ran into each other in the hallways of our university, once in a while Marija would stop and look at me and recite me a line from *Casablanca*. It was our inside joke. "But what about us?" she would say, looking at me teary-eyed, and I wouldn't answer with the most famous line but the one after that and would say: "We got it back last night." The "We'll always have Paris" line was embedded in silence and we swallowed it in a greedy gulp like the best spoonful of condensed milk in the world, sweet, gooey, and creamy.

She now stood in front of me in her black-and-white floral design dress with the bright yellow silky headband holding back her thick glossy black hair and uncovering her high smooth forehead. She was so beautiful that it didn't seem right. I felt shreds and shreds of my heart and memory become loose and fall off me like I was an animal shedding its skin. We were two little specks of sugary innocence, still left from the two cans of condensed milk, flying through the cold galaxies. What came soon after that was indescribable and filled with the stench of raw human flesh and deafening screams. Marija stood in front of me having walked through all that, with a glass eye and a yellow headband and an irresistible laugh. She said: "You either survive something like that or you don't, you know. And then if you don't die you might as well survive with flair." Then unexpectedly she embraced me with such fervor that I lost my breath. When I recovered it, we were both laughing, but really it felt like we were crying. Also like some new kind of laughter for people who had traveled to Apocalypse and back.

Marija sat on a bench in the fake street in the make-believe Paris and produced a perfect Gala apple from her purse and bit into it voraciously with a sparkling set of teeth. She offered me some and I bit into her apple, trying to match her hunger. It felt refreshing and soothing. I started to have the uncanny feeling that my person was finally starting to take a definite shape and contour. I was startled and surprised every second on that day, which seemed to last forever, and was irrevocably falling in love with Marija all over again. Marija said: "You know what people say, that you have to remember the past so you don't repeat the same mistakes in the future? Look... it's not true that people remember and then they don't commit atrocities anymore because they remember the past and don't want to repeat it. On the contrary, they have the model of past carnages and they keep perfecting that model... they do! What happens actually is that people become even more desensitized, they experience aesthetic pleasure, they cry, they feel good about themselves because they emote in front of a film about the Holocaust or the Rwandan genocide. That's not the kind of make-believe that we need, because it *is* real, it doesn't need to be made up, those horrors actually do happen to real people." She paused and breathed deeply. I took her hand and held it tightly. It was incredibly warm, like a bird that had just landed exhausted in my palm.

"I'm not saying it should all be forgotten," she went on with new energy and a swift move of her head, "but it shouldn't be remembered this way, like not forget it but not remember it, either. I don't know exactly which way. Tell the truth without telling a story, you know what I mean? I think they should

stop making Holocaust movies, and Rwanda genocide movies, and if anybody ever starts making a movie about the
Bosnian war again like Angelina Jolie's sappy movie about
Bosnian women in the rape camps, I'll set myself on fire right
in the middle of fucking Universal Studios. I think we should
start a new slate—a clean, fresh, sparkling new slate of life
and history—erase the memory of carnage instead of keeping it."

Marija circumvented time in her speech and never said
before what or *since* when, she just used the words *before* and
since and *after* indefinitely, letting them hang in a fluid past.
After our talk at Warner Bros. Studios she stopped using
those words altogether, shrouding us in a cooling silence
of forgetful dis-remembering. It wasn't really like forgetting
everything. You remembered it but it didn't touch you and
you said farewell to it. I also knew that when Marija said she
would set herself on fire she didn't use that as a metaphor
but would actually bathe in gasoline and strike the match. I
was praying that Hollywood wouldn't be so misguided as to
think of making another movie about the Bosnian war anytime soon.

When we were driving back to my hotel I looked at Marija
and her profile was a living statue. I couldn't get enough of
watching her, listening to her, breathing in her life energy.
The shape and sound of her letters that I had breathlessly
read in the Sarajevo hotel till dawn and then the last install-
ment only a month earlier started growing around me like

living creatures that explained Marija to me through a fantastical pantomime. Now it all came alive as I was watching her
shift gears, look in the rearview mirror, look at me and smile
her movie-star smile, listen to her languorous voice, like no
other voice I knew. "Marija, what kind of things were you
sending to Hassan?" I asked suddenly. "What human rights
and postwar materials was he talking about?" She didn't
turn around to look at me, but stared straight ahead at the
winding road: "Information about the war criminals, those
who are still running free. And accounts of women from the
camps. So the world knows. That's all. I gathered hundreds
of stories from women who had been in the camps when I
was in the rehabilitation center in Sarajevo. At first I didn't
know what to do with them, but then I thought they had to
have told them to me for some reason. I wrote them down
almost despite my will, mechanically, and when I got out I
thought that at some point when I felt a tiny bit more normal
I was going to reveal them to the world. I think they actually
helped me recover. Most of them were more horrific than my
own. I'm telling you, I was among the lucky ones. That's all."

Her face was smooth, not a line, not a single frown or
wrinkle, almost like the smoothness of death, only she was
so alive. "That's all," I repeated, and laughed. She had been
doing both humanitarian and investigative work, even though
she hated both those words. Marija lived and acted outside
the boundaries of common words. She had clues and hints
of the whereabouts of Radovan Karadzic, one of the three

masterminds of the genocidal war, who had also happened to consider himself a poet while killing Bosnians. "Whatever was lost in world poetry was gained in the art of genocide," joked Marija unflinchingly. I shuddered. Her two goals were justice and truth; that was all. She had some clues as to where Karadzic might have been hiding. A woman she knew had recognized him in a village near Belgrade. "Only after that I received death threats while in Sarajevo. So I'm going to stop my search for Karadzic and only worry about my son from now on. He could be in real danger. As for the rat Karadzic, he will eventually get caught and be brought to justice, I know it. For now we have to get my son and bring him back here as soon as possible, you see that, my dear Lara, don't you?"

The dark universe that had opened to me as I went down the steps into the passages of Sarajevo with Natalia only half a year before was now becoming darker, as if a sun eclipse was threatening to darken the entire planet. I had anticipated this new and final adventure—my American years with Marija, a new world, a new me, a new life of fullness—as the other side of grief and death. But right now it still all tasted of raw blood and I wasn't ready to face the uncharted terror. I was still so new to Marija's world and there was so much that didn't make sense. When I asked her about the trip to Sarajevo, the notes she left for me with the woman in that broken-down neighborhood, she said she had no idea I was going to go to Sarajevo, she had just left the notes of the women's stories in a hurry for Ferida to pick up and send to the Helsinki human rights committee and by mistake included notes from her diary, too. "The woman must have gotten confused and thought you were Ferida, since you were the first person to come by," she said. "Who is this woman, Marija?" I asked, feeling sick from so much confusion and secrecy. "Just some woman," she said and then was quiet for a while, and I could tell she was hiding something. The letters that she sent Hassan, she said, had indeed been meant for me. She had wanted to make sure I got those notes. She wanted to prepare me about the child, she explained. "And plus, I don't know, I somehow wanted to delay our meeting, I was buying time until I was fully formed, you know, ready to face you and to face myself as reflected in your eyes, Lara!" She abruptly pulled onto a side street lined with elegant white houses and sycamores. She looked straight at me as if truly trying to reflect herself in my eyes. I only hoped the image reflected back to her was as beautiful and majestic as I saw her in that moment.

"Look, I lost my parents, both sets of grandparents, I lost all my homes, my pathetic little country and my beloved native city, I lost the wholeness of my body, part of my mind and my soul, I lost an eye and am trying to regain my lost son. Why the hell do you want to know all of this stuff, all these little details? What does it matter?" I felt like dying with shame and sadness for having disappointed Marija. I remembered what she had said earlier how everybody's suffering was their own and nobody traded theirs for anyone else's. I remembered my own agonizing days torn between grinding and banal divorce proceedings, my destructive infatuation with Karim, the fear of losing Natalia, the struggle to keep my job and get tenured, and throughout it all the unbearable sadness at the thought I had lost Marija forever. I said looking straight at her with renewed courage: "Because all of the big stuff you just mentioned is just too big for me right now to comprehend, maybe with time...it's the little things, the little details that help me understand you and what happened to you and who you are now. For instance, I imagine you and your parents and Farah and Kemal all crammed in your blue Fiat, with whatever you could gather from the two houses piled up in the car, on your way to Semizovac driving at a hundred thirty kilometers an hour through intersections and sniper bullets..."

"And driving to our death," she concluded with a bitter smile. Her words fell between us with a heavy thud. Then she let go of the bitter smile and the dark thought. She shifted into the light and her face shone. "I never stopped writing to you, throughout everything. Even in the rehabilitation center when I was barely more functional than an amoeba I still wrote to you, for you, about you: poems, thoughts, fleeting sentences that came to my mind, songs, whatever...you were my thread back to life, you know that?" We embraced in the car for a long time and our tears blended as our heated faces touched in the bluish glow of the dusk on the sycamore-lined street.

She came to my hotel room and we sat for a while in silence on my bed holding hands and looking at the white walls. The red azaleas on the balcony were reflected in the mirror and a feeling of rosiness entered the room with that reflection. Then Marija said: "How is she?" And I knew she meant Natalia, I was catching on to Marija's puzzle system of dialogue. "She is wonderful beyond words! A star! And also fragile and strong. And funny, too. She went through so much grief with the divorce proceedings, she even had to testify in court. She was a kleptomaniac for a while, stealing from drugstores. But she is all right now. She is dying to meet you, asks about you almost every day. She came with me everywhere on my trip to Belgrade and Sarajevo." I started crying again, I had to make up for all the uncried tears up to that point in my life and also for what was going to come, which I knew was going to be beyond tears, right there in the last circle of hell where tears hang frozen on your cheeks like icicles. For the moment I needed Marija more than she needed me and I felt strangely soothed and puzzled by that.

Then Marija did something perplexing again: She got up and circled the room a few times humming an old Serbian tune, the tune of a Serbian pop star in the eighties, a song about loving someone in the spring and feeling reborn. She went to her white purse, carefully searched through it, and produced a photograph. "Here, look, that's him!" This time I knew who she meant: the boy, her son, born in 1996. The photo was of poor quality, with pale colors, and showed a tiny boy with a round head and very short haircut in the arms of an older woman with a scarf wrapped around her head and her face turned away from the camera, in a garden next to a well. I couldn't make out the features of the boy other than that he did not have three heads and displayed no evident signs of monstrosity as I was imagining, and that he was small and round. I was intrigued by the well in the garden and wondered what part of Serbia, Bosnia, Croatia that could have been. Something reminded me of Baba and Dede's village near Dubrovnik. "Isn't he beautiful?" Marija said with a sigh, and there was a completely new Marija emerging in that sigh and that statement, elastic and mellow and matching the silky headband on her head. I couldn't bring myself to say anything, but I didn't think anything in that picture was beautiful. "I know what you are thinking, Lara. But the thing is, this creature is now on this earth and I am his mother and he is there and I am here." I on the other hand thought the "creature" that came out of a monstrous act could only be a monstrous creature just by the nature of its conception and any contact with and sight of it would only rekindle, refresh, restart the oozing of the wounds, the gashes, the broken optic nerve, oh the unbearable crushed optic nerve. I just couldn't tolerate that.

"I had no idea I was pregnant until almost the birth," she said. "That's because I had separated myself from my body. There was me—this abstract me—and there was my body—a blob of pulsing flesh. There was this woman...this woman who was caring for me and told me it was time to give birth... she knew it and I didn't. I had been vegetating for months in her bed, in her room with my belly growing into this big balloon of life. I didn't feel a thing throughout the birth, as if I had been under anesthetic, and it just slithered out, one second I was crouching and squatting in this woman's room, the next second something with a head and four limbs slithered out of me. I didn't want to look at it. I just asked her what it was. I told her to keep it, I didn't want it then but told her I would come back to get it one day and she'd be recompensed. I said I would go back for it. Just like that as you would leave and come back for a coat you forgot. Now the time has come that I want him back."

At that point Marija took off her yellow headband and suddenly with her black hair all over her face and the imperceptible crookedness of her left glass eye she looked terrifying. I was afraid of her. For a moment I wanted to run out of the room, all the way to Washington, DC, and to my Natalia. If only it could all have been a bad dream and Mark and Natalia and I were still happily together, and Karim had never existed. That same moment I thought: *How did I get myself into this? Wake up and run, Lara, run!*

"We have to go to Bosnia and get him, Lara, that's all, you have to help me and you have to come with me. I need you to come with me," Marija said very gently, almost like a lullaby. I sat on the bed transfixed, wanting to move and run away and not being able to take one step. What was Marija talking about? I wasn't going to go with her in search of the child that resulted from her tragedy. "Bring Natalia with you," she said.

"It will be good for her to see her mother's childhood places, to see something different from the Washington sidewalks." How did Marija know what was good for Natalia? I thought in a wave of rage, she had no idea about Natalia and the kind of person she was and what she needed and what she didn't. I had already brought Natalia to my childhood places once and had no desire to do that again anytime soon. I should have listened to my sister, she always knew, I should have listened to her premonition that this was dark, unbearable stuff, and that neither of us could deal with it. It was undealable.

Marija sat down in the armchair across from the bed and next to the window, and the last rays of the setting sun lingered on her. The sadness that spread on her was luminous. It was as if the moon had melted onto her face and her sadness were a separate creature. Here was Marija and here was Marija's sadness raining all over us and drowning us. It overwhelmed me, but I couldn't resist it. I knew I wasn't going to run away and I was going to go with Marija to Bosnia and to the end of the world and to the empty space in the sky that was left after the meltdown of the moon onto her face.

We slept in my hotel bed holding each other like two fugitives on the run. Marija's sleep was so deep and so dark that at some point during the night I thought she died. I lay unmoving until my body went numb for fear of waking her. In the short periods when I slept I had dreams that made Frida Kahlo's paintings of eviscerated hearts and bloody fetuses look like innocent still lives: pears and grapes and feathers on a country table. Marija's eyes kept opening up as if dark endless holes and armies of horrid creatures were coming out of them. Marija's limbs were falling off her like a doll's, and Natalia was holding one of her limbs and crying over it; the little boy with the round head in the picture was shrinking and becoming a spider. The well in the picture was bubbling with rotting bodies, the bodies of Bosnians killed in the genocide, and a yellow ribbon was tied to the well saying not to drink that water. I desperately wanted to hold the spider in the dream and protect it. Then I woke up with a jump and had to rush to the bathroom to vomit. When I came back Marija was sleeping in the same position I had left her, unmoved, almost without breathing. I fell back asleep next to her terrifyingly silent body.

At some point toward morning Marija made coffee and started talking about postmodern theory. I couldn't tell precisely whether I was hallucinating or dreaming or whether Marija's words were real and happening in real time in my hotel room. I thought I had said something like: "Are you kidding me, Marija, postmodern theory at four in the morning? Just shut up please and let me sleep!" She said postmodern theory claimed that everything was text, even us, humans were texts and what was the real, then? There was no real, only a concept of the real that was different for everybody. Everybody's real was different. But then, she said, if you had your optic nerve crushed under the back of a rifle, then you were not text anymore. Then you were a handful of screaming flesh and that was the only thing that was real. Postmodern theory was bullshit, she concluded.

When the bright irreverent LA sun shone its late-morning rays onto my face and I opened my eyes I had no idea where I was. Then it all rushed in: the previous day with Marija so jammed with surprises that it seemed like an accident in the cosmic calendar. I got up and looked for her but she was nowhere to be found. The room was picked up and seemed unused except for the bed I had slept in. The bed *we* had slept in. I felt heavy from the horrid dreams, exhausted from the nocturnal conversation about postmodern theory, with my head screwed on all wrong. Then it hit me: the pang of pain from Marija's absence. I didn't want her to be gone even though her presence made me experience psychic shocks that were the human equivalent of earthquakes of the degree of ten on the Richter scale. I felt a gaping hole so deep and so excruciating that I bent over and held myself in a folded position at the edge of the bed. Marija rushed in through the door with a tray filled with pastries and fresh fruit, in her black-and-white dress, the shiny yellow ribbon holding her freshly combed hair.

"Have you found a new religion? Who are you praying to, Lara dear?" she said laughingly. "Here, have some breakfast, you had a rough night, must have had bad dreams, huh?"

I wanted to kiss Marija's face and hair and scream with joy at the sight and the sound of her. Then she asked me: "So what do you want to do today, my dear?"

"Here is what we are going to do," I said. "We will have this delicious breakfast together, then you will go home, wherever that is, and pack a few things, and then you will take me to the airport. And then you and I will get on the first plane to Washington, DC. And when we are there, you will meet Natalia and we will make plans to go to Bosnia and get the boy. What do you say?"

The Wild West

MAY 2004

"No," said Marija later that day as she was driving me to her LA apartment. "On second thought, let's not go to DC right away. First we take a trip out west. We need it. Both of us. We need a winding-down time, we need some time to cross over and to discover America. Neither you nor I has any idea what this country is all about, Lara. Now that you are with me and I know you will help me out, we can take our time for a while longer, don't you think so, Lara dear? We'll go to Washington next week." "What about Natalia? She's expecting me home this week." Marija thought for a few seconds: "We'll make it up to her, she'll understand." How did Marija know that Natalia would understand? What did she know about Natalia? Nothing at all. Again, for another second I wanted to run away and forget that Marija was back, forget that Marija existed. But I might as well have forgotten that I existed. Maybe soon I was going to be whole and I was going to reach the stream of clean water and be renewed. A new Lara without cracks and with a smooth face and soul would emerge from the clean water.

I couldn't say no to anything that Marija asked for. Once on that ride, I couldn't stop. And when she said "Lara dear" with her elongated vowels the way she always used to, I had even less willpower to deny her anything she asked for. It wasn't that she imposed her will on me. It was the way it had always been since the day she stood in the door of our classroom in second grade: I wanted to do everything she wanted because I knew it would be a magical ride, whether we ran across Sarajevo in the summer or went to Persia on the miniature Turkish golden velvet slippers. I provided the politics of it, she provided the magic, she joked and I laughed. I called Natalia and told her I was going to take another week or more to be home, that I would come home with Marija and she was going to love her. "Really, wow! How cool," she said joyously, but then asked: "Is she all right, Mama, you know, you said she had been hurt…" "Yes, Natalia, she is fine, great actually. She is coming home with me and then we'll all go on a trip together. We'll go back to Sarajevo, isn't that exciting?" Natalia said not to worry, that she was fine, she and Dad were doing things together. "How awesome, we're going back to Sarajevo, Mama," Natalia said. I wondered by what miracle Natalia came so complete out of cracked and incomplete me, Lara Kulicz, by what miracle had she been left unscathed and was emerging stronger than any of us.

"You put all your love into her, Lara, she'll always have that, she is full to the brim, don't you know it?" Marija said with her usual wisdom about life. "And you think a trip out west is going to give us the final understanding of the mystery of America?" We were flying again in her red Corvette. "America is not a mystery, it's a project of displaced people with a short-term memory that is still in the works. America destroys and creates itself simultaneously in an ongoing process. And yes, I think going out west, seeing the frontier, might be of some help to us. We are frontier girls ourselves, aren't we? If anything it's fucking stunning, you'll love it, I promise."

In this Balkan version of *Thelma and Louise*, Marija and I drove for hours and then for days across high plains, through canyons and alongside turbulent waterfalls, across orange deserts, through brooding forests of spruce and shimmering light-green aspen, on hairpin roads along several-thousand-foot drops that made your head swirl like you were drunk on absinthe. We were running away from our pasts but also thanks to the distance we could better understand them. We relived our childhood, our teenage and college years, and stopped at the brink of the day when we parted in Belgrade right when the war had started. We reached that point several times from different perspectives and every time we got stuck there. We rewound everything and played it backward and forward and invented new scenarios. What if I had stayed with Marija, gone with her to Sarajevo, forgotten about

Mark? "You would have never had Natalia!" Run, run, Lara, run from the past, you're in the Wild West now, no need to tiptoe around what-ifs! "Yes, but I would have had another Natalia, I wouldn't have known about this Natalia and it would have been just fine. And maybe you and yours would have been safe," and my voice would drop to almost inaudible on the last words as if stepping on minefields. "Because you were the holy mother of Christ to protect us all from the rage of the Republika Srpska? You might have been dead, too. And then what?" We would burst out laughing at points of memory where most people would have lain on the ground and howled in misery. "We are crossing over," Marija would say as if we were going to witness a cosmic event. "We're reaching the frontier," she would say with an alluring smile. The frontier was anything from a run-down gas station with an orange awning in the literal middle of nowhere of endless expanses of rocky land and big vaulted sky to lines in the past that neither of us was ready or willing to cross but were tiptoeing gently around in a carnivalesque ballet of swift forward steps, pirouettes, and swift steps backward.

"Everything gets muddled up in the war, yet you get to the ultimate truths about people like in no other situation. There is a fierce clarity about the war, you get to see humanity all bare, like an X-ray, just the skeleton, the bare bones of humanity, who people really are," Marija said at some point as we were driving past pueblo settlements and

Indian reservations, layers of frontiers and past wars for ter-
ritory. "Maybe it's all about land," she went on. "Marija, it's
about power," I ventured on the lines of my incorrigible lifelong political training. "You're such a politician. Of course
it's about power—land is power." I wasn't going to give up
so easily. Something in the fiercely violet sunset descending
upon the layers of mountains gave me the stubbornness to
stand up to Marija's theory, as if I had any stake in winning
this argument about the real cause of wars. "No, it's never as
concrete as that. It's the abstraction of power, the thrill, and
the rush that comes with the subjugation of one human being
by another. Land is a pretext. Even oil is a pretext. There
is enough land for everybody on this planet—look at this," I
said, proud of my theory, extending out my arm to the high
plains and the indomitable mountains in the distance, all
empty, all uninhabited, all ready for the taking.

Marija was quiet for a while, a silence akin to death. Then
she stopped the car at another gas station, put her head on the
steering wheel, and repeated five times the word *subjugation*.
A torrent of sobs erupted from her like the flood of doomsday.
The sobs were a creature in themselves, taking full possession of Marija and tearing every bit of her reconstructed self
apart. I was afraid that parts of her were going to fall off like
in my nightmare, as if she were splintered by a bomb from
within: limbs, organs, body parts shattered across the rural
gas station as in the most atrocious of horror movies and in

the midst of it all the wicked and immortal glow of her glass eye staring in grotesque immobility at everything. Some men in cowboy boots stared at us as they were filling up the gas tanks of their enormous trucks. A woman truck driver got out of her truck and moved slowly toward our car. Marija's sobs were unstoppable. The woman truck driver was tiny and red-haired and reminded me of Sally Bryant.

"Sweetheart, do you need some help?" Her low voice trailed sweetly in the cool air of that spring somewhere in the Wild West, where two refugee women from the Balkans were lost and trying to make sense of lands, frontiers, memories, their own lives, and the desert ahead of them. Marija stopped her sobs instantaneously. She looked up at the woman and smiled. There was the Marija of my childhood again sitting next to me on the school bench and playing with toy Turkish slippers. I couldn't keep up with Marija, and again I thought maybe I wanted out. The past was intolerable and we would never be able to cross over that frontier. I wasn't made for that insanity, I hadn't started the Bosnian war and it wasn't my fault that Marija went through what she had been through. I missed Natalia, I missed sanity and normality. I missed my corner of the stupid Washington duplex, safety and peace. The expanses of red rocks and the huge edgy rocks and drops terrified me like prehistoric monsters. "Thank you, we would like some help, yes, if you don't mind," said Marija in her sweetest voice.

The red-haired woman truck driver, whose name was Pam, told us to follow her gigantic truck to her little adobe house in the desert. I drove Marija's Corvette while she was fixing her tear-smeared face and combing her hair. Pam fed us cactus stew while her Chaco Indian husband worked on an ancient Chevrolet convertible with wings like the cars in the seventies. Everything seemed stuck in previous decades except for the cell phones and the computer. Her twin boys played on the dirt floor with miniature trucks while their mother fed to them bits of dried beef and cactus from the stew. They were four years old yet tiny as toddlers. The entire family was small, the house was small. It felt cozy and safe to be there.

We found out we were in a pueblo and the lunar landscape surrounding us was made of mesas and ridges, canyons and dune fields. The sagebrush and the juniper bushes spread luscious and delicate perfumes in the dry quivering air. "I too have a son. He is eight years old," Marija said, leaving me with my mouth wide open, cactus stew dripping on my chin. "He is very tiny, too, he is smaller than he should be for his age." The Chaco man spoke softly with an unexpectedly thin voice. His name was Hope and also Crazy Bull because he had left his reservation in New Mexico years ago and went around the country talking about the poverty and desperation on the reservations, trying to raise money and consciousness of the plight of his people. He told Marija that

249

small boys are good, they will never be too arrogant, but kind and gentle. Marija grinned with pleasure. "Yes, I know, that's exactly how my son is: blond and small and very gentle." I wanted to say that she had hardly even met her son, that she had no idea whether he was sweet and gentle as a lamb or violent as a crazy bull. But the certainty in Marija's voice and expression was so indomitable that the words died on my lips and for the first time, Marija's fantasy of her own sweet, tender blond boy entered my spirit as well. For some inexplicable reason the image of that boy fit perfectly with the dune fields and the juniper-delicate fragrances and the cactus meal in Pam's small adobe house.

Marija had dropped her past somewhere in a red desert in the Wild West yet she also carried it. She was inventing herself and her past as she went along, but the little boy in the house with the well was at the center of everything, an unmoved point in the darkness like a lighthouse for lost ships. "That's good," said the truck driver woman, "boys are good. They are fun to have." She gave them each a piece of dried beef in their tiny mouths, which opened up for the food like hungry birds. "Where does your son live? Does he stay with you?" Pam asked. "He is far away in Bosnia, in Sarajevo, at the end of the world, really," Marija answered casually, like she had known and raised this mystery son for her entire life and as if Sarajevo were just next door. "You've been through something, haven't you, honey?" said Pam with no preparation. "I can tell. I've been through stuff, too," she added.

COUNTRY OF RED AZALEAS

"People say it gets better with time, but it doesn't really. You just learn to live with it, whatever it is, with the stuff that hurt you. With your wounds and scars I mean." People were like the landscapes in that part of the world, in constant metamorphosis, becoming something else before your eyes, from rounded orange desert rocks to luscious aspen forests, to edgy gray rocks hanging above your head, to high plains and dark lakes to desert again. The desert and the orange rocks and the mesas and the sagebrush were our favorites. This was *our* America. Pam gave us her own and her husband's bed to sleep in that night and she and Hope and the children all slept on different sofas in the tiny main room. Even though everything was tiny, there was room for everybody. The lands out there were endless, uninhabited, and wild, but the adobe houses were small and self-contained, they held us in, they made us feel safe and whole. During the night, the two boys crawled into bed with us and cuddled against us, between Marija and me. Their bodies were fresh and light, velvety and soft, they whispered words in a language that could have been Spanish, but wasn't really, maybe Navajo. Marija and I each fell asleep holding one of the twins. It felt perfect for a night.

"This is a new generation of boys who will make the world a better place: these twins, my son, the new boys of this century." Marija had a habit of talking in the middle of the night. She wasn't sleep talking, she was awake and would start up a conversation in the dead of the night. I learned not to answer, and after a while she would go back to sleep. Marija's sleep was forever compromised so she took me with her on long conversational rides that ranged from theories of war and warfare to French movies to nouvelle cuisine to fashion to child psychology or modern architecture. She made up for lost worlds at night and the rides were exhausting. But during our road trip through the Wild West, no matter how hard and troubled our night rides through past and future universes might have been, I was always happy to find her still next to me in the morning.

"My son is blond," Marija repeated in the morning at the breakfast table with the Chaco Mexican American family. "That's nice, blond is always beautiful," said Pam. She was leaving that day for another week of driving transports across the country. She held her boys each on one knee through breakfast and fed them again like a mother bird would feed her chicks. "You need to go see your son, wherever he is," Pam said. "I hope my boys didn't bother you during the night. They're used to always sleeping next to someone, usually it's their father and me, but if someone else visits, they have no problem climbing in bed with them. They are funny that way." The boys said, "The ladies smell nice," and I was surprised to hear perfect little English words come out of the boys' mouths almost in unison. Marija laughed and said she enjoyed their presence in bed, it was comforting, and it made her think of her son. Marija spoke of her son with the assurance and knowledge of a consummate mother. If she had deserted him once because she hadn't even been aware she had given birth to a live creature eight years ago when it happened in some woman's house near Sarajevo, she was now giving birth to this blond son again and again in Pam and Hope's house. He was as real and as alive as the dark-skinned twins sitting on their mother's lap across the table. Upon departure Pam gave us a quilt in shades of orange and light green; it had the colors of the landscape and was soft and feathery and smelled sweet like some kind of hay or lavender. We gave her money and chocolate and she took it with a smile. Her husband came out from under the Chevy he was fixing and wished us a good trip. We left the small family standing in the road against their tiny adobe house with cacti and orange earth and red flowers around it. We wanted to take them with us, we wanted to stay with them forever, for some reason it broke our hearts to leave the pueblo family with the twins in the adobe house. We couldn't stand any more departures, separations, good-byes, but we had to go on.

"People killed each other over land and gold and supremacy in these parts not too long ago," Marija said as I was driving her Corvette this time on the way to Utah. "I can still smell the blood, it's as if the orange desert rocks are this color because of all the blood impregnated in it. I want to find a piece of earth where no blood has ever been shed, a clean and virgin piece of land. Then I want to buy it." She was smiling and radiant like the first hours after our LA encounter.

We went on the lookout for a virgin place where no blood

was shed. We acquired no better understanding of America but we found a zone of the earth where no memory of ours could implant itself and grow roots and bring our past into the present like an inevitable cataclysm. We needed to understand history and the need for blood now more than ever. Was it for power or for land that people killed and destroyed each other? Was land power? Or was power just a rush for an abstract sense of subjugation?

"You and I don't know anything about America, Lara. All we know about America is from the movies. It's all stereotypes and clichés, and a few memorable lines uttered by Gary Cooper, Humphrey Bogart, or John Wayne." Marija laughed. I was getting used to her unpredictable passages from the darkest depths to frivolous talk about Hollywood actors or movie scenes. At some point in the trip I wanted to know what had really happened during those days in July but could not ask Marija directly. By now, I had read her notes so many times that I knew parts of them by heart, but still only really understood the aftermath, the recovery period. I wanted to go with her as deep as she would take me and feel at least part of her pain. Then maybe she would feel a bit lighter. And she wanted to know about Karim and all the rest. We both knew that the telling of our darkest places was now as necessary as the road taking us through the lunar landscapes we traversed. The stories were completely out of sync with one another, but they were each our own stories.

"It was my idea to leave Sarajevo," Marija said, almost

screaming through the hot wind of our ride. She kept reminding herself of that like a punishment. "I thought we would be
safer and we went right into the devil's mouth and the devil
chewed and swallowed us all and spat our bones back in the
surrounding hills. The UN said it was a 'safe zone' and stupid me, I trusted the UN. There was actually a resolution
with a number attached to it that declared it an area of safety,
meaning where people could take refuge and be secure from
harm. The best lesson I learned was that whenever the UN
declares something safe, you should run in the opposite
direction. I was to blame for the massacre of my family and
it's up to me to decide whether I can live with that or not."
Her voice trailed in the wind, it sliced the quivering dry heat
like a sharp blade, it circled our heads like a famished vul-
ture, it rested on my heart.

"You and I can never get away from the Balkans, you
know that, right, Lara dear?"

"I thought we just did, Marija dear. This is not the fucking
Balkans and you know it," I went on with conviction. "For all
the bloody episodes in these parts, for all the feuds, the massacres, in the end they got it right. Or they got it better than
our people. Do you see anybody running for refuge in the
other direction, from here to there? Do you know anybody
from New Mexico or Utah immigrating to Bosnia or Serbia?"

"It's just that they have more land, that's all, look at all
this! There's enough for everybody. In the fucking Balkans
everybody's crowded on top of one another until you want

to kill your neighbor and their mother. And anyway it's the fucking Wild West. Why do you think they call it Wild? These are lands acquired and built through the power of the guns. First taken from the Indians, then from the Mexicans, it's what Westerns are made of. And none of that will ever change the fact that I am responsible for the death of my family." She slammed on the brakes at a dusty tiny gas station. I restrained from saying anything. What could I have said, a meager: *No, Marija, you didn't kill your family, the Serbs of Republika Srpska killed your family and hurt you and the UN tricked everybody because they were incompetent and evil and you are no more responsible for what happened to them than Pam's twins or Sally Bryant are responsible for the Bosnian war?* She had probably heard all that from Sally Bryant, from Ferida, from women in the rehabilitation center and countless other people.

"It dragged out for a while," she said, nonchalantly filling up the gas tank. The sky was always impenetrably blue and immense and the dry air scratched your lungs. Marija, wearing a yellow dress, looked majestic framed by the blue sky and the red awning of the gas station. I had no idea that if you survived the worst you could emerge as a thing of beauty. Indomitable and frightening, but beautiful nevertheless. "I said let's leave Sarajevo, and let's go to the country, it's safe there, that's what I said. And we all went to the house in the country where we thought it was safe. Just like we think it's safe out here. And before we knew it they were butchering us."

I thought I heard hyenas in the distance, saw vultures circling above, felt scorpions swarming at my feet. Nothing was safe. The gas station with the red awning was shifting in the sun and the immobility of the place was hypnotic. Life hung on so little. A scorpion, a man with a gun, a crater opening up, at any moment we walked a thin line across the abyss. It was all just a matter of where you found yourself at a particular moment in time.

"I killed a man in the ambush," she said with a weird grin looking at me across her red Corvette. "And it's the best thing I have ever done. Only that it cost me everything." The man in the red pickup truck next to the red awning of the gas station was smoking a cigarette and looking at us. We looked foreign. We were Balkan, we came from recent wars and fresh massacres. Just like everybody who came from a place with a history of massacre, only the layout of our land was different. And we had an accent.

Marija said she had also saved a young girl's life in what she called the ambush. She killed the man that had attacked the young girl, the daughter of their neighbor. She killed the man with a gun that she found on the ground. And the girl survived, she ran and disappeared. The next soldier got Marija. Other soldiers, too, were there for the revenge. The soldier beside the one that Marija had killed grabbed her and then all the rest. Her parents and grandparents were all lying on the ground at that point. Both her maternal and paternal grandparents. All six closest people of her family, an entire family erased from the face of the earth in a matter of minutes under a ferociously blue sky, like the wide vault above our heads in this desert land with a gas station with its red awning and its red gas pumps. A hundred years had passed between the killing and the soldier grabbing Marija to avenge the death of his buddy. An entire geological era passed when the earth dried up, then flooded, then froze, then burned, then the cacti bloomed again shamelessly out of the desert sand.

She was in the woman's house when she woke up with the crushed optic nerve. The woman had found her in the evening still breathing on the ground next to her massacred family as she crept out of her house a bit farther down the road. She practically dragged Marija to her house and she was still alive when she got there though bleeding profusely from her eye. The woman took care of her and her wounds day and night. Until the birth, the woman from Semizovac kept moving her from town to town, from house to house, like she was in an unclear chase by someone. She was Bosnian Muslim posing as Serbian. The woman who had saved Marija's life was acting Serbian while running away from the Serbs and she was dragging Marija after her. She sang Serbian songs throughout all the moves and the rides. The woman went from place to place, driving her ancient Yugo car that occasionally dropped off parts along the way, with Marija bleeding all over the backseat. Finally the woman found a recently lived-in house on the non-Muslim edge of a town. They stayed there for a while and seven months later it was where Marija gave birth, while the woman cleaned her up and sang Serbian songs at the top of her lungs to make sure the remaining neighbors or any Srpska soldiers passing by thought they were Serbs.

"Land and women have always been for the taking," she said looking up at the sky as if defying it. She lit up a cigarette next to the gas pump. In the quivering heat of the desert we could have all blown up at the mere spark of a cigarette. Life hung on a tiny gesture, on a silk thread, on a snap of one's fingers. At Marija's side, I, too, was part of generations of avengers, war starters, desert fighters, and killers. It felt cool like fresh springwater. "I am probably the only civilian woman in Bosnia who killed a Serbian soldier. I deserve a fucking medal!" Marija's voice and laugh were raw and unforgiving. I felt incomprehensible joy at Marija's news that she had killed a soldier. Women of the Wild West had killed attackers and killers before us in the heat of an ambush, not thinking twice, not praying or hesitating. Out here in the Wild West, the cacti were sharp as blades, their flowers luscious as bleeding hearts.

"How did it feel to kill a man, Marija?" I noticed that the

man filling up his truck looked at us. The gun rack was filled. He heard my question to Marija. "It felt right, it felt damn good to kill the bastard." The man stared at us again and muttered something. It looked like he was going to take out his gun and shoot at us. This new Balkan *Thelma and Louise* movie might end right here, with the two girls shot at a gas station near a canyon, their brains unromantically splattered all over red gas pumps. But instead the man let out a sinister laugh. We climbed back into the convertible without even opening the doors and screeched out of the gas station in a cloud of dust.

When I put Marija's wallet back in her bag as she asked me to, I thought I felt a gun. I did! And I pulled it out and looked at it wide-eyed: a small handgun, almost pretty, almost feminine. "That's right, Lara dear, it's a gun, I always carry a gun with me now." I gently put the gun back into Marija's bag. I had nothing to say. The ride was smooth again and now we were crossing back into Colorado and passing by the shimmering aspen forests. We greeted the light greens with joy, we had bled enough, we had had enough of the oranges and the reds of the arid desert.

Marija found a piece of land in the Wild West and bought it. We now had our own sliver of American land. We felt like bona fide Americans. On our way through the western landscapes we'd passed by a place in the Rockies that had a FOR SALE sign. It was a mixture of desert and pasture, forest and plain, rock and meadow, it had everything. And a lake farther up that glistened in the sun. A forest of aspen trees with glimmering tiny emerald leaves framed it. There was a tiny log cabin sitting on that piece of land like an old sage. It was as easy as buying a pair of cowboy boots at the general store. Marija paid part in cash and part with a check. She carried a big chunk of cash in her large white bag right next to the handgun, along with a mini *Webster's Dictionary* and the picture of the blond son standing by the well. "You couldn't do this in the Balkans. Only in America! We just got a bit closer to the meaning of America, didn't we? We own a tiny portion of it now. It's all in the ownership, right? Possession is fifty percent of the law, isn't that what they say in America?" Her laugh resonated across the variegated landscape like a magic song.

We stayed for three nights and three days in the log cabin. We slept on the floor in sleeping bags and Marija cried the whole time. The rooms smelled of pine and we could see a piece of a sharp peak and ponderosa pine forest from the cabin window. "We never had a chance to say good-bye," she said lying on her back, staring out the small window at the shard of raw blue outside. "You know, Mama and Papa, Kemal and Farah. The night before, Papa played the flute, he went through some of his classical repertoire from Haydn to Mozart to Strauss. He even played Ravel, and I had never heard Ravel on the flute. It sounded unearthly. We felt almost safe. Kemal smoked his last pipe. Farah drank her last coffee. Mama sewed her last embroidery stitches. Papa played

his last tune. We went to bed. We heard voices at night but
we thought it was the UN peacekeeping soldiers. We went
back to sleep, all in one room. I had a dream about children playing in a garden outside of Sarajevo. The dream
was beautiful but in it something felt rotten and hideous.
There were only children in this area of Sarajevo, no adults
anywhere in sight, and something terrifying was lurking in
the background, a slimy headless monster. But when I woke
up I refused to pay attention to the bad parts of the dream and
just remembered the beautiful part about the children playing in a blissful garden. It reminded me of us three playing
around Kemal and Farah's house in the summer. I thought it
was a sign that peace would come soon. In the morning we
were all restless. I said, 'Let's stay for another few days, we'll
be okay, after all they declared this to be a safe zone.' It was
the first time I didn't follow my intuitions and premonitions
and decided to listen to the party line, the news, the dirty war
communications. I should have known better. In the morning, they broke down the door and barged in. We saw the
Serbian uniforms, and Mama said she hoped it would be fast.
They dragged us all outside. Farah and Kemal were caught
by surprise but Mama and Papa knew what was happening.
I had the time to hold Mama's hand one brief second, right
before they tore us apart from each other. For some crazy reason I was wearing your turquoise necklace. For all I know
it saved my life. The soldier that I killed was our next-door
neighbor in Semizovac. You might have even seen him that

summer when you and I went there for one weekend when we were in college, remember? The girl he attacked was our other next-door neighbor. So much for love your neighbor as thyself."

She had said everything almost in a whisper yet incredibly clear in crisp words like crystal beads bouncing off the walls in the log cabin in the mellow light that came through the tiny window. I thought she had fallen asleep because she lay without moving for what seemed like a long time. Then Marija cried, for three days and three nights. This time she didn't cry with torrents and sobs like she had before. Her cries were now mellow and rhythmic like a song to sadness. A serenade to the world's most inconsolable sadness. She cried through her sleep and through the gulps of water I made her drink, through every moment of those three days she cried to the point where I thought she would die from crying. At some moments her cries were intolerable and I thought it might be better for Marija to die. I thought it would be easier for both of us and that she could never survive and bear all that grief for the years to come. But on the third day she stopped as abruptly as she had started. By then I was so used to the sound of her song to sadness that I almost missed it. I had never known such turmoil of mind, soul, and body as during those three days and nights. Yet when Marija stopped it was like she had woken up from the deepest sleep on earth. She was steady on her feet, determined in her actions, and clear in her speech. And she could always smile. We went for a walk on one of the trails near our cabin that morning. We climbed next to sparkly gurgling streams and majestic ponderosa pines through slivers of light and reckless blue. "We have never been here before, I am sure of it. All this is new, a new day," whispered Marija, and her face shone with beauty and love. I took her hand and we embraced in the shifting light, enveloped in the ponderosa pine scent. Marija's eyelashes fluttered against my cheeks like silk butterflies, everything melted in the spruce and ponderosa greens. Her lips were soft and honey-sweet as I remembered from our childhood. We had never been there, maybe there had never been any bloodshed where we stood and embraced, maybe we started a new America.

We decided it was time to go back to my other home in America. On our drive home, it was my turn to talk. Marija wanted to hear everything. I would tell her about Karim, Mark, and the trial. I didn't really feel like sinking into all the mire of my past and reliving the guilt, the breakage, the fear of losing Natalia, and the shamefulness of Karim's betrayal. But to her it was calming to hear stories of love and betrayal, divorce and legal proceedings, couples' misunderstandings and family feuds. It was like watching episodes of *Dallas* when we were young: the heartaches and family upheavals of the rich and famous from the perspective of our Communist Yugoslavia. My sagas meant to her a normal life in times of peace. Only that paradoxically enough, she considered my divorce, love affair, and custody trials with the same weight and grief as her own past. It didn't make sense to me, but to Marija it meant that everybody lived with their own burden depending on their circumstances and destiny. Despite her rationality and atheism she was a fierce believer in destiny. The drive was long, and the swaying American highways made me begin to fiercely miss my corner of banal living in my soon-to-be-lost American apartment. The quick pit stops with bearded truck drivers staring at us, the overweight waitresses with badly bleached hair, the smell of hot dogs or fried chicken in the early hours of the morning made me queasy and sad about living in a foreign country. Sometimes I remembered that Marija carried a dainty gun in her white glossy bag and that made me feel safer and more grounded. Maybe I was more American than I thought. I knew that if it came down to it and if we were to be accosted, insulted, attacked in any way, she would have no hesitation about using it.

"You needed all that, Lara, you needed to cross into some kind of delinquency and deep heartbreak, you needed to break at least one of the fucking commandments. You needed to be bad for once in your lifetime, you had always been so good. Marriage, adultery, justice, it's all sort of mythic. It made you stronger, it didn't break you." She left the sentence hanging in the rawness of the night on the American highway because she knew that of the two of us, despite all the heartbreaks, I was still the unbroken one.

In the motel rooms as we were getting closer to the East Coast we watched all the John Wayne, Clint Eastwood, Gary Cooper movies we could find, the old black-and-white ones, the colored ones, and the newly colorized ones. Once in a while, just for the hell of it, we rooted for the bad guys, for the ones who were out for money and only out for themselves, who killed and raped women and children and hung their male enemies on a lonely tree in the desert. But then we always went back to rooting for the good guys, because really they were still bad, but they never hurt women and children. And their reasons for being bad were nobler, the love of a sultry woman, an ancestral killing of a mother or wife, the haunting memory of the burning of a village or a hidden treasure. In the end they were all out for treasures, land and money. And it all hung on the women in the end. It was an ancestral, biblical universe with the sexy glow of Hollywood cinematography and the classy nonchalance of Hollywood stars. Justice and revenge hung in the movie frames interchangeably and were always diluted in the long shots of cowboys riding into the sunset, the classic ending. "All we know about fucking America is from the fucking movies, but now we are landowners and nobody fucks with us," Marija said again and again one night, as we got drunk on miniature bottles of whiskey and vodka from the little cabinet with refreshments. We laughed ourselves to sleep the way we used to in our Belgrade college years, during our Milko period, the way we did on the night we met Sally Bryant. In the end we rooted most for the women in the movies, the lustful ones, the virtuous hardworking ones, the tough and sassy ones, the unforgiving ones with a gun, the trashy madams, the angry wives, the naive daughters. And to that gallery of western women, we added two Balkan girls with a Slavic accent, fierce in their revenge and precise in their aim, landowners in the American West and riding into the sunset in search of a blond boy.

Country of Red Azaleas

SUMMER 2004

When we returned to Washington, it was already summer. The duplex on Connecticut Avenue had been sold and my tenure had been denied. Welcome back to Washington, DC! I had to laugh. If Marija could laugh, so could I. According to Mark we had gotten a great offer for the duplex and there was no way we could refuse it. Or that he could refuse it. I forgot I had given Diana Coman power of attorney in my absence and she really did use it and signed the closing documents in my stead. When I called her she sounded cheerful and proud as if we had won the jackpot. Which it turned out we sort of did. Apparently a French couple working for the French embassy fell in love with the house, outbid all the other bidders, and put down their deposit in cash in a day. I was getting a little bit more than four hundred thousand dollars as my 50 percent share on the sale.

Mark was happier than I had seen him in a long time,

and he even hugged me when I walked into the duplex filled with cardboard boxes to the ceiling. He looked straight at me, which hadn't happened in a long time. It felt like a new reunion, a new beginning overlapping the final end of our marriage. It wasn't sad anymore, but freeing and soothing. A mellow wave of understanding and resettling moved between us in the early-summer heat. After the year of battles and glacial treatment, Mark's hug and warm welcome were more of a shock than the four hundred thousand dollars that landed in my lap. Peace always came at such a high price but it did come once in a great while. Natalia was at her most cheerful in the multicolored flowery dress that Biljana had gotten her in Chicago and was doing somersaults throughout the emptied-out portions of the duplex. Life was a never-ending carousel and the most important part of my ride was yet to come.

Marija had a way of gliding through rooms and spaces like a magic force, and she fluctuated between making herself overwhelmingly present and making herself unheard, unseen, nonexistent. She was a Cheshire cat, now she was nowhere to be found, and now she startled you sitting in an armchair and smiling as if she had been sitting there her entire life, like in an old family portrait. Although she had never met Marija before, Natalia became friends with her within the first minute we entered the house. And so did Mark to my utter shock. When I introduced Marija to Mark upon our arrival I saw a flicker of recognition cross his face. Life often stood in the way of being noble and generous. For a moment, Mark and I clung to our first encounter in a Belgrade tavern, all under Marija's presence. And that moment was not wrought with sadness, pining, nostalgia, and all the other emotional wreckages from my past life with Mark in the madness of the divorce period. It felt like a friendly handshake taking place in the virtual space of our common memory and mediated by Marija's flesh-and-blood presence in our house. Mark found just the right tone and demeanor with Marija, and even apologized for the mess. The finality of our life as a couple came with a new lightness and just the necessary amount of coolness to our relations. The new kind, polite, and classy man in our soon-to-be-forsaken duplex was now a good roommate and an excellent conversationalist.

I knew, however, that the old history of Mark having brought Hassan over to the States instead of Marija was still hanging in the air among us like a bird of prey ready to devour every bit of our newly acquired peace and harmony. And even though Marija's being was fully possessed by the thought of her son, I felt we needed to clear the air of that ominous presence. To my great surprise it was Mark who brought up the subject one evening over dinner, since once in a while we actually all ate together as if we were still a family. And who was to say we weren't, marked by cracks and wounds as we all were, but somehow now tied to one another even more, precisely because of all the wounds!

"Marija, I talked to Hassan the other day and he was happy to hear you moved here. He asked me to send you his best wishes, you know he..." Mark stuttered like he hardly ever did, he paused, he left the sentence hanging, and he seemed vulnerable, even confused. The air froze in the room for a second despite the warm summer day.

"It would be nice to see Hassan again at last," Marija said without a shred of irony or resentment. "And you, too, Mark, it was a good thing you brought Hassan over to the States. You had no way of knowing..."

"I wish it had all been different, Marija. If I could, I would..." Mark halted and to my shock I saw tears in his eyes. I looked at Marija and her smile looked like tears, too. I followed the exchange between them like a stranger in my own house with a sense of relief and puzzlement all at once. The two of them needed to confront each other just like that and tear up the evil bird of prey feather after bloody feather.

Marija leaned over toward Mark and gently touched his hand as if consoling him. I felt a deep scratch of jealousy in my throat. I wanted to scream to Marija and say: *He is not the one who needs consoling, you are the one who needs mending and consoling.* Instead I stuffed a piece of blackened salmon in my mouth. I drank from my wine and stared at Natalia quivering with emotion beside me. I completely missed the remaining conversation between Mark and Marija. By the time I had finished my salmon, their words sounded like fast-forwarded bits of an unintelligible language. My thoughts were louder than the outside world and the conversation going on in the room right next to me.

"All we have is the present, and my son is in the present," I heard Marija say. "I wouldn't have had him if I had come..." Her Cheshire cat smile lit up the room for a brief moment, carrying with it desperation, resignation, and bitter irony all at once.

"But at what price, Marija! At what price! I would have never had your courage!"

I had never seen Mark so human and so unraveled. If it hadn't been for Mark I wouldn't have had Natalia, my thoughts resumed, as if wanting to compete with Marija, and then I just thought *The ifs don't matter anymore.* Natalia looked up and took turns examining each one of us. Then she giggled and asked for the honey-and-almond cake that Marija had made for us. Mark stood up in a flash to bring it to the table.

During the following weeks Natalia moved between us with the grace of a ballerina, tiptoeing her way in and out of all family interactions with a sly smile. I may have thought that reading and discovering some of the world's worst horrors in Marija's notes from Sarajevo were going to break her, but they seemed only to have made her stronger, with a maturity that still held the last sparkles of her childhood. She and Marija were made of the same metal: the bending and unbreakable gold of the stars.

I took the news of my denied tenure with a shrug. A

brief moment of sadness at the word *failure* written all over my career crossed me. But mostly I felt unexpected relief. At least now there would be no more waiting and guessing. The news came in the form of a letter that was waiting for me on my desk, together with all the other mail collected in my absence, including a letter with Tunisian stamps. I didn't bother opening that one, but I did open the envelope with the letterhead of the university. It announced that the vote had been "unfavorable" for my tenure and promotion. It was when I read that word that I laughed. *Unfavorable*, a word of diluted negativity, was priceless. Why couldn't they just say: *You did not get tenure*, or *The vote for your tenure and promotion was negative*, or *You failed, your academic career is finished*? That wimpish *unfavorable* evoked a scene with people sitting in front of a meal they didn't like and turning up their noses at the sight and smell of it. Maybe to get tenure everything was supposed to be the other way around, maybe I had gotten it all wrong and I should have done a lousy job teaching, not done any research, and pretended not to see my colleagues when they passed me in the hallway. Maybe you weren't supposed to be good to be promoted, or maybe you just had to be a man. What was the difference, really, between here and good old Yugoslavia, I asked myself without bothering to find an answer.

Marija was more upset by the news of my denied tenure than I was. She suggested I appeal it, or sue the university. I should go ahead and hire a labor attorney, she advised. That only made me weary, to think of throwing myself into a new litigation procedure with those same colleagues of mine who had already been inappropriately involved in the messy operation of my custody and divorce trial. The most important thing, I told Marija, was to unravel the logistics of adopting her son and bringing him to America. I was now ready to throw myself into someone else's tragedy and misery. I asked her to please not mention my tenure and suing anymore, I might even get out of the academic line of work altogether and work for a nonprofit organization for women's rights or something noble like that. Then I told Marija of my plan to see my attorney and get her advice on the matter of her son. I knew Diana had worked on some cases of adoption of orphans from Romania. Every time I mentioned the boy, the son, the little round-headed child in the blurry picture that had become a tiny spider in my nightmare in the LA hotel, Marija stretched and relaxed and moved like a purring cat. I kept thinking: How was she going to look at him every day of her life without being reminded of that day, how was she going to pull any love toward that child? And invariably, every single time, Marija heard my thoughts and answered me directly, without me having uttered a single word on the matter: "I think about that day all the time, Lara. But the sperm and the egg that merged and produced this child didn't know what was going on when that happened. I look at the two things," she'd say, "the violence and the child—as separate. He could have been born just as much as the result of overpowering and tender love as of a hideous crime, it makes no difference to him—or to me." Her voice would wind down in a melodic way, her face acquiring again that lunar sadness that transfixed me like a supernatural force. "I can't go on with my life until I have that boy. It's just how it is. He must be lonely and scared in the care of that woman, with no children to play with, stigmatized because of his origins."

Diana Coman told us we had to go about it via the regular adoption route, and not try to claim the child on the basis of Marija's biological maternity. First, she needed proof that she was the biological mother. Who was going to believe her? And to start the process of showing biological parentage based on DNA testing across two continents would have been too daunting and most likely not successful. When Diana said that, Marija became fidgety like I hadn't seen her yet since our meeting in LA; she wrung her hands and cracked her knuckles. When I looked at her, I saw the full horror of that day in July 1995 displayed glaringly on her face. The gushing of blood, the obscene panting, the muffled screams, flesh, organs, guns, screams, begging for death, sighing for death, screaming the sharpest scream across the black earth. It all passed for one second on Marija's face like an apocalyptic cloud. The next second it was gone and a strange light, a blueness and rosiness, spread over her like the sky becoming uncannily clear after a devastating tornado. Red azaleas flooded the world in a fierce desire to make it bearable, livable, and possible again. Both Diana and I were heaving from what we had just witnessed and couldn't say a word. It was the first time I had seen Diana Coman undone. Tears flowed down my face. Tears flowed down Diana's face, the air in the room felt damp with sadness. And then Marija spoke: "All right, tell me what I need to do and I'll do it. That's all."

Diana devised a plan. She knew people who knew people in Sarajevo at one of the adoption agencies. She also knew a couple of Bosnians in Washington who worked at the Bosnian rehabilitation center and who could give her invaluable information about the adoption of children who were born during and after the war. Apparently they were a special category, the "war children." She was going to do all the paperwork as if it were all a regular adoption. But the woman who had raised the child needed to get involved, too, and to go along with the plan. Over the next few days Diana drafted papers and made phone calls while Marija was on the phone with people from Sarajevo, sometimes hiding in my study or in the bathroom to talk, not even letting me overhear the conversations. Sometimes her voice was shrill, sometimes plaintive and defeated. But always she kept on moving forward. There was no stopping Marija from getting what she wanted. Once I heard her talking to the woman who had the child, something about compensation. One evening I heard Marija cry on the phone, begging the woman to let her son talk to her. And then I heard her say in the sweetest Serbian, "I will see you soon, my love." Still, she needed a location, so she could find the mystery woman.

Mark happened to be home from work the day the three of us were leaving on our Balkan adventure and he offered to take us to the airport. Despite all my expectations, Mark and Marija had developed a warm friendship during the weeks in our house starting with the evening of our mythic dinner. Brief and achy waves of jealousy went through my body occasionally. Mark's idiosyncrasies started irritating me all over again like in the period preceding our divorce, while they didn't seem to bother Marija a bit. I didn't want to share Marija with Mark, or really with anyone other than Natalia. It seemed that love hardships and breakups had made me brittle instead of stronger. At the airport, Mark embraced and kissed Natalia tenderly and asked her to send him a postcard. He hugged Marija and wished her good luck with her search and then he turned to me and said "Good-bye, Lara," as if it was adieu and forever. It melted all jealousy and revealed to me the puzzling paradox that I had been right both to marry Mark in the fall of 1992 and to divorce Mark twelve years later. I leaned over and hugged him with no regrets.

When Marija, Natalia, and I landed at the Sarajevo airport, Marija turned pure white and I thought she was going to drop dead the next second. She stood in the middle of the airport, her eyes closed and breathing very slowly. It wasn't the shock of being on native land—she had visited Sarajevo a couple of times since the war. It was the weight of what was ahead of us. I observed as she breathed deeply, opened her eyes, and regained her color and her force.

Natalia seemed to be as much Marija's daughter as she was mine. She understood Marija's brief journeys to the edge of life and death, and would take her hand and hold it tight. Ferida waited for us at the airport with Mira. Ferida cried and hugged both of us effusively, a different Ferida from the controlled and almost aloof woman Natalia and I had met on our last trip. After I'd traveled back and forth out of American and French airports, the Sarajevo airport now seemed like a little toy version of one. The customs police were tired and old-fashioned, the security machines and checkpoints obsolete, the whole place unusually drab and nearly deserted.

We discovered that the woman had left her Sarajevo apartment right before we'd arrived and left no trace. She was supposed to call Marija as soon as she knew we were there, but this never happened, nor did she answer her phone in Sarajevo. Marija was growing more agitated, holding her nervousness under layers of maternal anticipation. Sarajevo shone and hummed that summer of our return with the enthusiasm of reconstruction and the pride of hosting international tourists. We moved through the city of our childhood like a colorful caravan of reckless refugees. To Marija and me, who hadn't witnessed the processes of its reconstruction over the years, it seemed almost fake, a movie set, a bit too glossy, a bit too colorful. Tarik the copper vendor was still selling his shiny coffee- and teapots at the same corner, only his face was wrinkled and his hair white. We drank little cups of dark, grimy coffee at the café next door while talking with Tarik about the business and the reconstruction, and avoiding the topic of the war, which Marija refused to discuss. We drank our coffee, ordered a baklava, we smiled at each other and just said nothing. Somewhere in another life, two adventurous girls chased each other and a wild ray of magic all through those streets and sloping alleys, up and down cobblestone steps, in and out of hidden courtyards. They stopped at a street corner, ate their fruit spoils for the day, ran some more, brushed by rows of stone houses with red flowers hanging from their windows, and ended up in an enchanted courtyard crossed by a tiny gurgling stream and surrounded by fruit trees and pines.

Natalia, ecstatic, absorbed the sounds, smells, and sights of Sarajevo in the summer with the pride of recognition. She and Mira ran carefree ahead of us, still reminding me of myself, Marija, and Biljana at their age. But the reminiscing broke. Everybody in Marija's family was dead. Marija's face was reconstructed. Sarajevo had been blasted to smithereens and its soil swallowed ten thousand dead. The surrounding hills were crowded with orderly white tombs in new cemeteries, myriad white tentacles moving toward the sky in a pointless prayer. Yet here we all were. Ferida with her daughter, Mira, born in the midst of the war in a basement in the dark, Natalia born on the very same day, Marija desperately and yet lovingly searching for the child born out of the blob of darkness that befell her the fated July of 1995.

We were all staying in Ferida's apartment, where she had

given birth to Mira nine years earlier. The building, near the Howard Johnson hotel where the foreign journalists had been lodged during the war, was now renovated, but the bullet and shell marks remained, dotting the exterior, a sign of remembrance. Marija thought it was bullshit, that it all should have been renovated and covered up and made to look new and fresh. "People want to start over and go on living—if they survived, if they are still alive—why stick the painful memories under their noses every single day of their lives?" she would say. Ferida seemed to agree with her. "I don't need to be reminded. I remember everything pretty damn well. This is for the tourists," Ferida said, "so that they can look and shed a tear and take a photo on their cell phones; it's to make the foreign tourists feel good about themselves." Marija and Ferida both laughed heartily, but I failed to get their humor. I didn't see how the tourists were made to feel good if they saw the bullet and shell marks on the sides of buildings in Sarajevo. "It's like a sign of sympathy or something, to remember the 'wretched' war victims, it's like the tourists who visit these faraway places such as Bosnia and see their war ruins are courageous and compassionate, you know what I mean? Maybe you've become too Americanized, Lara, and you can't see these subtleties any longer," said Marija.

Ferida served us some fruit and cakes from the kitchen. Mira and Natalia whispered in a corner of the room as if they had known each other since birth. Which in an indirect way they sort of did. Marija and Ferida and I laughed until Ferida

stared at Marija and I realized it was only then she noticed
the glass eye. She stopped short. "That's right. When all of
me is rotting in the ground my glass prosthetic organ will
still be as good as new," and she burst into a deep laugh.
"They did a good job, didn't they? A complete makeover,
Hollywood-style." Ferida confirmed that she had seen worse,
that Marija was lucky. But I couldn't understand the meaning
of luck like that. Marija and Ferida continued to recount war
stories like soldiers sitting by the fire. It was only then that I
heard the full story of Mira's birth in the basement of Ferida's
house. It seemed like the birth from hell, yet both Ferida and
Marija were having the time of their lives remembering the
details. They talked about their friend's sculptures displayed
in the basement, horrid and stunning at once, thin spiraling
pieces of metal with recent bloodstains and multimedia materials wrapped around or hanging from the metal and giving
the illusion of sad monsters. There were musicians with vio-
lins and guitars and one of them brought a keyboard while
another one brought a tuba. Ferida had baked bread by putting together several rations of flour. They'd even salvaged
some eggs, and vodka. "Somebody must have paid big money
on the black market for those eggs," said Ferida.

"And then the ad-hoc band started playing waltzes,"
Marija reminisced. "Of all the choices they could have made,
they decided to offer a medley of the best-known waltzes:
Strauss, Chopin, Tchaikovsky, Shostakovich." Marija became
immersed in her own storytelling and I feared the new rush of

her memories. "We danced as if our life depended on making those waltz steps in the crammed damp basement. Everybody was crying and dancing. Even my parents were dancing and my father played the flute." Marija's face was smooth as ever, almost too smooth; it took on a serene expression, like overly blue skies before a storm. "Even now I can't believe you delivered my baby from the sheet of instructions that my husband had left for me in case he was on call at the hospital when the baby came, which with my luck it turned out he was," said Ferida at a point of hilarity. Together they recounted the birthing instructions with peals of unrestrained laughter. I thought of my own luxurious labor and delivery of Natalia in a clean hospital room with Mark holding my hand and the nurse wiping my forehead. This, compared with Ferida's adventurous and almost comical wartime labor and delivery, even more in stark contrast with the birth of Marija's son somewhere in a dark house, in loneliness and in a semiconscious state. Yet it was this same visceral and primal experience that tied us. I finally was coming to understand Marija's desperate search and yearning for her son.

The morning when Marija announced that this was the day we were going to fetch her son, we all ate our breakfast in silence. Mira and Natalia were talking about pop music stars in the conspiratorial tones they had adopted. Ferida was feverishly writing bits of a poem on a paper napkin all the while gulping toast with cheese and a hard-boiled egg and pastrami. Marija drank her coffee in silence and ate all the berries at the table before either of the girls had a chance to touch them. I had forgotten how Marija devoured fresh fruit. She looked radiant; she was wearing the turquoise pendant I had given her when we parted in Belgrade, which was now more than ten years ago.

"So what shall we do in town this morning?" I said, daring to break the silence.

"We're not going into town," said Marija.

"What do you mean? Where are we going?"

"To Semizovac, that's where."

Semizovac, near Srebrenica, where Marija's family had lived and where they had returned upon Marija's suggestion and where they had been killed and where all the unimaginable rest had happened. My mouth literally hung open and Ferida's eyes were wide with disbelief.

"It's fine," she said. "It's all fine, I'll be fine," she repeated. "I'm made of steel, didn't you know? And five percent glass." Marija laughed one of her laughs. Natalia looked up and stared at her with the same fascination she always had for her.

"We are going to the place in the picture, Lara," Marija said sternly.

"That's where they've been living all along?" Ferida asked.

"Off and on," Marija said in a relaxed manner. "That was where they were when the photo was taken. Then she moved to Sarajevo for a while. And now they moved back and forth to the countryside. I went back to her house in Sarajevo and she had instructed a neighbor to give me information about her whereabouts. She had left a note with a different phone number and her new address. Apparently she'd been receiving threatening phone calls, too. Welcome home, right? And she wants the money, of course."

I bombarded Marija with questions. "Wasn't this all prepared and set in the adoption process? Why didn't they give you the information at the adoption agency?"

"Oh, Lara, you've become so American. All the legal procedures in America don't count for much of anything over here. Have you forgotten where you've left? It's her right to have the money. I don't care about it, she could have left my little boy in the street, right, but she didn't." There was no arguing with Marija. On this day when she would claim her son, her face was perfectly made up and her hair flowed in black luscious waves as always. We would drive in Ferida's eight-seater van. Marija told us she wanted everybody to be together, we were on a pilgrimage of sorts. In preparation for our trip, she put a big stack of cash in her white patent-leather purse next to the dainty gun.

But it wasn't enough, Marija said. She still needed more money to compensate the woman. The five grand in her purse wasn't enough. "We'll get it somehow," she said nonchalantly. "Today. Anything can happen, you know, I need to get there as soon as possible." And then worry about her son spread over Marija's face like a translucent spider's web, making her look unreal in the morning sun that streamed through the apartment's windows. I knew right then and there that Marija would rather die ten times before she would let go of that mystery son of hers. Ferida and I had no choice but follow every single one of her wishes. Even if she had never explained what might possibly happen within these next few hours or a day, and why she was in such a mad hurry.

"Look," Marija started in an unexpectedly serious tone as if about to reveal an important secret. "This boy is one of those kids who around here are called 'the rape babies' and everybody knows it. In America they call them with a nicer, more dramatic name, they are 'the war babies,' but here they call them for what they are: children born out of mass rapes. Many of them were taken by the state and put in seedy orphanages like the one in Zenica up north of Sarajevo. Others were taken to Serbia by their Serbian fathers or by those who thought they might have fathered them during the rapes. This woman, for whatever her faults may be, took care of my son when I abandoned him like hundreds of other wretched women did in those days. Only she didn't abandon him, nor did she give him up to some orphanage. She was even able to get a fake birth certificate for him, stating it was actually her child. And do you realize what this meant? It meant she was probably thought of as a victim of rape, too, which she never was. She was willing to take on that stigma just to save my life and the life of my son."

Marija stopped to light a cigarette, which I hadn't seen her do in weeks. She reminded me of the Marija of our university years. Mira and Natalia stared at us from their corner of the room cuddled into one another amid the Turkish cushions as if to find refuge from our conversation. The talk of rapes and "rape babies" seemed to have brushed by their girlish faces and left them darkened with premature aging. Ferida, though, looked at me and waved her hand, after which she said casually: "She's heard it all, don't worry." I calmed down thinking that Natalia, too, had sort of heard it all, or at least read it all. I had no idea by now whether that was good or bad, it was how it was. An ambulance siren sliced the silence. Marija's smoke filled the room.

"Why did this woman become so wrapped up in you and this child, Marija?" I ventured. Marija sat unmoving, without blinking, as if she hadn't heard my question. She continued to smoke and for a second I had the uncanny feeling that nothing had happened at all. That we were all young and no wars had swept over us.

"Remember the girl whose life I told you I saved by killing the bastard who was trying to rape her?" Marija said without flinching.

"Yes, I do. Does this girl have to do with something?"

"She is this woman's daughter, that's what she has to do. We were all neighbors, and the daughter happened to be near our house that morning. After I killed the soldier, she managed to run home and told her mother about it. The mother took her to her sister's house at the other end of the town and from there they escaped to Sarajevo. That evening, once it grew dark, the woman came back looking for me and found me in a pool of blood in our front yard. At first she thought I was dead, but it turned out I wasn't. You know the rest."

After Hollywood, the Wild West, the three days and nights in the sound of Marija's epic sobs in the log cabin in Colorado, very little could still shock or even surprise me in Marija's continuously unfolding story.

"So she has this undying gratitude for me because I saved her daughter," Marija continued. "She promised she would do everything to save me. When I had the baby she vowed to keep him, even though she'd been left dirt-poor after the war. And she did keep my child. Just like she dragged me from house to house during those days trying to hide me and my bleeding self. She sang bloody Serbian songs and pretended to be Serbian for my sake. Her husband and son had all been killed during those sunny July days and she hasn't found their bones yet to bury. Like I said, killing the soldier was the best thing and the worst thing I had ever done."

Then she smiled to herself the saddest smile I had ever seen. One life had ransomed another, and for that, sometimes it paid to kill someone. It was like the Wild West, only it was happening now in our little drab corner of the Balkans.

"It seems like the fuss we've made with the adoption papers, and the fuss I've made with that stupid search for Karadzic, were a mistake. The woman says some Serbian authorities and some Serbian thugs, which really is pretty much the same thing, found out about the boy."

"I get it." Ferida, no stranger to postwar mystery, now understood. "It's possible they could actually take him to Serbia, like they've done with others of these 'lucky' rape babies."

"It's very possible," said Marija in a calm voice. "The woman told me there had been a bunch of Serbian guys stalking her apartment in Sarajevo, and then there were the phone calls. With me coming and going back and forth to Sarajevo and visiting her over the past couple of years, somebody must have guessed it's my child. You know, many of the soldiers who raped us are still around, some were Bosnian Serbs and some were our neighbors. Some are still on the prowl looking for the children they engendered or even for their mothers, to punish them for having reported the rapes to the state. We are still not safe, you know, all the glitter and shimmer and color and tourists you see in the historic Sarajevo—it's only one side of it." Marija wanted to make sure I understood that and held no illusions about our dear Sarajevo, nostalgic as we might have been for its prewar beauty and vibrancy. "There is still a silent, invisible war going on. At least for some of us. I need both of you on this trip. I need you to help me get this money today and get my son. Today. I have an intuition and I have to follow it like it's now or never. It has to be now."

Marija spoke in a detached way, like a lawyer or a politician. Her tragedy had not destroyed her. She had all the poise and logic needed for the hardest tasks, including an "invisible war." She survived and emerged shinier and stronger. I was ready for everything next to her. The morning light burst into Ferida's apartment in dazzling shards that blinded me for a second. I knew that something new was going to start in my life like never before.

We climbed into Ferida's eight-seater van and flew around Sarajevo all morning and afternoon collecting the necessary funds. Marija, Ferida, and I managed to gather the necessary ten thousand dollars in cash. We went to every friend and source we knew in Sarajevo, Belgrade, and the United States. Biljana and Mark sent money through Western Union, while Ferida and Marija, who looked like burglars on the run, gathered bundles of cash in canvas shopping bags. It felt like a mafia movie, one about desperate women trying to recover a child conceived out of war and violence who was still not safe from war and violence. Sarajevo was ablaze that day, alive in the dazzling colors I remembered from my childhood. The utopian city of my youth had again come to life in our mad race for money to recompense the woman who had saved Marija's life and her son's. I asked Marija again why this nameless woman wanted money, anyway, if Marija had already saved her daughter's life. "Money helps," she said. "I owe her that, ten times this much. This way I know she'll be set for life."

We got out of the van and walked through the city. The silks shimmered on the vendor's street counters; the coppers glowed with wicked reddish tints in the sparkling light. It now seemed partly unreal, and dark shadows of what Marija had called "the invisible war" seemed to move through the crowds and behind the luscious silks. I started looking behind me, worried that we might be followed. Men who seemed or sounded Serbian scared me now more than ever. Marija on the other hand, once in action, acted and looked as if she was living the adventure of her life. She was girlish one minute, stern the next, a dazzling bundle of contradictions as always. Marija joked that she and Ferida had robbed a bank. Marija compared us to Butch Cassidy and Sundance Kid, then to Bonnie and Clyde, and I wondered whether it was maybe her uncanny reliance on movies and Hollywood that had given her the strength to survive the most outrageous blows of fortune. I had never thought of Hollywood as therapy for traumatized people, but maybe that made sense. Everything was possible in times of war or peace when you were Marija, I thought, as we counted and stashed the bundles of fifty- and one-hundred-dollar bills.

By the end of the afternoon, we got back on the road with our bundles of money, all wrapped with elastic bands and stuffed in Marija's backpack. Marija insisted on driving the van this time, saying it relaxed her to be at the wheel. I sat next to her, and the two girls were in the back with Ferida. At first, when we left Sarajevo, it felt like an exciting adventure, some kind of a road trip with laughter and bubbly conversations back and forth between the two of us in the front and the girls and Ferida in the back. It was after we got onto the winding roads out of Sarajevo and began to head toward

Semizovac that Marija became a menace. She sang Serbian songs in a deep low voice, like a cabaret singer. It made my skin crawl to hear her sing like that and made me want to get far away from that person I loved so much and yet who chilled the blood in my veins with her macabre whims and her roller coaster of mood swings and the heaviness of her past. She had told me once when we were in the Washington, DC, duplex that having gone through what she had turned her into something of a repulsive monster and that once they found out her story, most people wanted to run away from her, fearing they might be contaminated by her black destiny. "That's why I don't want to tell my fucking bloody story to anyone," she'd said, laughing. Marija started passing every car in sight like a race car driver on the winding serpentine roads leading to the dreaded village. The girls in the back were squealing like they were on an amusement park roller coaster, while Ferida and I exchanged worried glances.

It was still afternoon and the sun was blazing like an angry blob of lava above our racing van. I realized it was a sunny day in July. Maybe the memory of another sunny day in July was scorching Marija's psyche. She gave the finger to a truck driver that she passed, then she rolled down her window and spat out her gum while her hair rose wildly in the 120-kilometer-an-hour speed. We were on a mad race to hell and Marija was our doom and our salvation at once, a goddess of death and life, with the face of a statue. Drivers stuck their arms out of their car windows and made obscene gestures at us, people stared at us from in front of their houses as we passed them by raising clouds of dust. They raised their fists at us and promised revenge. Marija got all the more excited. She turned on the radio and blasted a rock station one minute and sang at the top of her lungs the next. She sang those Serbian songs again and again. It seemed so wrong. Like so much else on that ride. "Why am I singing Serbian songs, right? Why am I singing the songs of the motherfuckers who crushed us Bosnians and killed my family and raped and maimed me? Right, that's what you are wondering?" I was praying that the girls in the back couldn't hear her. When I looked back at them, they were cuddled into one another, holding hands, terror on their pale faces. The raw truth pulsated like an angry viper in the stuffy air of the van. "Open the windows for God's sake," I yelled, "open the fucking windows, Marija." Marija did nothing of the sort, though Ferida opened the window on her side. "It's because of the woman from Semizovac," Marija stated. "She kept singing the bloody Serbian sentimental songs over and over again while she transported my shredded self in her rattling car. One night when she went delirious I got it why she was singing those songs, and I picked up on her delirium so I started singing, too. These had been our songs after all, too, hadn't they, in the good old days of Tito and 'mother' Yugoslavia we all spoke the same fucking Serbian language and sang the same stupid drinking songs. We had just as much right to the goddamn hills and fields and the language and the songs."

As we approached Semizovac, Marija drove the van right into a ditch. We scared a few cows that were grazing in the field and a bunch of kids playing by the side of the road. The girls started crying that they wanted to go home, they both had bruises on their arms and knees. Ferida's nose was bleeding and I had a bump the size of a walnut on my head from banging it into the door. Only Marija came out unscathed and looking like a mythical Fury, with her hair disheveled and flying out in all directions, an expression of rage on her face that chilled my blood. We left the car in the ditch and walked by the side of the road like a caravan of doleful refugees in our own country. I thought Marija was finally having the breakdown to end all breakdowns, the one that Sally had warned against, when her past would come rushing in like the biblical flood sweeping everything in its passage and leaving only devastation and corpses behind. The sun was setting and the air was getting chillier. A mixture of beauty and ominous silence spread around us as we walked through the countryside. The hills surrounding us pulsated with rotting bodies. No one spoke. We entered the village and Marija stopped in front of a larger stone house painted in light pink: Chez Sonia. She stood in front of it and began laughing hysterically. Ferida whispered to me that the place had been turned into a rape hotel during the war. We tried to drag Marija away from the site but she wouldn't budge. She just stood there laughing. Laughing, I now understood, was Marija's way of sobbing the bitterest tears in the universe. Then she opened her purse, the patent-leather white purse that carried her pistol, and she shot at the walls and the windows of Chez Sonia hotel three times. The sound of shattered glass reverberated through the heated air. She put back the pistol as if she had just taken out a Kleenex to wipe her nose. Some people came running toward us and we stood in front of Marija trying to protect her. But Marija became composed and sweet, smiling at the people and asking them if they had heard any shootings. The people looked as puzzled as we did. Marija changed the subject and asked them if they could direct us to the address where the woman lived. There was a sudden silence that seemed to envelop everything and I stopped hearing what Marija or anybody else said for a few moments. It was not as if I had gone deaf, but as if the world itself had become deafeningly quiet. Then it all erupted again with brutal loudness: the voices, the cars on the road, the airplanes, the motorcycles. "It's past the tracks, straight up the road, then there is a dead end and the house is right there," was all I heard. "Past the tracks, past the tracks," something important was always "past the tracks" or "past the corner," and always there was a "dead end," I thought. I had had enough of that movie. I didn't want a dead end, but a new beginning. When I looked at Natalia, she took my hand. I wanted to ask her forgiveness for everything—for the way her father and I ended up, for having brought her into a horrendous world, for belonging to a brutal country. But she didn't need my apologies. She already understood. She was happy to hold my hand.

We walked for another full hour, much longer than the kind people who had given us the directions told us it would be. It was sunset by the time we arrived at the small stone house. There was the well in the middle of the front yard, just like in the photograph. A creepy feeling spread all over me. The girls were intrigued by the sight of the well in the middle of the yard, where there was also a flower and vegetable garden. The haunting nightmares that I had in the LA hotel room rushed back and all I could see and think of were bodies of Bosnians rotting inside the well. I reached out toward Natalia and Mira and tried to stop them from getting too close to the well, and just then there was a sharp scream that sounded almost playful. A tiny round-faced blond boy emerged from the side door of the house and behind him stood a middle-aged woman wiping her hands on her apron, her hair held back with a yellow scarf. The boy was no three-headed monster but an angelic malnourished golden-haired boy taken by surprise by the visit of strangers. He was an older version of the boy in the picture, but more beautiful and wrenchingly alive. His watery blue eyes sparkled in innocent amazement. For a few moments the air was motionless and clear, and there were no sorrows, no regrets, and no floating sadness. Everything stood still in suspension. Then I looked at Marija, and that was when life burst in. She was the old Marija, except that she was moving very slowly. Her hair shone in the dying light with sparkles of bluish black. In slow motion, she moved toward the boy whose name I didn't know. Why did he have to be so blond and so terribly blue-eyed? I looked toward Ferida for an answer. But she was standing a few steps behind me in a state of stupor. Marija picked up her son and started laughing with her million-dollar laughter.

Two unhinged corners of my soul suddenly came together. Something shifted back into its place. I saw Marija and me dancing a slow dance over meadows and cities. I saw us gliding through the white snows of the Sarajevo winters and running through the apricot orchards of summer. It had been her all along, the one I had been waiting for. The long journey strewn with war and divorce, of misguided searching and incomprehensible suffering, could only take me back to her. I understood all of her tears when we hugged that final day in her apartment on the day the war started. I rewound our phone conversations from the Sarajevo bomb shelter to my duplex on Connecticut Avenue. My own unexplained longing and the nagging sense of something amiss all throughout my years in Washington, throughout my marriage to Mark, and even when I'd numbed myself into oblivion with Parisian love. The love for Marija had been there all along. At this most incongruous moment the worst and the best of life was gathered in one gleaming image in a Bosnian village. And Marija knew it at the same split second that I did. She turned to me, smiled her most radiant smile. "His name is Marijo, imagine that!" she said, and stretched out her hand beckoning for me to join them. Natalia came over to complete the circle and for the first time ever it felt like a real family. As I looked up and saw the woman who had raised Marijo wipe her hands again on her apron, the gesture triggered another afternoon in Sarajevo. On that drizzly November afternoon last year, I had brushed by Marija's son and this same mysterious woman without having any idea of who they were. The woman in the run-down house in the unreconstructed neighborhood of Sarajevo, the one who had handed me Marija's stories and notes! "Just some woman," Marija had told me when I'd asked about her identity when we first met in LA.

As everything stood poised in perfect harmony and the light of the setting sun quivered in delicate pastels, Marija said: "Good-bye, Lara dear, for now. I'll need to stay in Sarajevo for a while longer. I have to close all my accounts here with this wretched country before I leave for good. I'm here now, and no one can hurt my boy. He's safe. I'll stay with Ferida. Marijo and I will come to your America soon enough. Our America, I should say. I will get to know Marijo first in his world, and then we'll make the huge leap to America. We're a family, you and I, Natalia, all of us, what the hell. It won't be long." I stood motionless staring at Marija holding her son in her arms, the angelic boy who looked nothing like her. "What about us, Marija?" I said, without thinking. She laughed, I cried. Marijo the blond son laughed, too, a reverberation of his mother. The last sun rays flickered, leaving us and the garden and the well with sparkling water in the grayish light before complete darkness began to set in. Dusk was rushing on silvery wings and enveloping us. The idea of another separation from Marija weighed on me, and I had to sit down on the wooden bench in front of the house. I was surrounded by the smell of jasmine and honeysuckle. Marija put down her glowing golden son with exquisite gentleness, sat beside me, and embraced me. Her long eyelashes fluttered against my tear-soaked cheeks, just like they had when we embraced under the ponderosa pines in the Wild West. "We are home, Lara dear. We'll always have each other and Paris be damned!"

She laughed her beautiful laugh. The sound of my name in her silky voice sparkled. I stood up from the bench, ready for our adventure even as tears streamed down our cheeks. Marija's lunar sadness glided from her face onto mine. I was being bathed in the fluid sadness that had belonged to Marija for so long. Marija, my one and only love. I was going back to *our* America, and together we would be in a place where cacti bloomed out of orange dunes and red azaleas hung from the windows of adobe houses.

Acknowledgments

This book would not have seen the light of day without the intuition, support, and insightful guidance of two brilliant women: my incredible and vibrant agent, Anne Edelstein, and my equally incredible and passionate editor from Twelve, Deb Futter. Each in her own elegant and thoughtful way has led me toward the final artistic product that is *Country of Red Azaleas*. Thank you both for embracing my book with love and meticulous care!

In order to weave the complicated fabric of this novel I have gathered many wrenching and amazing stories of survival, and talked to many people who have offered me priceless insight and information and have guided me along some of the dark paths of memory of the Bosnian war during the early nineties. I wholeheartedly thank Kemal Kurspahic for meeting with me on several occasions, visiting my university, sharing with me startling and unforgettable stories about living and reporting under siege in Sarajevo during the years of the war. I want to warmly thank Nermina Kurspahic for hosting me in her lovely house in Semizovac one July afternoon on the commemoration of the Srebrenica massacre, sharing her stunning stories and delicious fruit and opening her heart and house to the curious stranger that I was. You both have greatly inspired me.

I want to thank Dijana Milosevic for the inspiration and insight she has provided for me for years with her stunning work as director of the DAH Theater, sharing war stories and her lucid perspective on the war. I thank her also for connecting me to the unknown woman from the Women in Black group who welcomed me in her Belgrade apartment. I thank this anonymous Serbian woman who in the hallway of her apartment handed me in silence and pride the invaluable document that is the collection of testimonials, gathered in the book *Women in Black: Women's Side of War.*

I am thankful to the Bosnian poet and peace activist Ferida Durakovic, who met with me in Sarajevo and shared her own story of survival and those of many other women, as well as her poetic vision of the war and the postwar period. Many thanks are also due to Sonja Biserko, who received me warmly at her office of the Helsinki Committee for Human Rights in Serbia and shared invaluable insights and information.

I owe heartfelt thanks to Catharine MacKinnon for her brilliant, poignant insights and valuable information about the sexual violence against Muslim Bosnian women during the Bosnian war of the nineties and the glorious victory she obtained for the Bosnian women victims of the war in the trial of *Kadic v. Karadzic.*

ACKNOWLEDGMENTS

I am grateful to Washington and Lee University for the ongoing support with research time and funding, Lenfest Sabbatical and summer leaves and grants that have facilitated the completion of this book. In particular I want to thank my friend, colleague, and dean, Suzanne Keen, who has offered continued support of my creative projects throughout the years.

I am grateful to Paul Friedrich for having read and offered helpful feedback on earlier versions of the novel and for his unflinching support of my creative work. As always I thank my mother, Stella Vinitchi Radulescu, a brilliant poet in her own right, who is both my greatest supporter and my most lucid critic and who inspires me endlessly.

About the Author

Domnica Radulescu is a distinguished professor of French and Italian literature at Washington and Lee University. She came to the United States in 1983 as a political refugee from Romania soon after she had won a national literary prize for a collection of short stories. She is the author of two internationally praised novels, *Train to Trieste* and *Black Sea Twilight*. *Train to Trieste* has been published in thirteen languages and is the winner of the 2009 Library of Virginia Fiction Award. She has authored, edited, and co-edited numerous books on theater, exile, and representations of women and is also an award-winning playwright. Radulescu received the 2011 Outstanding Faculty Award from the State Council of Higher Education for Virginia, and she is a Fulbright scholar. She is working on her fourth novel, *My Father's Orchards*.

Bibliography

Bilic, Bojan, and Vesna Jankovic (eds.). *Resisting the Evil: (Post) Yugoslav Anti-War Contention*. Baden-Baden: Nomos Verlagsgesellschaft, 2012.

Boskailo, Esad, and Julia Lieblich. *Wounded I Am More Awake: Finding Meaning After Terror*. Nashville: Vanderbilt University Press, 2012.

Caruth, Cathy. *Unclaimed Experience. Trauma, Narrative and History*. Baltimore: Johns Hopkins University Press, 1996.

Drakulic, Slavenka. *They Would Never Hurt a Fly. War Criminals on Trial in the Hague*. New York: Penguin, 2005.

Filipovic, Zlata. *Zlata's Diary: A Child's Life in Wartime Sarajevo*. New York: Penguin, 2006.

Galloway, Steven. *The Cellist of Sarajevo*. New York: Riverhead Books, 2009.

Helsinki Committee for Human Rights in Serbia and Sonja Biserko. *Annual Report: 2010. Human Rights Reflect Institutional Impotence*. Belgrade: Helsinki Committee for Human Rights in Serbia, 2011.

Jankovic, Mirka, and Stanislava Lazarevic. *Women in Black: Women's Side of War*. Trans. Dubravka Radanov. Belgrade: Women in Black, 2007.

Kurspahic, Kemal. *Prime Time Crime: Balkan Media in War and Peace*. Washington, DC: United States Institute of Peace, 2003.

Kurtovic, Larisa. "The Paradoxes of Wartime 'Freedom': Alternative Culture During the Siege of Sarajevo." In Bilic and Jankovic (eds.), *Resisting the Evil*, 197–224.

Macek, Ivana. *Sarajevo Under Siege: Anthropology in Wartime*. Philadelphia: University of Pennsylvania Press, 2011.

MacKinnon, Catherine. Personal interview, June 29, 2011.

Pervan, Nenad. "Hair in Sarajevo: Doing Theater Under Siege." In Kevin Wetmore (ed.), *Portrayals of Americans on the World Stage*. Jefferson, NC: McFarland, 2009, 179–191.

Power, Samantha. *"A Problem from Hell": America and the Age of Genocide*. New York: Harper Perennial, 2002.

Stiglmayer, Alexandra (ed.). *Mass Rape: The War Against Women in Bosnia-Herzegovina*. Lincoln: University of Nebraska Press, 1994.

Trebincevic, Kenan, and Susan Shapiro. *The Bosnia List: A Memoir of War, Exile, and Return*. New York: Penguin Group, 2014.

Umar, Ayesha. "From Bosnian Rape Camps to the U.S. Court: The Story of *Kadic v. Karadzic*." https://www.academia.edu/629451/From_Bosnian_Rape_Camps_to_the_US_Court_The_Story_of_Kadic_v._Karadzic. May 7, 2011.

Visniec, Matei. *The Body of a Woman as a Battlefield in the Bosnian War*. In Cheryl Robson (ed.), *Balkan Plots: New Plays from Central and Eastern Europe*. London: Aurora Metro, 2002, 14–66.

———. *The Word* Progress *on My Mother's Lips Doesn't Ring True*. Manuscript courtesy Matei Visniec, 2009.

ABOUT TWELVE

TWELVE was established in August 2005 with the objective of publishing no more than twelve books each year. We strive to publish the singular book, by authors who have a unique perspective and compelling authority. Works that explain our culture; that illuminate, inspire, provoke, and entertain. We seek to establish communities of conversation surrounding our books. Talented authors deserve attention not only from publishers, but from readers as well. To sell the book is only the beginning of our mission. To build avid audiences of readers who are enriched by these works—that is our ultimate purpose.

For more information about forthcoming TWELVE books, please go to www.twelvebooks.com.